BETRAYAL

REVIEWS OF CHRISTINE PURKIS' BOOKS

Jane Evans

'*Jane Evans* is a gripping, rewarding read.'
Lynn Guest, Historical Novel Society

'Christine really takes the reader viscerally into the hard, cold,
muddy life of the drovers.'
The House Historian Wales, Twitter

'*Jane Evans* is a vividly drawn and fast-paced tale,
combining historical detail with engaging character.
It has a broad scope and is nonetheless grounded in
place and time, a story of Wales in the wider world.'
Myfanwy Alexander, author

The Shuttered Room

'A real breath of hot, French air comes with this
fascinating novel set in the south of France…
A captivating story by a talented writer.'
Books for Keeps

Paddlefeet

'An engaging, imaginative fantasy story… An excellent read.'
Kit Spring, *The Observer*

'A truly magical book.'
Book Recovery 8–12

Dark Beneath the Moon

'An interesting and complex book… with
beautiful descriptions of the local countryside.'
The School Librarian

BETRAYAL
CHRISTINE PURKIS

Peggin's journey from maid with the
Ladies of Llangollen to Pontcysyllte –
a short distance but at great cost.

y Lolfa

For Mopsa

First impression: 2023
© Christine Purkis & Y Lolfa Cyf., 2023

Cover image: Sergey Dolgikh (girl)
Cover design: Sion Ilar

ISBN: 978 1 80099 319 8

The publishers wish to acknowledge the support of
the Books Council of Wales

Published and printed in Wales
on paper from well-maintained forests by
Y Lolfa Cyf., Talybont, Ceredigion SY24 5HE
e-mail ylolfa@ylolfa.com
website www.ylolfa.com
tel 01970 832 304

Prologue

1784

Fʀᴏᴍ ᴛʜᴇ ꜰɪʀsᴛ moment Luca Begg held his baby in his arms, she was his chuck, his lambkin, his little grub, his Aggie. Every evening when Evercreech's Entertainers had finished the show, he took her after feeding and rocked her in his arms, sitting by the fire outside their tent. She was flopsome and heavy, still sucking, her lips searching until she found her own thumb. They were the best of times: Joe, six years old, cross-legged at his father's feet, feeding the fire with sticks, Luca's wife Nelly sewing glass beads onto her tumbling costume, and baby Aggie suck-sucking as he stroked his chin over her soft baby hair.

When Aggie's legs dangled over his and her hair was springy as moss, she was still his 'suck-a-thumb'. 'Pa' was her first word (though Nelly swore it was 'Ma'). From her first steps, she would take his hand and walk with him to the practice field: Aggie small, wide-legged and rolling as a drunk; Luca tall, with a sideways lean and a limp – noticeable on the ground, vanishing when he performed as an acrobat or walked his beloved slack rope.

At only two years old, Aggie helped chalk his feet, smacking the white dust from her hands when they were done, hunkering to watch. In his tatty hose and vest, he danced the slack rope just for her.

Hand in hand, they would walk home. Home was the tent, wherever – up or down the country – it might be pitched.

'What will you be when you's growed big, Aggie?' he'd ask her.

'I'll walk the rope,' she'd answer. 'And not fall never.'

Luca Begg was two acts in one man: a slack-rope walker and the seventh 'brother' in the Flying Fantinis acrobatic act. The name of the act was taken from his Italian mother, who had come to Britain three decades earlier with her parents' act and fallen in love with an Englishman who performed with horses. The finale to the show was the Fantinis' pyramid act – a row of three, two on their shoulders, the sixth on theirs, balancing a chair on his wide forehead. Luca leaping from the trampoline and executing a forward roll mid-air to land perfectly in the chair was the breathtaking climax.

Never in the three years since the Fantinis had perfected the act had Luca Begg overshot, but one night a trailing foot caught the chair, unsettling the pyramid. It wavered, before crashing like a tree in a storm. The unfortunate Luca landed on his head with a sickening crunch. After all the years of training: falling this way and that, with a shoulder or an arm taking the impact, but not the head. Never the head!

Luca lost the use of his legs, and with it his livelihood and life as he had known it. Joe tried his best to look after his father's needs. Aggie watched him from underneath scowling eyes, biting at the skin round her thumb till she bled.

Luca turned his back and told her he was dead.

And then he was. Drowned in the swollen leat on Christmas Eve, 1787.

Ebenezer Evercreech, the owner of the Entertainers, had had his devouring eyes on Nelly well before Luca Begg's accident. Dressed in his purple velvet coat and three-cornered hat, with his wigs and his long sallow face, his craggy forehead and aquiline nose, he was a frequent visitor afterwards. Nelly's third pregnancy, undetected by him until she was near the time of the birth, was a nuisance but something he could reconcile himself to. He was a patient man. An absence of a couple of days, which is all his ladies needed, could be accommodated. Nelly's Joe, a sensible lad, would be able to look after Aggie and the baby when his mother had recovered.

Nelly's labour was shocking, long and loud. Even the horses in the practice ring, where Joe dragged Aggie while the birthing was in progress, laid their ears back and snorted in fear. Nelly was left pale and feeble with eyes for the baby alone: a scrap of a thing from the start, with a bluish tinge to her and a faraway gaze.

Aggie did not like to linger in the tent with her pale mother and her pale baby sister. Sometimes she would go with Joe to watch him practise his juggling act, but juggling bored Aggie, and Joe didn't need any chalking. She preferred watching the horses, with their dark eyes, soft quivering lips and knowing silence. They did what they were told, galloping round and round the ring with their necks arched and their coats glossy, but inside they were different – raging. She saw that in the little flame in their eyes.

Four months after the baby was born, in the short, dark days of winter, Evercreech came to the tent. This time he did not take off his hat nor shoo the children away, but instead sighed and announced that he was sorry, but it was time to part ways. Realistically, Nelly wasn't ever going to tumble again. Look at it from his point of view. Times were hard. The cost of keeping a family of four who could contribute nothing to his coffers was, regrettably, no longer possible. He would take them to a place where Nelly might find the Christian goodness she deserved: Chirk, the parish where she had been born – albeit on the side of a road. Nelly's mother, also a tumbler in a troupe of entertainers, had been travelling to Wrexham for the Saint David's Day celebrations. The ease and speed of Nelly's arrival had happily been no impediment to the tumbling act in the Wrexham festivities.

Evercreech himself drove them in his cart all the way to the parish priest's house in Chirk.

The priest, an elderly man with thin, snowy white hair revealing a pink scalp and sad, watery eyes, took them in – being, as luck would have it, in need of help. In spite of his kindness and the good food he provided, the baby died. The priest said she was too good for this world, which Aggie doubted.

For three whole months Aggie had Nelly to herself. Together they scrubbed the grates and polished the brass, laid the priest's fires and washed the priest's clothes.

One early March morning, stretching up to dust the clock on the mantelpiece, Nelly was seized with pain which doubled her up and took her to her bed. By the evening, another baby had arrived – a shock to Aggie, though Joe rolled his eyes and told her she was a ninny.

The priest was as surprised as Aggie. She saw him counting on his fingers and a frown creasing his forehead.

'You told me your poor father died in August a year ago, Aggie!' he said.

'He did. I was four!' Aggie said, as Joe dug his fingers into her arm. 'Ow!'

The priest's surprise turned quickly to shock, then outrage. They must go! Forthwith!

'And use the back stairs!'

No one explained. The priest called Nelly a Jezebel, which confused Aggie further. However, being a Christian man, he promised through his spluttering that he would make 'arrangements'.

What those arrangements might be, Aggie didn't know until she met Nelly, holding the baby, on the back stairs. It was right at the point where the stairs curved round, with a little window looking out over the adjoining stable and courtyard towards the church tower.

'What arrangements?' Aggie asked.

'I'm to go to the poorhouse with Baby, Aggie. A home for women like me, down on their luck. Just until I can get myself up and going again. Joe is apprenticed to a button maker in Oswestry, so he'll be employed and looked after.'

Aggie backed down a stair. Nelly shifted the baby to her other arm.

A crow landed on the roof of the priest's stable outside. Through the rippled glass it cawed silently.

'Am I to come with you?' Aggie asked.

Nelly bit her lip and closed her eyes.

'But what is to become of me?' Aggie cried.

PART I
Aggie

1

I STAYED WITH Mrs Price, the old woman what bought me from the priest, for five long summers, five long cold winters and more before I left. She said I did wrong things but so did she. I knew slippin' away. Done it all my life. I weren't goin' to see Mrs Price, nor the girls, nor Mister Gulliver from the church nor none of 'em ever again. I went where my feet took me, to fields with sheep what don't care who you are nor what's happened to you nor about none of your business. I went where the river went, 'cos it knew where it was goin'. Rivers do. It roared louder than the roar in my head. And when my river met the bigger one, they went on together and I was with them, on the bank, jumpin' roots and ditches till I was weak and my legs draggin' and the dark was swallowin' everythin'. I found a dry place under a hedge and curled up in leaves. Dry and safe and hidden till the hedge-pig came scuttling down the lane, with the garden boy chasin' behind.

That little critter rolled up in a ball like me but I didn't have hedge-pig prickles so the boy – a bit older than me – hauled me out instead. He asked my name and I said, 'Beggin' pardo', sir.' He must 'ave heard 'Peggin'. It stuck.

'Peggin!' He had a ferretin' cosh in his hand and I know what a thrashin' feels like, so I didn't say nuffin'.

'Moses is my name. I'll take you to the Duckies.'

'Duckies' is what I heard. Later he told me he said 'Duchess', but his voice was all funny, like singin'. She weren't a duchess but a Lady, and so was the other one she lived with. They had the same name: Beloved. They seemed old to me, but their hair weren't shorn and short then like it was later. More rolled up, out the way. Duckies was what they were to me. Dowdy Duckies. Where the big one waddled, the other one followed.

That first time I saw them, they was bent over rakin' the path neat, snippin' at plants, makin' everythin' how they wanted to see it, not how it was.

'Ah, Moses. What have you got there?' The big Duckie stood up. She weren't that tall, but looked fat from good eatin'. Moses pulled me forward.

'Peggin, Ma'am. I found her in the hedge.'

'Did you now?' The blue eyes of the fat one was laughin' and the thin one was soft in her face.

'Peggin. That's a pretty name, to be sure.' She was lookin' at my bare feet. She was all bundled up in a coat and her boots was big and stout.

'You must be frozen. You're hungry, are you? Moses, take Peggin to Mary in the kitchen. Give her food and footwear. We'll be coming directly.'

Mary was tall with big, strong hands. She needed both to lift the black kettle from the hook over the fire to make tea. She cut bread, holdin' the loaf to her chest.

That crusty splittin' sound made my stomach ache, and the warm smell inside that kitchen had me grabbin' for it.

'Wait, would you?' Mary said. 'I've butter and cheese.'

I tried to eat like I had been told, takin' one bite and chewin' over and over. That were hard when I was wantin' to gobble fast as I could.

The butter was yellow and sloppin' in milk. Moses fetched the cheese from a little cupboard what had holes in the top part like mice holes. When he opened the back door, the fire went sideways and cold air chased in, but it was lovely and warm in that kitchen. My feet and legs were itchin' badder than anythin', but I didn't care. If you rub itches, they'll be worse, I knew that. But you can't stop yerself, so I ate with one hand and scratched with the other.

Mary don't miss a thing. I knew that from that day. Her nose goes pinched, then her mouth goes pinched too, then she does what she needs to. She took a pot down from the shelf above the fire. Then she took a big black knife from the block to get the bung out. Bits of wax fell all round her shoes. She gave the pot a sniff.

'Would ya let me, now?' she asked, lookin' straight at my feet. I stuck them forward. Her mouth went sideways and she whistled and put the pot on the table. She tipped water into a bucket. When I put my feet in, it didn't hurt 'cos the water was cold, the fat soap wasn't gritty and Mary was gentle that time. Moses took the bucket outside when the water was black. He looked at the water and made a face, lookin' at me with his mouth goin' down to make me laugh, but I didn't. Next, he turned away so I couldn't see and turned back with a crust of bread in his mouth turned into a grin. I snorted, like a laugh wantin' to get out but me not lettin' it.

'Is it a cold you're hatching there, Peggin? Poor lamb.' Mary said, pattin' my feet, which was all red now, with her own apron. Lovely that: eatin' bread while she greased my feet till they was shinin', with me on the box stool and Mary kneelin' there and callin' me her lamb.

When the Duckies came in, Mary stood up and went to talk to them over by the window. She had to lean down to hear what they were sayin'. Moses was sittin' at the table but soon as they came in, he put his hands down out of sight and jigged his leg up and down real fast, lookin' from them to me, and his eyes were all worrit.

They came and stood round me and I stayed sittin' on the box stool.

'How old would you be, Peggin?' the soft Duckie asked.

I didn't have to say nuffin', 'cos they answered themselves.

'Do you think she's eight?'

'She might be nine.'

'Or older?'

They bent down again, six eyes starin' at me.

I was ten 'cordin' to the old woman what sold me, but I didn't say. Those Duckies didn't know children.

'Where do you live now? Where are your mother and father? Are there any siblings that you have?'

'Sibbins' is a word I didn't know so I said nuffin', just kept shakin' my head.

'Is anyone looking for you? Will anyone be missing you?'

If you squeeze yer face up hard, it looks like cryin'.

The two Duckies looked at each other like they each knew what the other beloved was thinkin'.

'Mary, I'm certain you can find tasks for Peggin, as you are still without a second pair of hands after the last disaster!'

All three laughed and that was that.

They turned to Moses, leg still jigglin'.

'Ah, Moses,' the fatter Duckie said. 'You did the right thing bringing Peggin to us. Would you pass on a message to your father? We're reconsidering his position. Frankly, the garden is missing him. Tell him to be at the back door at seven tomorrow morning and Mary will give him back the key for the tools.'

Moses moved fast as a fox. And there I was, not knowing nuffin' about these people, but feelin' warm and fed and safe. When my head was heavy and my eyes was closin', I folded my arms on the table.

'They're the best!' Mary said, shakin' me awake. The Duckies had gone. 'Always thinking of others. It's nine sharp they retire and that is that. They'll be needing nothing else tonight. Books and each other is all they'll be wanting. Come follow me. I think we'll find you something better than the table to sleep on.'

She took my hand. Hers was so big and mine fitted inside, so small.

The room she led me to weren't that warm but it had walls and a door and a roof and windows. On the shelves there were big bottles lined up, which bubbled and belched away without stoppin'. Mary made a bed under one of the shelves: just a cover stuffed with straw with real sheets stitched down the centre. Mary said they'd been 'sides to middled'.

'Can you stitch, Peggin?' she asked. 'Did anyone teach you to do that?'

I shook my head. Safer.

'Do you know your letters, Peggin?' she asked, shakin' out this wool cover, all criss-crossed with yellow lines that had twists on the end. 'There's holes in this where the puppies chewed it, but it's clean washed and it'll have to do you,' Mary said, throwin' it over the sheet. 'Do you like dogs, Peggin? I hope you do. There's dogs everywhere here, and cats. And there's the fowls in the yard and soon we'll have a cow! Did you ever milk a cow, Peggin?'

I shook my head.

'Well, no matter. We'll hire a girl for that. You might help her with the churning and the like. Or you might help in the house. Cleaning and scrubbing and so on, and laying fires, if I showed you first. How about it?'

That little bed looked so soft, tucked in the dark under the bubblin' bottles, with the air so appley. I yawned real loud.

'Bless you, Peggin! And here's me rattling on and peppering you with questions, and there's you desperate for sleep. But you saw the colour of the water, my girl. What would be the point of putting you between clean sheets without washing you up first? Come with me to the bucket, and then I'll put you in a clean shift of mine for now. There's salt and a cloth there for your teeth.'

Mary weren't so gentle when I was standin' in me nuffins and the water was cold and the soap scratchy. And just when it was over, she started on my hair, tuggin' and pullin' till I thought I'd be bald when she let me go. I didn't cry out and when she finished, she hugged me to her and that was nice.

She lit a candle to take me back to my nest, which made everythin' flickery orange and the dark darker than it was and big black shadows slippin' over the walls. I didn't like it so she blew the candle out and they disappeared.

'I'll not leave the candle now, Peggin. We don't want the house up in flames, now, do we?'

It takes longer for bad things to slip away from your mind but the bottles bubblin' and the apple smell disappeared them in the end too.

I didn't tell them, but I did have a Ma – once. She give me to the priest and he sold me to the woman. I watched for my Ma every day. She never came. But a girl can't go on just waitin' and hopin'. If Ma didn't think about me then I wasn't goin' to think about her.

2

THOSE DUCKIES WOULDN'T do nuffin' that was wrong. I learned that from the first few weeks. Only good things. Like the next day when I was standin' on a box by the sink in the scullery, washin' the turnips which Moses' father Walter had just dug up. I looked up and there was an old, old woman starin' in at me. I screamed, 'cos she might have been a witch come to get me. I'd picked up a turnip so I was ready, when Mary came rushin' in, with the dogs barkin' and runnin' behind her.

'Jesus, Mother of God. You had my heart racing there, Peggin!' she said, openin' the back door. 'Get back, back!' She was kickin' the dogs away 'cos they was hungry to eat that old witch up.

Turned out she was Mad Annie from the hovel down the valley and the Duckies gave her money and food when she needed it.

'They're a thoroughly decent, Christian pair!' Mary added, and her face was all smiley and her voice soft.

As far as I could see, those two Duckies never went nowhere, though Mary said there weren't an inch of Wales their feet hadn't stepped on.

'Their roaming days are behind them, for they have found what they were seeking in Plas Newydd. Known and revered far and wide – and deservedly so, for they're generous, learned… they're the best of women!'

She talks like that, Mary does.

She went out, steppin' into the chaise which came from the village. She came back with boots and a dress, not new but new to me, pretty blue with checks. Mary dressed me up and sat back on her heels, smilin' so I could see all her teeth, and then she hugged me. She was the best, Mary. No one was ever so nice to me.

One day I'd been out to the wood pile to get sticks. The driest grass and littlest twigs to stuff into that hole under the bigger twigs, the black chunks of coal on the top. They had a special glove for the coal but it came up to my elbow so I used the tongs. Just like the pretty tongs in the sugar bowl, which I had to polish till I saw my face upside down.

Moses was in the kitchen talkin' to Mary.

'I asked Mr Edwards at The Hand, but he don't know,' I heard him say.

'Keep asking,' Mary told him, and then saw I was listenin' and went quiet.

Later, Moses was helpin' Walter, his dad, in the garden, bankin' up potatoes. I was just wanderin' through – 'explorin'', Mary called it. They both looked the same, only Moses was smaller: black hair down over their eyes so they was always puffin' at it. Soon as Walter went into his brick shed where he kept his flowerpots and tools, I came up behind Moses.

'Who's Mr Edwards? You bin checkin' on me?'

He shook his head quick.

'I know you're lyin'.' I pulled the fire tongs out fast from behind my back and bit him on the arm – black, witchy fingers clackin' at him.

'They told me to find out who you are.' His voice was mousey. 'But I can't.'

'I'm me and I'm here. And that's all you need to know,' I said, all fierce.

Fire tongs is nothin'. He could have knocked them out of my hands but when Mary told me at supper time fire tongs must not be used outside the house and the coal hole, I knew she'd seen me. Her face was stiff.

Every time the dogs barked, I was ready with the knife or the wood, or whatever was in my hand. People was always comin' by, too: the butcher, the fishmonger, some girl with milk or the eggs, Walter with the vegetables, the post boy, someone with a message from a neighbour. It ain't easy to live that jumpy.

3

G WENDOLYN ARRIVED AT Plas Newydd the next year.
I heard Mary tell Big Duckie, who'd come into the
kitchen dressed ready for the garden.

'She's 14, her mother's just died and she's five sisters! The
father's a waster and they're dirt poor.'

Big Duckie shook her head and her lips screwed up like
those words hurt to hear.

'I brought the guest list down, Mary. I'll leave it here on
the mantelpiece. Come on, Gypsy! We've work to do!' and she
left, still shakin' her head. That dog followed her everywhere.
She didn't need to tell it nothin'.

If we'd guests comin', that would mean laundry to be done,
fires to be laid and a whole day of jobs. Egg-collectin' I liked,
'cos it could be stretched out, sayin' you were huntin' a broody
that Moses said he'd seen under the hedge.

The sky was blue, the sun on the window.

'I'll get the eggs, shall I?' I said to Mary.

'Bless you now, Peggin. We've just hired Gwendolyn to
do that.'

'I don't mind!'

I knew the right basket, the one with the hooped handle
and round like a nest.

If I went round the front of the house, I'd find the Duckies
at work and they'd see me and have me helpin'. Safer to go

round the side and leave the Duckies to their arches and views. What's the point of views, makin' what you see so perfect all the time, like pictures and not like it is? If a tree wants to go one way, why make it go the other?

At the back of the house, behind the fowlery, the land went down sudden like an edge. Most days the wind blew strong, whistlin' round the corners and tossin' the branches of the trees like madness. But this day, when the new leaves were all limey, there weren't no wind and everythin' was louder: the chop chop of Walter diggin', a dog scratch-scritchin' at its fleas, an old horse cloppin' down the lane with the cartwheels turnin' in the mud. Behind that and the scuffin' and soft bumblecooie noise of hens searchin' for grubs was a new noise. I put the basket down on the grass at the top of the bank and went over the edge. It was steep. Even with legs bent, I had to run; a tree arched over the river saved me a wettin'. Weren't no distance from this bank to the other bank here, with the water tumblin' down between two rocks. I threw a stick in, watchin' it hurtle down the water and then slide off sideways into the calm place, circlin' round and round with no way back. I was searchin' for a stone to throw to help it out when a big girl with gold hair and pink cheeks came leadin' a cow down to the water on a rope.

I'd seen her before when she arrived, but I'd not spoke to her. She didn't see me. She was talkin' to the cow but I didn't know what the sounds meant 'cos it was Welsh, like singin'. The cow stopped and the rope went tight and the big girl said, 'What's the matter?' in English words. I jumped up and she jumped too, and so did the cow.

'Oh! I didn't see you!' she said, pattin' her chest.

'Gwendolyn? I was comin' for eggs.'

'Eggs are my job. But first Beauty's coming for a drink from the Cufflyman – that's the name of the river, isn't it, Beauty?' she said.

Plain stupid to talk to a cow what can't talk and wouldn't know and wouldn't care. Beauty flicked her ears and walked up to her knees in the mud, stretchin' her neck till those big fat lips touched the water. She sucked long and loud.

'That's our milk, that is,' Gwendolyn giggled.

'I'll get the eggs,' I said.

Gwendolyn couldn't stop me 'cos Beauty was still drinkin'.

'You don't know what to do,' she called out after me.

'I do.'

And I did. I knew about eggs from before.

'Did Gwendolyn show you how to mark them?' Mary asked when I got back. The kitchen smelt like it was the inside of a pie and the ceilin' was the crust. 'We've a system, you know. A way of doing things.'

They all had ways of doin' things except me. I went crossways when they was goin' in a straight line, like on that blanket Mary gave me for sleepin' under, with the holes where the puppies chewed it. When I went to sleep, I pulled the twists apart and in the mornin' I swizzled them up again.

The best hidin' place at Plas Newydd was in the barn, where the cats curled up in the sun. A cat can spring from sleep to hunter in a squeak. It crouches, it quivers, then it pounces – but that don't spoil the fun. A cat plays over and over: lettin' the mousey go just so it can pounce all over again. I like cats.

My second-best hidin' place was on the roof beam in the garden house. It was easy to get up there, just climbin' up the rope and walkin' along the thin part careful, one foot in front of the other like on a line, but I'm good at that kind of thing. Above the shelves, the beam was wide enough to lie on. I couldn't sleep in case I rolled off, but there was lots to see. Walter was in and out all the time and I know for what, 'cos he kept bottles under the flowerpots. Gardenin' was thirsty work. When they was empty, he went to the village to top them up.

I was up there one day 'cos Mary was looking for me to do somethin', when Walter comes in, has a drink, holds the bottle up to the light and shakes his head. He checks the money in his pocket and says to Moses, who's just comin' in, 'Off up The Hand, boy. Keep an eye out.'

They talk their Welsh up and down, but I heard him say 'The Hand', anyway.

Soon as Walter has gone, Gwendolyn's in there and so's Moses and they don't say much before they're kissin' and he's got his dirty hand up her skirt, and that's enough. I feel squirmy and bad so I cough really loud, and they spring apart and I jump down, laughin'. Gwendolyn's face goes so red.

'Don't you say anything to anyone,' Gwendolyn says, fierce and then soft. 'Please, Peggin. Just harmless fooling.'

'I might and I might not.'

She clamped her mouth shut so her lips were all disappeared into her face, and went.

Moses gave me a look from under his black thatch but his eyes were half smilin'. I shrugged.

'I knowed her from ages back,' he said. 'From the village. I don't even like her much.'

4

I GOT GOOD at things the longer I knew how they were.

There was a lane run right down to the village past Plas Newydd. Mostly it was horses and riders that came down our lane. Sometimes a coach came this way, though usually the visitors came the longer way round, where the lane was wider and not so steep. If you flatten yourself to the hedge, the worst that can happen is a splatter on your skirt when it bowls past, leaving hot horse stink and your ears ringin' like bells.

I was out blackberryin', further up the lane than usual so's to be right out of sight, nor hear them shoutin, neither. Mary was huntin' for me 'cos it was stitchin' and conversation time with the Duckies. If I filled my bowl with blackberries, Mary wouldn't be so cross. The worst she would do is shout. She never hit me, not even when I did something bad, like when she found the Duckies' seal tooth that one of the visitors gave them under my mattress. I took it from the little table in the library. It was so cold and hard and smooth and it just fitted in my pocket. I took one of Tatters' kittens to bed with me once, but Mary told me it was cruel 'cos the kitten was just born and needed its mother. That silly kitten mewed and yelled like I was going to murder her. Tatters got in such a state she ran about and tripped Mary up, so she fell and hurt her back.

'Jesus Mary Mother of God!' Mary shouted, her face all red and her eyes flashin' and vexed. 'You'd try the patience of a saint, Peggin. And if the Ladies would let me, I'd have your guts for garters, so I would!'

Gobs of spit landed on my new dress, which Lady Fanshawe had sent over for me 'cos I'd growed faster than a beanstalk, Mary said. 'And now you'll be doing all the work till I sort myself out.'

Mary's mouth was pinched and the nose with it, and when the Duckies heard the noise upstairs, they come runnin' to calm her down.

They said I was to come to them from now on to learn my letters and stitchin' and conversation at the same time. They'd threads and needles and Big Duckie would read while I stitched and then we would talk: how would I like that? I lied and said that I would – very much.

So there I was, a real distance from Plas Newydd that day, wonderin' why all the best, biggest blackberries can only be reached by the birds. I should have been sittin' on the hard stool, pokin' my needle into the hoop while the Duckies droned on and on, and I'd be fallin' asleep and would have to prick my finger to keep myself on the stool. I'd only got as far as H, with so many letters to go. Little Duckie sat near me with her inks and her paper in front of her on the table, light fallin' square on the paper, drawin' her maps. She was so patient, she made me feel like screamin'. That scream would be desperate to escape the room, shatterin' the coloured glass in the top of the window.

Talkin' was worse, 'cos they'd ask somethin' and I would begin to answer, and they'd be interruptin' all the time – which was somethin' I must never do – tellin' me to put sounds on at the end of words that didn't need to be there at all.

'*Ing*, Peggin, *ing*: sew*ing*, read*ing*, yawn*ing*.'

So there I was in the lane, right where it flattens round the fields, when I saw this really fat, ripe blackberry just past where I could reach, wavin' at me.

If I threw my shawl over the thorny brambles, surely I could reach it. I was just shakin' the shawl off my shoulders, movin' the basket from one hand to the other, when a chaise came round the corner – just the one horse, but it was goin' fast so I had to throw myself into the hedge. Instead of bowlin' past, it slowed down till the carriage was right by me and the little window opened and a man called out. I thought he was going to say sorry, and ask if I was alright.

'Plas Newydd?' he said. 'Are you the child from Plas Newydd?'

My heart was jumpin', but who did I know who could afford a carriage? I could always throw the blackberries at him if I had to, and run. But I was caught in the brambles.

'Please sir, yes sir. I am, sir.' I was all meek while I unpicked myself.

'How would you like a ride home, eh?'

I'd never been near enough to a carriage to see myself in the shine. He didn't look so bad. I'd be alright. This was my chance to ride in a carriage and I might never have that chance again! He folded down a little step and stretched out a hand, clipped nails and dark hairs on his knuckles. He never minded the blackberry juice on me. I sat on the little seat and he sat opposite beamin', with his white wig tipped on one side so I could see his own dark hair underneath. He weren't that old. He banged the roof. The strange thing was that he didn't go fast down the lane to the house but told the driver to pull up just short of the turnin'.

'Give the horses a rest here, eh?'

This didn't seem right. I got jumpy inside but didn't move. There I was, sittin' in a carriage which was all red and stuffed hard like the Duckies' pin cushion, opposite a man with whiskers and a tight jacket. You could hear the horse's harness jingle and the sparrows in the hedge.

He leant forward. His tongue went lickin' over his lips like I was good for eatin'.

'What's your name?'

'They call me Peggin. If you've come to get me...' I was edgin' towards the door, sittin' with my feet ready to run, but there was no handle that I could see, just a leather strap.

'No, Peggin. Nothing like that.' When he smiled, he pulled his chin into rolls of pink flesh. 'Peggin. Pretty name... Peggin, I was wondering if you could shed some light on the dear Ladies. People are interested... I'm a writer, you know. A newspaper man. I was hoping for your help. Naturally, you would be rewarded,' he said, feeling in his waistcoat and pulling out a coin.

'Know the Ladies, do you? Know their story?'

'I don't know nothin', sir. I'm only a maid.'

'Light the fires? That kind of thing?'

'I can lay a fire, sir.'

What did he want from me? I shouldn't have got in that carriage. I knew that now. The old woman who bought me warned me about men and their money, though she never knew what was goin' on right under her nose.

'Lay the fire in the Ladies' bedchamber, do you?'

'Not the bedchamber, the other girl does that.'

That wasn't true. I had done it, but there was nothin' I was goin' to tell him about that: not the four-poster bed with the curtains and the wood carved into creatures and leaves all twirlin'. I wasn't going to tell him nothin', him with his words polished so they slipped out not seemin' what they were, but his eyes sharp as thorns.

'Share the one bed, do they, the Ladies?'

I didn't like this. I wanted to say, 'So what if they do?' but instead I said, 'I could send the chamber girl out, sir, if you'd wait a moment.'

He gave me this look and his tongue went from one side of his mouth to the other. Should he? Shouldn't he? He knew he weren't going to get anythin' from me. He leaned out of the window and pressed the handle down.

I jumped out and raced across the yard, screwin' my nails hard into my hands till I was cryin'.

Mary was pluckin' a goose, squeezed between her knees, on the back step. Tiny white feathers floated round her like it was snowin'. I blurted out the story.

'You didn't tell him anything, did you?' Mary said, pressing her lips together, with little lines cutting down her forehead.

'I'd nothin' to tell.' She looked at me and saw it was true.

She left the goose hangin' out of the bucket, its long neck drippin' blood on the cobbles.

'Watch for the dogs, Peggin,' she called. She'd a face like a storm comin' and feathers stuck to her arms. She picked up the cleaver lyin' by her side next to the goose's head, which looked up at her, still not knowin' what was to come, nor what had just happened.

Stitchin' was forgotten that day. Mary was pleased with the blackberries, poppin' one into her mouth before she took them to the Duckies, givin' me a little squeeze as she passed.

'I'll explain your absence. They're very understanding, so they are.'

When she came back, she said, 'The letter H will still be waiting tomorrow. Come Peggin, you can get those little fingers to work. Pull out all the feather ends, now, like I showed you. We don't want Lady P cracking her teeth on a quill end, do we now? And tell me all the words you know that start with H. Begin.'

'There's *horrible* and *hate* and *hurt* and...' I liked that job, better than squeezin' the pus from spots or splinters.

'I was thinking of things like *horse* and *hazelnuts* and *hope*... nice words... *happiness*...' Mary said, pickin' up the cleaver, placin' the goose's feet on the wooden stool she'd been sittin' on and bringin' it down: crack. Two pink feet dropped to the cobbles. She picked the head up and dropped it in her pot, followed by one of the feet.

'*Hiccoughs*, *headache*...' I said.

Mary flicked at me with the second foot.

'Get away, you old misery guts! To the scullery now and start on those potatoes. Get the eyes out, now, like I showed you... we don't want eyes in the potatoes when we're serving the guests tonight: the Wynns, the Goddards and the Duke of Wellington himself! How about that? It'll be the best china.'

There were always guests comin'. Pity for us, because we had all the work to do, and no rest: polishin' the silver, food to prepare, layin' the tables and then cleanin' ourselves and puttin' on starched pinafores in case we might be seen. Mary always took the food into the dining room with Jeremiah the new butler, who wore trousers to the knee and long white socks. His shoes were like mirrors.

I just kept out of the way and no one came lookin' for me.

Not until after I sang 'The Cruel Mother', and I never had time to think of the consequences.

5

ONE DAY A cart came into the yard with somethin' tall sticking up at the back, covered in a tarpaulin.

The Duckies were in a frenzy of excitement and so were the dogs.

'Our aeolian harp has arrived, my beloved,' Big Duckie said. 'Our gift to each other!'

Little Duckie squeezed her hands together under her chin as though she was prayin'.

'Bring her in!' Mary said, grabbin' at the dogs and shooin' them into the scullery so she could pin back the door. My job was to keep them shut in as the men carried the harp into the house. The dogs and I stood at the door listenin' to the men strugglin' and pantin' and Mary shoutin', 'Mind the paint!', 'Mind the bannisters!' and the Duckies' distant voices shoutin', 'Up here!', 'In the window!'

When the cart clattered out of the yard, I let the dogs out and, after lunch when the Duckies were in the garden, I offered to black the grate in the library and polish the tongs, though a fire would not be needed, this being the summer.

I opened the door and there was the harp, set right in the window, its tall wooden frame like a tulip flower with strings top to bottom. Mary came up the stairs behind me, opened the window and stood back holdin' her finger in the air, her head on one side like she was waitin' for somethin'. A gust of wind lifted the curtains and the air around me was filled with music notes, which was soft then loud then soft, high and low together, strange and beautiful and sad all at once. Mary was noddin' and smilin' at me.

'Hear that, Peggin? The wind is the musician here. Wonderful, isn't it, though?'

'It sounds like a ghost,' I said.

'Get away with you, Peggin,' she said.

The next day was a rare one, when the Duckies went off with Mary in a carriage hired from The Hand. I don't know where they were goin', but they wouldn't be back till late. This was my chance.

I found Gwendolyn washin' out the milk churn in the cow byre. She was always nervous when I was there, as though she was not sure what was goin' to happen. This time I was very friendly.

'Can I help you with that, Gwendolyn? You'll not be wantin' to spoil your hands.'

She looked up, wonderin' which way it would go, but saw my face all concern for her. That put her in an easy mood. There's nothin' like two girls chatterin' to make them close.

'I'm not liking that Moses boy any more!' Gwendolyn said. 'He come after me with a big brown slug and I thought it was a dog's doings and he threw it at me and it was horrible. I don't know which is worse, a slug or dog doings? I never really liked him,' she said, lookin' at me.

'Come with me, Gwendolyn,' I said when we had righted the churn on its stand. 'I've somethin' to show you.'

Moses was wheelin' the pea sticks out to make a fire in the courtyard. 'Where you off to?' he asked.

'Wouldn't you like to know?' I smiled. Gwendolyn just put her nose in the air. A rotten plum hit Gwendolyn in the back. It was hard not to laugh.

Inside, we crept up the stairs and I tapped on the door. You can't be too certain. I made Gwendolyn wait outside while I went in and opened the window and closed the velvet curtains round the harp so it couldn't be seen, and the long window at the end so the room was dark. She came in but I had my fingers on my lips. I cupped my ear and made a frightened face. That sound was just like a ghost, all low and moanin', and the curtain made it softer too. Gwendolyn went pale and trembly in an instant, turned and ran out of the room, patterin' off down the stairs with a big plum splat on her back.

The trick had gone just fine. I pulled back the curtains and started singin':

There was a lady lived in the North
Oh, the rose and the linsie, O
She fell in love with her father's clerk
Down by the greenwood sidie, O

Where that song come up from, I couldn't say, but this voice from behind me made me jump. I hadn't thought the Duckies would be back so early.

'Peggin! What a beautiful voice. I had no idea!' Little Duckie was standin' in the doorway with her hands clasped together. 'What is that song called? I'm not familiar with so many Welsh songs, more Irish.'

'It's "The Cruel Mother", ma'am. It's English, I think. I used to sing it with… my father.'

I don't know why I said that, probably because she'd caught me out like that. I don't even remember my father so how could I have sung it with him? She didn't tell me off, nor ask why I was there, nor nothin', just came into the room removin' her hat.

'How lovely that is, and the memory of your dear father. I have no memories of my own.'

I didn't say nothin'.

'Poor Eleanor has a migraine again,' she said, 'or I'd have brought her in to hear you. Another time.'

6

'A BATH, A hair wash, new clothes,' Mary told me, luggin' the iron bathtub into the back kitchen a few days later. Gwendolyn had not talked to me since I'd scared her witless. When I told Moses, he laughed till I thought he'd burst.

'Those are the orders from upstairs,' Mary said, sloshin' the water into the bath from a jug of hot water filled from the copper. She was strong, was Mary. 'They've company tonight and you are to sing for them. I never knew you had a voice on you, Peggin!'

'Me? Sing? Never. On my life, I can't!' I said, but Mary took no notice. She pulled my work dress off careful enough, but she'd not the kind way with the soap she had when I first arrived. She never hugged me to her like she had when I was smaller.

'It's a sad song is it, this "Cruel Mother"?' she asked, as she tugged at my tangled hair.

'It is.'

'Keep your head still, will you, Peggin? Did you have a mother now, Peggin, that you remember? I hope she wasn't cruel. Look at the state of you! I'll be quick as I can. Nothing lasts forever.'

She picked up her metal comb and started her torture. I kept still as she told me to.

'Do you not want to tell your story, Peggin? Is that it?'

She stopped her combin', so I spoke.

'My mother was cruel. She sold me to an old woman to be rid of me, so I might as well be dead. I sang with my father when I was small. I'd take the pennies in my pinafore.'

'Oh, that's nice now.' Mary's face was all soft.

'But that was before he took to the drink… he's dead now.'

'Ah, but you recall the song… Do you want to sing it to me like a practice before you sing in front of strangers?'

I cleared my throat.

'The Cruel Mother.'

There was a lady lived in the North
Oh, the rose and the linsie, O
She fell in love with her father's clerk
Down by the greenwood sidie, O

I didn't do all the verses 'cos the water was cold and scummy. Mary was shakin' her head by verse two.

'Same old story,' she said, helpin' me out of the bath, holdin' out the cloth to pat me dry. 'A man taking advantage of a poor love-sick lass.'

'She's the cruel mother!' I said. 'She killed her babies. And she's going to hell, which is what she deserves.'

'And the man gets off scot-free!' Mary said. 'Ain't that the way. But that's a gorgeous singing voice you have there, Peggin. That's a gift from God, so use it well.'

From that time, I was maid in the day and entertainment for the guests in the evening – men and women, mostly women, though the men liked me best. Their eyes went tearful and they shook their heads when I sang. It was the men who asked for more.

'Sad or happy?' I asked, though I knew they'd say sad. I could do 'Over the Hills and Far Away', but they always chose 'The Lunatic Lover'.

Those Duckies were proud of me like I was their own, like the harp or the books or the food Mary cooked with the vegetables from their own garden – though Walter grew those, and God.

The fuss from those frizzy-haired ladies was nice, and whiskery old men patting my hand and stroking my hair till I felt like Flick or Tatters or Gypsy, or whatever the dog or cat the Duckies had at that moment.

I didn't care how important they were, nor what they done, nor whether they was a Lord or a Sir or a poet or a soldier, 'cos I was the one who made the song in the room.

And then it was all over. Off came the pretty dress and it was all back to normal.

'Peggin, do this. Peggin, do that.'

More and more, as I got older.

7

THERE'S MORE YOU can do and less you can do when you grow. You find that your skirts is short so the snow nips your ankles and you've those sores up your legs and on your heels again. Your boots pinch and your hands and arms stick out of your sleeves. Your clothes wear so thin you can see through them. When you catch your skirt on the door handle, carrying the coal to the library, it rips; you're to blame and your punishment is cutting the patches out and stitching, squinting to sew small and neat enough for the work to pass Mary's testing eyes.

'You're turning into a clumsy careless girl now, Peggin, with your mind always whirling ahead of you. You're not 10 now, you know.'

Then Sara came and everything was worse. I had to move out from under the shelf of bubbling bottles to sleep in the same room as her. She was 12 and I was only a few years older by my reckoning, but she was small and nipped about, bobbing and Ma'aming all the time, so everyone loved her. Her eyes were green and her hair like beechnuts, which is better than mousey like mine. And Mary was kind to her like she used to be kind to me.

'Don't you be lifting that heavy bucket now, Sara. Peggin will do that for you. She will be showing you how to lay the fires, now, and polish the fire tools and the fender, so.'

When Mary gave her a squeeze, holding her close, my heart went fast and I wanted to be where Sara was, and I wanted to hurt Sara so bad.

Sara was scared of me. I don't know why. I didn't give her no reason; she just was, right from the start – forever trembling and saying, 'Sorry, Peggin,' all the time.

One evening there was a fire in the chimney when we were all in bed. Mary told us the story the next morning 'cos we had to spread sheets over everything in the drawing room and roll up the carpets. Big Duckie had been reading a letter which made her so mad she threw it in the fire and once it had caught light, it blew up the chimney, where it became stuck, putting the whole chimney in danger. Big Duckie screamed and screamed, but Little Duckie leapt into the grate, stuck her hand up the chimney and pulled the letter out.

'Such bravery,' Mary told us. 'Her arm is burnt and terrible sore. That letter must have been the size of a pamphlet to get so stuck! No doubt it was something about money, to make Lady Eleanor that mad! No, girls, I didn't say that. Just think, if Miss Ponsonby had not acted so quick, we'd all have been burnt alive in our beds!'

She saw me frowning.

'The Ladies, Peggin! They have names, you know.'

I wasn't bad to Sara at all. I was the one to show her how to make the sticks stand up in the kitchen grate, packing the kindling loose underneath, heaping the small coals on the top. When I sparked a flame from the tinder box for her, she jumped backwards as though I was going to set fire to her. The day after the practice, we had a fire to prepare for real.

'There's the library fire upstairs to lay, 'cos the Ladies spend the morning in there with their learnings and their poetry.

They like a warm room, but you must never ever touch their things, Sara, or they will go mad and torture you.'

I liked to make her eyes go terrified.

Out we went to fill the buckets with coal and wood, stuffing our pockets with moss for kindling; in we went, scraping the mud from our boots at the kitchen door. Up we went to the library, which was cold and quiet with the rain slashing on the windows. The Duckies wouldn't be outside on a day like this. Even so, the light coming through the coloured glass at the top of the window made everything weak pink and yellow. Sara had never been in here before and she gawped at all the books and the shelves like a simpleton, with her mouth open.

'Have you never seen a book before?' I said. She closed her mouth. I could have told her the harp was a ghost, but I didn't. Her eyes went huge when I opened the window just a crack to make it sing.

I handed her the brush and told her to sweep the ashes into the burlap bag. Cold was blowing down the chimney and the raindrops pocked the hearth. When it was clean as an old fireplace could be, I told her to take off her shoes and her dress.

'Go on, now, do as I say.'

'Yes, ma'am.'

'And don't call me "ma'am" 'cos I'm not. Just Peggin.'

There she stood in her shift with bare feet, her top half disappearing up the chimney.

'Look up. Can you see the sky?'

I picked up the brush with the long handle and tickled her ankles. She jumped clear off the ground, then bent down with her beechnut hair black.

'I thought it a rat!' she said. She was white and all shivery. 'I'm not fond of rats.'

'Just stand and reach as high as you can with this brush.'

What's a bit of soot anyway? I didn't think there'd be much after the sweep had been but I certainly didn't think Sara'd fuss so, sobbing and spitting as she put her dress back on, running away down the stairs with her shoes in her hand.

Mary said Sara didn't tell tales, she didn't need to; it was quite obvious what a mean, nasty girl I was.

'As ye sow so shall ye reap, Peggin. Remember that!'

'What did I do? What?'

Sara was snivelling by the sink and rubbing her hands with an old rag.

'Nothing, Mary. I did it myself,' Sara said, looking down, not at me, though I was staring at her.

No one believed her. Mary said it was a spiteful, cruel thing to do. It wasn't! I was just making a bit of fun in a day that didn't have much fun in it. Even fun was serious in this house, although you could hear Mary singing and laughing with the Duckies sometimes, or a roar of laughter from the men in the dining room. I never heard the lady guests laugh. I suppose their wigs would fall off.

8

Six months later

YOU NEVER KNOW when the last time has arrived until you look back.

I was called for one summer evening when I'd been sweating all day in the kitchen, helping Mary with the pies and pastries. Sara and I were laying the table, with the silver and the glasses just so. Mary did the plates because she didn't trust me to get the little blue crest in just the right place. I don't know why – it's the simplest task. Little Duckie came in, her hair still in its papers.

'Ah, Peggin. You'll be singing for us tonight?'

It was a question, but not a question. She glanced over the table, checking everything was like she wanted.

'Flowers. We need flowers, Sara.'

The heat in the kitchen would have wilted the strongest flower. Sara's sister Elizabeth was coming to Plas Newydd specially to arrange the roses in the cool outhouse. Walter would pick them for her, 'cos of the thorns.

All the windows were open in the kitchen and the swifts were zipping to and fro outside, screaming 'cos they was free. Mary had the mutton and the fowl already cooked and standing. She slid the game pie into the range for browning, all washed with egg – a waste, if you ask me – and all the while she was telling me what to do.

'Wash yourself now, Peggin. Make sure you smell sweet. Do your hair, now. On with your dress. Mrs Gibby's given it a press.'

Mrs Gibby came in from the village once a week to do the ironing – after I tried once but burnt my hand so bad that it came up in a blister, which popped and bled white blood onto my dress. It wasn't me they were worried about: the dress was burnt through and only of use to the poor, who would not mind a hole in their clothes. This dress was tight over my chest, which was swelling out now and tender. It was hard to take the breath. I was practising how it would feel when I felt the material tear and my lungs filled a bit more.

Mary, who doesn't miss a thing, spun round, whacking the range door closed with her leg.

'I heard that. Oh, sweet Lord, what are we to do?'

She wiped her forehead quick with both her forearms – swipe, swipe.

'Take my shawl from the chest there. You're to keep it round you all the time, Peggin, and stand with your back to the door. When you've finished the singing, don't turn round, now, but back out.'

I would have said something, but her eyes told me to hush and not to point out that if I had the shawl anyway, what was the reason for backing out? Sometimes it's best to bite your tongue.

The candles and the lamps made it sweltering hot in that dining room, with the air like mutton fat, but I kept that shawl round me. Quite a time I stood waiting for quiet and the sign from one Duckie or the other. Those Duckies never dressed in fancy clothes – always the same, plain and comfortable with their hair rolled – while their friends had all manner of colours in their dresses, and necklaces and earrings which caught the candlelight. I was near to faint when I cleared my throat and they turned and looked at me and hushed. Little Duckie smiled but Big Duckie looked cross, with her bottom lip pouting out.

'"The Cruel Mother",' I said, clear and loud 'cos some of the guests were hard of hearing, and then I sang it like I had a hundred times. I finished:

God keep me from the flames in Hell
Down by the greenwood sidie, O

They clapped. One man tapped his glass with his fork and I smiled and nodded and kept my eyes down like I'd been told.

I hadn't had the nod from the Duckies to go before this man with white hair and a great domed forehead and a black flop of a tie at his throat asked, 'The tongue of the bell? Was that it, young muse?'

I didn't know it was me he was talking to. I thought a muse meant something to laugh at and it was a sad song.

'It's a question for you to answer, Peggin,' said Big Duckie. Her voice was sweet but I heard the hard underneath. 'Was it a tongue, now?'

'"Welcome, welcome, the tongue in the warning bell…" I don't know what it means.'

I did not expect them all to laugh at that, but they did.

And then they turned their backs and were having this conversation all about tongues and clappers and 'What did you call it now?', and 'Did you ever have occasion to call it anything? Ha ha.' All washed down with mouthfuls of the wine which had bubbled over my bed last year.

The red wine was dark as Elizabeth's rose 'arrangement', as Mary called it. I was thinking about those nights with the window wide and the air so very sweet when I saw Little Duckie was frowning and nodding at me. I backed out carefully, feeling for the door behind me.

Those Duckies were never far from a bell to call for this or that. That's the best part of being a Duckie. Even in the garden they had a bell. I was walking by it the next day, right by one of their arches which smelt like heaven – the bees thought so too. I stopped by that bell with just the tip of its ringer lower than the dull grey rim. Moses, who was as tall as his father by now, came walking round the corner that very moment, pushing a wheelbarrow with a pitchfork lying over it. No doubt he'd been called to clear the tree branches the Duckies were chopping off nearby. You would not think you could have a thought and act on it in the time it takes to slip behind the hedge, but I rang the bell hard just as Moses was one pace away. I skipped behind the privet hedge, just catching his face all startled.

Through the leaves I saw the Duckies look round. Big Duckie's face was red.

'Moses! Was that you? Ringing the bell is forbidden. You know that. Forbidden.'

Moses stood dumbly shaking his head. 'Weren't me.'

'I don't see anyone else about!' Big Duckie said. 'You are turning into a liar, Moses, as bad as your father!'

Both Duckies had put down their loppers. I think they were too hot and glad of a reason to stop.

Walter appeared from behind the ball-shaped hedge near the Duckies. He weren't too steady on his feet. 'I'm no liar and neither is my son!' he said, swaying like a tree in the wind.

'Right!' Big Duckie turned to face him. 'If you are no liar, Walter, where have you been? Eh?'

In his face I could see Walter trying to find a way out, but he never found it.

'I've had enough of the pair of you. Moses is a chip off the same block. You can both collect your wages and be gone.'

I never meant that to happen. I knew Big Duckie had a temper on her. I'd heard it and seen it before. But this was unfair. Little Duckie picked up her loppers and went on chopping. She knew how things were. I'd half a mind to step out and say, 'It was me.' I didn't, though, because where would I go? What would I do? There were chances round every corner for men. I must not feel bad.

Moses was my friend, though. I didn't want him to go. I went to the potting shed and stood in the doorway, watching him returning the pitchfork to its hook. He stuck his jaw out. He'd nothing to say to me.

'I'd have left the fork for them bitches to put back,' I said.

If only he'd spat at me or punched me, or something. He didn't even look at me, just lifted a flowerpot, took out a bottle, held it to the light and put it in his pocket. He collected his father's coat from the shelf, shook off the soil, pushed past me and was gone.

'I suppose your father has gone back to The Hand to get drunk!' I called after him.

Outside, everything was very bright, burning on the eye: the cobbles and the path and the swifts skimming the grass in the meadow. Moses was marching straight for the cow byre. I could have followed but I didn't. I just stood there till he came out, Gwendolyn running after him. She stopped and turned.

'You, Peggin. I hate you!' she cried.

9

I DIDN'T WANT anyone to hate me and now everyone did. Mary had had to find a new gardener and a lad '*tout de suite*', Big Duckie said. She set off to the village grim-faced, leaving me and Sara to do all the work. There were no guests that evening, but salad leaves with caterpillars to remove, radishes to cut, cold mutton which Jeremiah could slice, and a ham. The meat jelly must be spooned away and saved in the cold store, and there were eggs to boil and blackberries and apples to stew. Gwendolyn arrived with the butter but there wasn't that much because of the weather, and the pat was melting.

She gave the bowl to Sara, ignoring me.

'*Mae'n rhy boeth* – it's too hot,' she said, followed by some more Welsh words that made Sara giggle. I didn't like that so I told her to stuff her mouth or I'd tell the Duckies I saw her drinking the milk, and she'd had a white moustache to prove it. She huffed away, rubbing her mouth with little sideways glances at Sara, whispering words to her as she passed, looking straight at me.

'What did she say?'

Sara was slicing the radishes. 'Nothing.'

'Something about me?'

'No. Not you. Just… It's hot.'

I knew that wasn't it.

When Sara wasn't the new girl any longer, when she was a bit older, we grew closer. We were like bean seeds, one growing one way, one the other, ending up twisting round the same stick. We worked together. We slept together and, in that time before you fall into sleep, we'd talk. There's nothing like holding someone's stories.

In the dark when we couldn't see each other's faces, Sara grew chatty and she liked to tell me everything. I didn't trust her not to gossip about me so I didn't tell her anything I minded the whole world knowing.

'Are you Welsh, like Gwendolyn?' I asked one night.

'I am.'

'Do you speak Welsh at home?'

'Welsh or English. My father was English, but he's dead now. He went to war and he never came back to us: two girls and five boys and my mother… but she's dead now too and our brothers are gone, so there's just Elizabeth and me…'

'My father's dead too. My mother sold me to an old woman. I was a slave.'

'Slavery's terrible. That's what we Methodists think.'

The owls were hooting in the woods. If the wind blew right, you could hear the harp from our room.

'The Ladies are Catholic,' Sara whispered. 'Did you know?'

'I did.'

'They're Irish.'

I knew that.

'They ran away together from Ireland.' Sara dropped her voice to a whisper, though there was no one to hear but me. 'The talk in the village is they eloped.'

'What does that mean?'

Sara didn't know either.

'I know it's bad,' she said. 'Because the first time they eloped, they were caught and thrown into prison, but Mary helped them escape and they rowed over to Wales in a little boat with their dog. And they got captured by pirates who took their money and that's why they've got none.'

They were always worrying about money, that was true, sending letters every day and Little Duckie forever adding the figures in her books. Even Mary was worried, sitting at the kitchen table with her calculations, in a terrible mood. If you so much as dropped a teaspoon, she'd shout at you.

'You eejit! Now I've to start all over again!'

In all my years at Plas Newydd – seven – I'd never heard the story Sara had told me that night. There might be truth in it, or there might not. When Mary finished bargaining with the fishmonger the next day, she was in a more cheerful mood.

'Mary, did you row across the ocean from Ireland?'

'Row! Who told you that? We came in a regular ship. Row! That's a good one!'

'And were you captured by pirates?'

She shrieked with laughter. 'No, we were not! Though we had to wait to cross because the sailors wouldn't risk the journey with Pirate John Paul Jones about. Rumours or not, I don't know. We never saw them, thank the Lord.' Quickly she crossed herself, with her hands covered with fish scales from her scraping. Fish scales stick to everything worse than feathers from a fowl, but the worst part of a fish is their eyes and the way they stare at you, round and gluey like they're cursing you for killing them.

'What's elope mean, Mary?'

She turned on me fast, knife in her hand, arms shimmering with scales.

'Who's been saying what to you, now? Gossips and people taking an interest where they should not! Two friends retiring together is all they are and the best ladies in the world. I chose to come with them, I'll have you know, when I had good reason to stay in Ireland. I had a good position with Lady Betty, and my old mother is there still, God protect her and forgive me. Now get that fish wrapped in paper and forget things that don't concern you.'

I had it in mind to tell her it was Sara who told me, but there was no strong reason to and every reason not to. Gwendolyn was dancing around Sara; she was jealous of me now Sara and I were friendly. Just that morning Gwendolyn had bounced into the kitchen to invite Sara, in English, to the dairy to see the new cow, glancing at me and then speaking Welsh words very fast. They know I don't know what they're saying exactly, but I know the sense from the way they look and it ain't nice. I act like I don't care when people don't like me. But I do.

PART II
Joe

10

J OE BEGG WAS early for the meeting. Down on the riverbank, he dipped his hands into the cool water to pick out four large river stones to hold down the corners of the aqueduct plans and, though the stones weighed heavy in his pockets, he was pleased by his foresight.

He turned on to Llangollen bridge, pausing to look down on the River Dee, which was running fast after the unseasonal July rain. Bad news for fishing, the current being strong enough to take your legs from under you. However, as he hadn't the time to fish, that was barely of consequence.

A duck swam out of the reeds, followed by her brood. No longer downy, the youngsters were still small, struggling to follow their mother. The strongest one stayed as close as he could, chest and head stretched out; the two behind darted this way and that and were suddenly caught in the current and swept away under the bridge. Joe tensed, wanting to call out, to alert the mother, knowing, as he thought it, that would be to no avail. Nature's way. And yet, and yet.

Three siblings split, carried off in different directions by irresistible currents. How miserable they made him feel, these moments, facing his own inability to fulfil his promises, to find his sisters. At the moment he had not the time even to think of his wife and children. Success: that was Joe Begg's problem, forcing him to live his life forward with no time to take a backward step. One day, one day! He would fulfil his promise. With this meeting in front of him, he must be rid of all personal thoughts and be the clear, thoughtful, dependable, grateful man Mr Telford knew him to be.

The bell at the church of St Collen struck once. On the far side of the bridge he passed the Corn Mill, his last project. Those paddles he had helped to reconstruct must be turning at such a speed with the Dee thundering down so fast. An excellent job they had made. There was talk in the town of a woollen mill and a cotton mill too, and with the aqueduct, there would be no stopping the improvement of Llangollen and the people's lives in it. Joe's small part in it all was surely something to make his children proud.

Two hours later, in the back room of The Eagle, Joe stood in the shadows behind the sturdy oak support post, ready should anything be required. Mr Jessop and Mr Telford leant over the table examining the plans for the aqueduct. Both men had shed their topcoats. The windows were open to cool the air. Today, even the sound of the Dee did nothing to bring relief.

'Ready, I think, Mister Architect?'

'I believe so, William. Though I prefer the word 'engineer', sir!' Thomas Telford's voice lifted with a Scottish lilt.

Of all the ways of speaking Joe had heard, it was the Scottish he liked the best. He admired every part of this man who had taken him under his wing and given him opportunities he could never have dreamed of.

'I started knowing nothing, Mr Begg,' Mr Telford had said. 'You learn as you live... trial and no errors, please.'

Just as the great William Jessop had helped Mr Telford, so Thomas Telford had helped Joe. One day, he too might be in a position to show his faith in another human being.

From outside came the sound of a chaise, hooves clattering on the cobbles, bridles jangling, horses huffing and snorting. Joe glanced out of the window. Two men stepped out of the coach, straightened their waistcoats and exchanged excited looks. On the glossy carriage door was an unmistakable shield: three wolves on a white background, the coat of arms of Sir John Myddleton himself!

'Where are these plans, then?' Sir John, Joe presumed, strode into the room, throwing his blue topcoat and tall hat to Joe, who placed them neatly on the settle. Sir John tugged at the kerchief round his fleshy neck with fat fingers. What a waistcoat: thick with embroidered flowers! Clara would love that, the work in it. A vision of dear Clara flashed into Joe's mind, sewing that petticoat for her trousseau a few years back: such fine stitching, he could not believe it would be an undergarment, with only his eyes admiring it!

Mr Telford stood back. 'Come, Joe – you must be in on this, lad!' he said, beckoning Joe into the light.

Joe jumped forward, his face red, unable to believe he was found thinking of Clara's shift at such a moment.

'Joe Begg here – my assistant – will be involved from the start, gentlemen,' Mr Telford said. 'Mr Davidson, my second-in-command, is unable to be with us today. Busy on another of my little schemes.' He paused for laughter, but only Mr Jessop smiled. 'Joe may be relied on for the day-to-day running of the project, paying the wages, keeping the books, and so on. Naturally I will oversee the whole enterprise. Joe will be the bridge between us all!' He paused and winked at Joe.

The men circled the table, viewing the plans – stopped from curling up by Joe's river stones – from every angle. Details were explained, features pointed out, calculations decoded. 'In love with the impossible': wasn't that how Mr Telford described his passion? Joe Begg knew exactly what he meant.

The plan was of great beauty! Audacious! On paper it was feasible: those elegant tapered pillars – 18 of them, four in the Dee itself – linking bank to bank across the river; the arches, each 45 feet wide; the solidity of the canal they supported, matched, visually, by the solidity of the ground onto which the pillars must be built. The plans themselves were works of art: the elevations, the sections. 336 yards long, 12 feet wide and 5' 3" deep, 126 feet above the River Dee. The figures, so small and neatly written, were beyond imagining. Never could Joe aspire to the great man's genius and vision, but penmanship: that was something he could achieve with diligence and practice.

'We have the approval; we have the site.' Mr Telford's voice strained to convey his need to persuade but not presume. 'It will be a mighty investment, but with your endorsement, gentlemen, work could commence forthwith.'

Mr Jessop nodded his head in agreement. Mr Telford pushed his wire spectacles to the bridge of his nose. Sir John Myddleton tapped his teeth with the silver top of his cane. If his eyes were an indication, he'd been impressed.

'This would bring untold wealth into our district. Barges linking us to the Chester canal, opening up the northern markets, the ports – the world, by jingo! My mind is bursting with the possibilities!'

Agreement was reached and hands shaken – with Joe included, at Mr Telford's insistence.

Joe slipped away, rubbing his palms. To think that his hand had been shaken by these eminent, wealthy men of position and standing! He approached the bar with a grin on his face and joy in his heart.

'Jennet!' he called loudly, raising his hand. A few of the men from the town, drinking at the far end of the bar, looked round. Recognising Joe, they relaxed, raising their tankards to him.

'Serve Joe first.'

Joe touched his forehead with his finger.

'Good men.' Joe ordered brandy and five glasses for the toast. Grand to be in this position: a fulcrum. Lean one way and you were where you came from; lean the other and you were where you wanted to be.

'I'll be carrying them in, will I, sir?' Jennet said with mock deference. Sir! – Joe smiled at that! Yes: if Jennet handed the drinks round, he could drink to the success of the scheme with the other men.

'To the aqueduct!' Sir John proposed the toast as they clinked their glasses over the plans. 'The aqueduct!'

11

JOE'S ROOM UPSTAIRS in Mrs Evans' cottage was simply furnished: a bed, a ewer of water and a bowl, a cedar chest. What else does a man need? The ceiling was low. Even he, a small man, must walk with a stoop to avoid banging his head, as he had on his first night. He still bore the scar on his hairline. Once was the only lesson he needed.

He stooped lower to look out of the mullioned window over the river to the Berwyns. On this warm summer evening the hills folded into each other, green dotted with white sheep on the lower slopes, rising to the purple heather and hard outcrops of rock. He thought of Clara. If her nightshirt slipped, and in his thoughts he could make it do so, he could glimpse the pale curve of a shoulder or rise of her collarbone and that one dark mole. He opened the window on the hinge and secured it at the second notch. If it should happen to rain in the night and he did not wake, the second notch would keep the rain outside and not stain the floorboards, as a previous occupant had. Open like this, he could hear the twitter of the house martins swooping in and out of their perfectly engineered mud cups under the eaves. Had he been minded to, Joe could have reached out and seized the babies. In truth, the joy of the day was a glimpse of a wobbling head or wide triangular yellow gape.

Cool water on the neck and under the arms was bliss. Slowly, Joe unfastened the buttons on his britches. Never a day went by when he didn't finger those buttons, thinking of the days sitting at the long table with the other apprentice, George. What a distance he had travelled from there to here.

***

Of the Webbers' two apprentices, Joe was the quicker learner. He and George sat at opposite ends of the table in the workshop. Concentration and silence were the best conditions for making buttons. From the blocks of seasoned wood, Joe cut the squares, a precise job which he enjoyed, measuring and marking the wood with a nick.

Total absorption in the task at hand stopped Joe thinking of his mother and sisters. Gradually, the pain inside lessened.

After a couple of years, Joe could produce a button with the exactitude Mr Webber required, fashioning the stem, the shavings falling in curls to the floor. The hole through the stem for the thread must be precise also, finished with the finest awl. The light was poor, the window being at the far end of the room, but Joe knew by the feel exactly how it must be. Buttons, though small, were vital to every person who wore clothes with a fastening – a satisfying thought to Joe. He had no complaints.

Every Saturday evening the apprentices took a bath, and were inspected by Mrs Webber: fingernails, necks and behind the ears – any part visible above clothing. Sunday mornings they went to chapel, which fed Joe new and helpful ideas. His favourite hymn was by William Cowper:

God moves in a mysterious way
His wonders to perform
He plants His footsteps in the sea
And rides upon the storm…

When the preacher took for his sermon the text 'How unsearchable are his judgments and how inscrutable his ways!', Joe knew God was talking directly to him, making it easier to accept how things were.

Mrs Webber's food was the best he had eaten. Two meals a day, with meat or fish from the river and bread Mrs Webber made herself: soft on baking day, harder as the week progressed. On Sunday afternoons Mr Webber would take Joe and George fishing, showing them how to tie the stale bread to the hook and how to cast the line. Joe, standing braced against the force of the river, thinking of God planting his feet in the sea and riding the storms, experienced the greatest joy in his life, until it was surpassed by his first catch: a tug on the line, the fish breaking the water, the sinewy toughness of life in his hands, and the look in the fish's eye after he had brought Mr Webber's cudgel down on its head.

'No need for excess violence, boys,' Mr Webber said. 'A short sharp tap is sufficient.'

Joe was not a violent young man. 'Could you not let it die naturally?'

'A slow death or quick?' Mr Webber asked. 'Which would you rather?'

An unexpected memory of his father flashed into Joe's mind: Luca with his dead legs, roaring with misery as he wheeled himself on his makeshift trolley through the mud. Joe did not like or need to think about those times.

Mr Webber's eyesight was failing, his hands shaky. One day he knocked over his ink, staining wood and clothing alike. All Mrs Webber's remedies proved ineffective. Turning misfortune to opportunity, Joe discovered not only that buttons marbled with ink could be made desirable, but also a skill he was unaware of: his ability to write neatly and legibly.

When the accident happened, Mr Webber had been in the middle of an important letter on his wife's behalf.

'What can I do? This is urgent! Money is at stake!' Mr Webber flapped the paper in his hand, his grey curly hair bouncing like falling wood shavings. Joe took the quill from his hand.

'Tell me what to write, sir,' he said. He concentrated on the precision of the letters, not on the content, something legal about monies owing to Mrs Webber. Joe finished it, Mr Webber signed the bottom with his signature, and Joe blotted it with sand.

'Where did you learn to write like that, Joe?' Mrs Webber stood looking over his shoulder.

'Not from my mother nor my father. They didn't have need for writing. It must have been the priest when we were living with him. He made me copy texts from the Bible. I sat at his desk, but my feet didn't reach the floor and he didn't like me to tuck my feet up on the wooden bar. He taught me to speak nicely too.'

'He did a good job. You speak lovely, Joe,' Mrs Webber said.

Under the workshop table, Joe lay on his back, staring up at the slab of wood. Above the table was the space where he worked in the day, then above that the tiled roof, on up to the vastness of the dark, lit only by chinks of starlight. When he was at the priest's house, he had made patterns of the stars he could see from his bedroom window. Here, he would make those same patterns in his mind.

Thinking about the priest was confusing. Joe might have been fortunate, but what of his mother, Baby and Aggie? He had not prayed for them, nor thought of them, enough. True, his concern was to work hard so that one day he might have wages sufficient to find accommodation so that all the family could be together once more. This excuse did not satisfy him, resulting in a night of fitful sleep. When George shook him awake the next morning, the Webbers, ready for church, were waiting below.

Whether things happened by luck, design, divine providence or in an utterly random way, Joe found difficult to decide. The visiting preacher that Sunday morning, an old man with Old Testament sensibilities, chose as his text Ecclesiastes 5. Not a book that Joe had ever heard of before – their usual preacher kept to the New Testament.

"'Be not rash with thy mouth… When thou vowest a vow unto God, defer not to pay it; for he hath no pleasure in fools: pay that which thou hast vowed.'"

The preacher leaned forward, gripping his lectern with white knuckles as he began his sermon, repeating the verse, "Be not rash with thy mouth…" Words which bounced round the stone walls like thunder, meeting and mingling with the same words spoken a few seconds before. Joe had been rash with his mouth. He had made a promise which he had 'deferred to pay'. He was the fool. He had stood looking down into his father's hollowed eyes at the top of the hill leading down to the river. 'Promise me lad. Let me hear you.' 'Promise,' Joe had said – anything to be released from his father's presence.

'People of good character keep their promises!' the preacher thundered, shaking his lectern, his fierce eyes locking with Joe's own.

Joe shifted position. The wooden pew was hard. Joe had kept his promise to his mother, though. When she had handed him up onto the cart which was to take him to Oswestry, she would not let go until he had faced her, looked into her eyes and nodded in response to what she was telling him.

'You make a good life for yourself now, Joe. You are not to come looking for me. I don't want you seeing me in no Poor House. Promise me that, Joe.'

The nod was not enough. She held him until the driver shook the reins and when the cart moved away, his fingers were pulled from her grasp.

'I promise, Ma,' he'd whispered back to her. He did not know if she had heard.

'"Be ye kind to one another,"' the preacher bellowed, leaning forward in his pulpit. 'So wrote Paul in his letter to the Ephesians.'

A letter! Joe had not promised he would not write to his mother. She might not be able to read it, but she could find someone who could. He knew the price of paper but when he asked Mrs Webber the next day, she was astonished.

'Joe! I didn't know you had a mother still living! You never told me. Of course you must write to her,' she said. 'Where is she?'

'In Chirk.' Joe looked down, ashamed.

'Chirk is only 10 miles away! You've been here over four years now!'

'She went with the baby. We could not stay together. My sister Aggie was sent to a different place.'

'Lots of the tradesmen go to Chirk regularly – I will arrange for someone to take your letters. Oh, Joe!' To his embarrassment, Mrs Webber hugged him close. She was round and soft as a cushion. 'I have lost children myself. I know what it is to lose family.'

He was not ready to feel the warmth of her, nor smell her fusty clothes. As she squeezed him, he felt small, and in danger: a creature of bones all delicately and intricately held tight by skin, keeping him together as Joe Begg, apprentice button maker.

12

THE DAYS FOLLOWING Joe's letter to his mother turned to weeks. When the weeks turned to months, Joe's heart no longer quickened when he heard his name called by Mrs Webber. One day, walking past the workroom window, he saw the post-boy jump from his mule. Joe's heart jumped a few minutes later as Mrs Webber called him downstairs. She was waving a letter in her hand – but it was from her sister, a milliner in London, writing to keep her abreast of the new fashions there.

Mrs Webber pointed the line out to him.

"Covered buttons is all the rage." he read.

That very day, Joe took a wooden button and worked out a way of twisting and stuffing material around the surface. The colour of the silks transformed the room with their intense blues and reds and yellows. The wools held subtler colours, but more than the dull brown of the wood he had used before.

A man learns things about himself as he grows. Glue and twists of material were not so much to Joe's liking as design: the drawings, the measuring, the exactitude. Fabric was tricky stuff – he was not so greatly in control of his materials.

So absorbed was he in his new work that the message, delivered by a local drayman, was a total surprise. Joe was called to the front door to hear it himself. The man had been delivering beer barrels to the Trap Inn at Chirk and had been asked by the publican's daughter to convey a message, brought to her from Mrs Stebbings at the Poor House: Joe Begg, apprenticed to Webbers in Oswestry, should visit his mother as soon as he could be spared.

As it happened, Caleb the knife grinder, who lived nearby, was due to visit Chirk the very next day. Joe could be certainly spared, said Mrs Webber, kissing him on both cheeks.

All night, Joe lay tossing and turning in excitement and agitation. He wished he had something to take them. He sprang up. Buttons! He could take two of his finest covered buttons and show them how skilled he'd become. In the dark he tiptoed to the basket of finished buttons and felt for two of his best: plump and round with fine stems. He took them to a shaft of white moonlight by the window. One red, one blue, or possibly green.

Pulling into the forecourt of the Trap Inn the next morning, Joe jumped down, leaving Caleb to take the mule to the field behind the Inn. His hands were clammy with fear and anticipation. He wiped them on his jacket and felt the buttons he'd stowed there in the night. The sun had appeared over the hills, turning the leaves on the trees golden. It would be a glorious day. A big man with a ginger beard and wiry curly hair came round the corner of the inn, trundling a barrel of beer over the cobbles.

'Excuse me.'

The man straightened. His eyes were green and fierce.

'Do you know where the house for, um... the unfortunate...?'

'Poor House? Mrs Stebbings? Down there,' he pointed. 'Turn right and take the path on the left. Can't miss it.'

Joe gulped and fled, feeling the man's green eyes following him as he went.

The house stood on its own at the end of a lane, cowering under a ragged thatched roof, with low windows and a cracked, peeling wooden door. Chickens scratched at the mud in the front yard.

He knocked on the door and stood back, heart thumping, stuck between wanting to run and wanting to burst forward. His own mother might be just the width of the door away.

The door opened and stuck on the floor.

'Push. It sticks in the heat.'

He shouldered it gently at first, then with his full weight, nearly falling into a large woman in front of him when it gave. Her face was red and fleshy, her hands like paddles – not like Nelly at all. Her sleeves were rolled up and in one hand she held a pewter ladle.

'Mrs Stebbings?' The woman nodded once. 'I think my mother is here. Nelly Begg. And her baby – well, she'd be grown a little girl by now.'

'Joe Begg?'

She led him to the kitchen. Sitting at the table, chopping parsnips, was his mother. Joe stood uncertain until she looked up and gasped, colour draining from her face. Two other women worked alongside her: one young with a sad face, the other woman bent with the weight of years. Both gawped open-mouthed at Joe. For a long moment Nelly sat as though she'd seen a ghost.

'It's me, Ma. Joe.' He stood shifting from foot to foot, feeling all the eyes in the room watching him.

'Joe! My Joe!' Nelly jumped up, flinging down the parsnip and knocking her stool over. She ran to Joe, throwing her arms round him, hugging him tight. Joe stood, unable to breathe, conscious of the eyes still on him. He took his mother's hand and squeezed it tight. She stepped away, wiping her face with her free hand. Her hair was so thin, so grey.

'I gave up believing I'd see you again, Joe, so it didn't hurt so much.'

They stood, neither of them knowing what to do. His eyes flicked over her shoulder to the women she had left at the table. It was terrible, worse than he had thought, the bleakness of this room.

'We could go outside?' she whispered. 'I'll do some windfalls,' she said to the other women, picking up a bowl and a small knife.

Outside, a stool sat under a gnarled old apple tree. Nelly held out her skirt for fallen apples from the grass.

'Sit, Ma,' Joe said. 'Allow me.' He was glad to have something to do.

'Oh Joe,' she said, taking his hand when he tipped the apples into her lap. 'I can't believe this!'

Out in the sunlight her skin was blue, almost luminous.

'How are you, Ma?' Joe said, waving away a wasp he had disturbed.

She smiled and kissed his hand.

'I dreamt of this,' she said. 'In the early days. It was the best dream but when I woke, it was like losing you all over again.'

'I'd have come before, Ma, but…'

'I know Joe. And I meant it. See what a fine young man you've grown into.'

Joe swallowed. 'Where's Baby?'

'Baby?' Nelly laughed. Her teeth were gone and her mouth sunken in on itself. 'Iris now. Someone's gone to fetch her. She's haymaking in the field. She's a fine strong girl, Joe, though I'm not as strong as a mother should be.'

Joe pulled his hand free from her cold fingers.

'I thought I'd try and find Aggie while I'm here,' he said, looking over to the lane. 'Have you seen her?'

Nelly shook her head. 'Oh, Joe, Aggie ran away. I was too ill when we first got here to go and see her and when I was better it was too late. I don't know where she is.'

Joe's heart thumped, absorbing the shock. He had not thought much of Aggie, but had imagined finding her would be simple.

'Why did she run away? Where could she go?'

Nelly shook her head.

'I'll find her, Ma. I will. We'll all be together again one day. You'll see.'

Nelly's smile was the kind that wants to be a smile, but behind it lies a different feeling.

'I will, Ma. I promise.'

He was biting back the word, wishing he'd said, 'I'll do my best,' when a child appeared, cartwheeling round the corner of the house. Her cheeks were red, her grassy fair hair a wild tangle and her feet bare. He did not know her. And then immediately he did.

'Look, Baby. Your brother Joe has come to visit.'

'Iris!' she corrected her mother. 'I'm not a baby. I'm five! My name is Iris,' she said to Joe. 'I choosed it,' she said with a winsome smile, swooping down to pick up a curl of apple peel, which she wound round and round her fingers.

'See what I can do, Joe.'

She was upside down in a trice: handstands, forward rolls, leaping and twisting, finally coming to a standstill next to her mother, where she stood on one leg, picked up the other and held it straight in the air in front of her face.

'She takes after you, Ma,' Joe said, sitting on the grass by her.

'Don't encourage her,' Nelly said.

'I'll come for you soon, Ma. We'll all be together one day, you'll see.'

Could it have been his words that made Nelly choke so, holding her chest and coughing and coughing until the bowl of apples slipped from her lap one way, the little knife the other, stabbing the ground near Joe's foot.

Iris took no notice.

'Look at me, Joe. I can do the splits!'

One of Iris' legs slipped one way, one the other, a look of triumph on her face.

'Get up!' Joe said. 'Help Ma. Fetch water.'

Nelly shook her head, still heaving for breath.

Joe stood uncertain, then bent to pick up the cut apples as her breathing quietened.

'It's nothing, Joe,' she gasped. 'Don't fret about us. We're settled here. I help Mrs Stebbings out where I can.'

No sooner had Joe arrived than he was longing to go. There was nothing here to make him feel comfortable. He was turned upside down, pulled this way and that, and there was nothing he could do about anything.

'Come with me, Joe,' Iris said, taking his hand. 'She'll be alright in a minute.'

At the hedge behind the house, Iris lay down, squirming her way through on her tummy. Following was almost impossible, but Joe could not disappoint her. He struggled on, heaving himself forward on his elbows, twigs scratching his cheeks and snagging his clothes.

'You did it!' Iris said, executing four cartwheels as Joe pulled leaves from his hair.

'That's the other Iris! I choosed her name so we'd be the same,' she laughed, pointing at the old grey horse over the far side of the field. 'She knows me!' Iris said. 'She's old.'

Iris the horse was making her way towards them; her back sagged and her coat was dull and matted. Baby Iris pulled up handfuls of grass and buttercups, which she laid across her palm. 'Same grass,' she said. 'But she don't have to waste time biting it.'

The horse's eyes were milky; on one side of its muzzle flies lifted and settled on a livid-looking sore. One hand flat, offering the grass, Baby Iris fanned the flies away with the other one.

'My worst thing in the world is flies,' she said. 'What's your worst thing?'

'Squeezing through hedges,' Joe answered as she threw herself down, disappearing into the greenery.

Nelly was still sitting where they had left her, the last apple in the bowl. Joe helped Iris pile the peelings ready for the horse the next day. Mrs Stebbings came to the front door, banging a pan with a wooden spoon. She acknowledged Joe with a nod of her head.

'We'd best go in for food,' Nelly said, but Joe had no desire to go inside. He wiped his hands on his britches, and remembered the covered buttons in his pocket. He took one, the red one, holding it out to Nelly.

'Very nice, Joe,' she said, but Iris jumped forward, swiped the red button from his palm and raced off into the house.

13

JOE KNEW THAT Aggie would no longer be at Mrs Price's house on Bronygarth Road, but someone there might know where she had gone. Caleb had not finished his work, and Joe would rather be doing something than nothing.

A man standing in the shade in the forecourt of the Trap Inn whilst his sickle was being sharpened by Caleb directed him to the end of the village, where he should take the lane downhill to Bronygarth Road. The house Joe was directed to had two storeys, with small, blank-looking windows and a good slate roof. Turning at the gate, he could see the tower of the church over the fields, and beyond that the roof of the priest's house.

Hand on the gate, he hesitated. A terrible squawking came from the back of the house. Several chickens came hurtling round the corner, chased by a girl waving a basket at them. She stopped, staring at Joe with insolent eyes.

'Excuse me,' Joe said.

'I don't speak to no strangers,' the girl said. 'Unless you're come for eggs.'

She must have been Aggie's age, maybe younger. 'I'm looking for Aggie Begg.'

The girl narrowed her eyes. 'She's long gone.'

'I know. I wondered if you'd heard where she's gone. I'm her brother.'

'She ain't got no brother. She ain't got no one.'

'She has. I'm her brother Joe. Did she tell you she hadn't got a brother?'

The girl shrugged.

'Do you know where she's gone?'

The girl shook her head. 'No one does. And no one cares.'

14

JOE VOWED TO himself he would visit again soon, but next time he would take more suitable gifts than buttons. The week he finished making the building blocks, a spinning top and the stiff-legged horse for Iris was also the last week he worked with wood. Mrs Webber received good news. Her shriek from downstairs pierced the silence upstairs. A moment later she came rushing up the stairs, holding on to her cap with one hand, fluttering a letter in the other. A middle-aged man with intense eyes and greasy hair tied back at the nape of his neck followed her.

'Good news!' Mrs Webber's cheeks were scarlet.

The money Mrs Webber had been scandalously denied on the death of her brother several years before had finally come to her. Her nephew, Zachery – her sister the milliner's son, not her brother's, or all the money would have gone to him – had come to help her invest in a new enterprise. The inheritance was modest but sufficient to create changes. Roast beef and fine ale for everyone that evening!

'This kind of luck don't happen to people like us,' Mrs Webber said that night, blotting her mouth with a linen serviette. 'Where you're born is where you die, and that's the way of things.'

'But you were born to money, Aunt. Born a girl, that was your undoing,' Zachery laughed.

'And I ran away with the man who took my heart, that was my second undoing,' Mrs Webber said, looking fondly at Mr Webber.

Zachery was the innovator, the man with the ideas. Mechanisation, power, steel, industry were his currency: steel buttons were the way forward in this rapidly changing world. Machinery must be purchased. New premises must be found to accommodate this expansion.

Joe discovered he had a flair for turning Zachery's ideas into practical design. Steel circles must be punched out, a circle depressed in the centre of the circular button, and holes punched in that for the attaching of the button to the garment. He was the person with the greatest aptitude: his mind sharp, his muscles strong enough to operate the press, his eye clear to cut the steel, his hands steady to bore the holes in the centre of the buttons – two holes or four.

The noise in the workshop was intense, the heat fierce, the dangers obvious. Sacrifices must be made to progress. Now it was the sparks from the steel and the soldering Joe must watch. His clothes were peppered with holes and he carried the smell of burning everywhere. The steel button output was astonishing, the appetites of the markets insatiable. Profit was turned to wages. Joe and George were no longer apprentices but workers. The day was growing nearer when he might be able to rent a room nearby for his mother and Iris.

George, with no mention of a mother nor dependent siblings, spent his money on ale, supping with Zachery at the hostelry down the road. Joe preferred to stay in reading to Mr Webber from the Bible until his eyes ached with the flicker of the candles.

'Have you no liking for ale, Joe?' Mrs Webber asked one evening, busy at her crochet work.

'I'm saving. I want to fetch my Ma,' Joe said.

'Dear Joe!' she said, dropping her crochet work to her lap. No searching for premises was necessary, Mrs Webber told him. There was attic space above the new workshop. It would give her joy to be able to provide accommodation for Joe and his family for a modest rent, and it would only take a few days to make everything ready. Joe wrote a letter to Nelly, telling her to expect him in about a week's time. He would be coming with good news. As he dried the ink, breathing gently over the letters, he imagined Mrs Stebbings holding the paper in her big red hands, reading it to Nelly. Iris might leave off her exercising and stand and listen. He sealed the envelope and went straight to give it to Caleb, who was going to Chirk the next day.

15

TEN DAYS LATER, armed with two of his new metal buttons, Joe clambered into Caleb's cart to set off for Chirk. The mule was a slow beast and felt nothing of Joe's hurry as it climbed the hill outside Oswestry. At the Trap Inn, Joe jumped down and walked briskly along the lane to the Poor House. Oh. Confound it! He'd forgotten the toys for Iris. Next time, he said to himself, whistling as he walked, mimicking the birds in the hedges. April was a goodly month, the air filled with song, the trees and hedges bursting with fresh green buds. Before long they'd be reunited as a family. Aggie would join them when he found her, and find her he would. At six years old, Iris would be able to help Mrs Webber in the kitchen, or even sweep the workshop or check the buttons for faults – more likely to find them in George's basket than his own, he smiled. Six, the same age as Aggie when they were split apart. He should have searched for Aggie before – though how, he did not know. One step at a time: and you, Aggie, are the next step, I promise.

He lifted his head at the path up to the house. Such a low, dark, depressing place, especially so on this fine spring day with the forsythia bursting yellow, and the celandines under the hedges. He stopped at the front door, which was open a fraction. He pushed it open and stepped inside.

'She's gone,' a voice called from the dark hallway.

'Gone? Gone where?'

The little bent woman he had seen on his first visit came towards him, feeling her way along the wall. Her head was level with his waist, and Joe was a small man.

'Cough... took to her bed, and the next day... gone.' The woman blinked her pale eyes at Joe.

Mrs Stebbings came running out from the kitchen, greasy hair escaping from her bonnet, face red and sweaty. The hands that took Joe's were calloused like a man's.

'I sent word...' she said, her voice defensive, 'but you did not come.'

'I had no word. I would have...'

'Course you would. I know you would.'

Joe was shaking with shock.

'Come through, now. There's a chair in the kitchen. I'll get some water.'

Wooden shoes on wooden floors. No colour anywhere but steam wreathing round the kitchen from a vast pot bubbling on the stove.

Joe sat, taking the tankard he was offered. It smelt of metal and old mouths. He could not drink.

'She's dead?'

Mrs Stebbings nodded. 'Gone to a better place.'

'Where is she?' Joe whispered. His hands slipped into his pocket, fingering the flat buttons, circling them between his fingers.

'Behind the church. We've a special place where the ladies from here move to their final resting place. It's an arrangement I have with the priest. He's a decent man.'

Joe's thoughts flashed to the thin-faced priest they had known, his shoulders speckled with dead skin.

'And Baby – Iris?' he gulped.

Mrs Stebbings frowned. 'The man took her.'

'What man?'

'Iris' father sent his man to collect her.'

The next thing Joe knew he was on the floor with two toothless women over him, one slapping his cheeks, the other smoothing his hand between her own rough fingers.

Joe struggled to his feet.

'Her father's dead!' he said. 'Drowned, long ago.'

His mind filled with an image of the cart and of Luca, face down in the river. He had never seen it for himself but he was told that Ivor the Strongman had had to be sent for to haul him out.

'Who sent for her? Where is she?'

Mrs Stebbings shook her head, anxious. She had helped write the note herself. She should have made sure, but the man who arrived to take Iris a few days after Nelly died said he was Evercreech's man; Lodo was his name, and the poor child had nowhere else to go. Nelly had told her, so pale and almost with her last breath, that a man would come for her.

'She meant me. Me!' Joe shouted.

Mrs Stebbings shook her head. 'She said a man.'

The old woman stood in the doorway, clutching the doorframe, listening.

'Did she say anything to you, Nora?' Mrs Stebbings asked.

'Entertainers... markets and that. Always upside down, that little one!' she replied.

Joe was shaking so badly he had to drink. Mrs Stebbings held the mug steady as he gulped the water, sluicing his body. By the time he had drained the cup, his hands were round hers.

'Thank you,' he said, standing up. 'If you should hear anything of my sister Iris, please tell me. I'm at the button factory in Oswestry. The new one. Your letter must have gone to the old one. I shall go to the churchyard before I go back.'

'She didn't leave anything. They don't here,' Mrs Stebbings called after him.

Joe knew where the poor were buried from years before. The other baby. The one with no name. Under the yew.

He looked up. There was the red-brick priest's house across the field. That was the window he had looked out from each night before he went to sleep, to say good night to the baby. Nelly would be buried on the north side, where the shadow of the church fell, where the ground was humped but no headstones marked the buried lives. One mound of bare earth rose from the ground. He felt in his pocket, took out one button, turned it over before kneeling and pressing it into the earth.

'One day, Ma. I'll find them. Both of them. I promise.'

Now Nelly was dead and everything worse than it ever was, both sisters scattered and he hadn't an idea where. Baby Iris gone with Lodo to her father? Lodo was Evercreech's man; Evercreech had been such a frequent visitor, and whenever he'd arrived at their tent, Nelly had sent the children away.

'Take Aggie to the horses, Joe...'

Joe kicked at a crust of dry earth. The heaviness inside threatened to unbalance him. He might fall, one way or the other, if he did not think himself steady with every fibre of his body. He rubbed at his wrist. He'd not done too well so far. Now he had the weight of a double promise. He curled hands into fists. 'Just you wait and see!' he said, out loud so his ears could hear his words.

Caleb was busy at his whetstone. The cart was empty, the mule tearing at the grass, flicking away flies with his long ears and thin tail. Being a market day and a warm one, men sat in the courtyard round trestle tables. Joe had pennies in his pocket. Ale would wash the metal taste of the Poor House away, or numb the pain.

Inside, Joe waited, steadying himself on the wooden counter with a strange sensation of floating, his ears ringing with a loud noise of nothing at all. A tall young girl served him. Her face was red, her eyes clear and grey, a perfect almond shape, and her lips outlined like a bow. Her neck was long and white with a tiny black mole above her collar bone. A pulse throbbed blue beneath the skin. Joe did not know he had lifted his hand until she batted it away.

'Hey!'

'I'm so sorry,' he apologised, snatching his hand back and curling his fingers in shame. 'Everything so…' How could he explain? Too real. Too distant.

The publican, the giant with the orange beard and angry eyes, loomed up beside Joe. 'Everything alright, Clara?'

'Yes,' she said quickly. 'It's nothing.'

In those hands, Joe thought, he'd be beaten to pulp.

'I apologise,' he said again. 'My mother's dead, I…' He gulped his sadness away.

She shook her head quickly. 'I'm so sorry about your Ma.'

Joe slipped his hand into his pocket and brought out the second metal button.

'I made this,' he said. 'I was going to give it to my mother… but I want you to have it.'

Her smile broke his heart – so sweet, a row of perfect teeth. He stumbled out of the inn, tears trickling down his face.

PART III
Peggin

16

EYES ARE CHILLING things, dead or alive. A fish stared up at me from a bed of ice in the bottom of the stone sink. You can close a dead person's eyes so they can't look at you anymore. That's why we got eyelids. But a fish don't have eyelids.

I was rolling my sleeves right up for the scraping job, knowing how fish scales can be washed from skin better than brushed from cotton. Sara was flicking the ice from the fish and pulling out bits of the straw they were packed in.

'It's a Feast Day, is what it is, girls.'

Mary stood behind us, peering over our shoulders to make sure we were both 'hard at it'.

'St Brigid, and she's the saint that my mother called me after. It's tradition.'

'So why's you not called Brigid?' I asked. The fish was melted enough to pull it free from the ice, but stiff as an icicle and cold, so cold. I held it up by the tail and picked up the short knife with the curved blade where it had been sharpened for years on the stone. Mary loved to talk and tell you things, especially about her Ireland. Set her going, and she'd never notice the scales falling on the floor, nor the gash in the fish's side where I had the knife angle wrong.

'A fair question, Peggin. Brigid is in the parish records but it's Mary I was known by. Brigid herself was known as Mary of the Gael – don't ask me why. February 1st is her Feast Day and the feast will be special. The dear Ladies always honour my day!'

The bell from the breakfast room rang above the mantelpiece. Mary bustled away.

'We don't have saints in chapel,' Sara said. Picking blackened leaves from the cabbage is not being 'hard at it' the way she was doing it. 'Do you have saints in yours?'

I wasn't chapel, I knew that, and I wasn't Catholic either, but I didn't know what I was. The old woman never told me when she dragged us all to the church every Sunday.

Sara's eyes were forever flicking over the comings and goings outside the window. The courtyard was white and slippy with the cold, the trees beyond waving their black branches in the air like they were desperate.

Immediately pink spots glowed in Sara's cheeks, I knew who was coming.

'Mo-ses!' I said, all sing-song. Sara frowned and pulled the leaves off twice as fast.

His knock was always the same. Three hard raps with his knuckles on the kitchen door.

My hands were frozen blue and sticky with fish, but Mary hurried back down the stairs.

'Now, who can that be, do you think?' she said, as she always did, even when she knew who was there. I thought it was so she could say, 'Ah, it's you!', like she was surprised. 'I thought it the post-boy.'

A rabbit dangled from Moses' hand, head down, blood dripping from its mouth. He said nothing.

'I'll pay you, Moses, when you bring me a brace of pheasants like we agreed.'

The moment the bell from the library jangled, Mary was heading back to the stairs.

'That'll be their letters ready.'

Moses was grown big as a man, with his dark hair and muscles. He was now employed by the Ladies to keep them supplied with game and had a gun loaned by the Ladies and a dog, Jock – a stubby little creature, white under the mud, and always panting hot even when there was snow on the ground. Jock was left outside, for he'd chase the cat and send her crazy. Moses came in, slapped the rabbit on the table and with a sly tilt of the head towards me and a wink, he was gone.

Sara hadn't moved.

'He nodded at me, did you see that, Peggin?'

The fish was done and I got busy stoking the stove with more logs and wondering where the draught of cold air was coming from, blowing the smoke away towards the stairs. At the same moment I realised Moses must have left the door open, the cat streaked past me, rabbit in its mouth, making for the door. That cat was a big Tom, his ears flat on his head as he glanced at me to see what I dared do, just as Mary came running down the stairs with the letters.

'No!' she screamed, flinging herself at the door. 'You eejit, Peggin! Get after him!'

And that's when she kicked out at the table leg like she wanted it to be me, but harder than she meant to, howled and collapsed into the chair, rocking to and fro with the Duckies' letters still in her hand.

There weren't no point in chasing that cat. He'd be long gone and Mary knew it. I kept my face blank but Mary gave me such a look.

'Let this be a lesson to you, Peggin.'

'I'll never kick a table in my life!' I said.

It was a risk, but she burst out laughing.

'Oh, sweet Lord. Ah, well. What's done is done, no use crying over spilt milk. Rabbit's off the menu but I'll make do with the fish and – the new gardener, what's his name now? Stour, that's it. He can bring me a chicken.'

And with that she was up, limping out of the room.

Mary ate with the Duckies to celebrate her Feast Day. The rest of us ate earlier in the kitchen, round the table wiped clean of the day's cooking. We always sat in the same places, Sara next to me. When we were alone, before the others arrived, she was close and we would talk but as soon as one of the other girls came in, she'd move her chair as far away from me as the leg of the table would allow. Her sister Elizabeth, who did the flowers, sat opposite me but turned towards Sara always. Her black darting eyes, her curly hair and her face freckled like an egg made her prettier than Sara, and she'd far better table manners than her sister. Golden Gwendolyn sat next to her, as near the dishes as she could be to help herself to anything that might be left after serving the rest of the table. Stour, the gardener, came in late, sat at the far end and shovelled food into his mouth as though that was its only purpose. He curled over himself and ate with his spoon, not wanting us to see his dirty hands.

Jeremiah the butler, who thought himself above us, usually sat at the head of the table, but today he was serving the Feast Day celebrations upstairs, so we had no one to give us stern looks nor dampen the chatter. Not that I was included much in the talk, which was mostly in Welsh, with the three girls – heads together – in high spirits. I didn't care at all. They did it to make me mind so I didn't. Every now and then Gwendolyn would turn to me and say, 'Oh sorry, Peggin. We were just saying...' and then make up some nonsense and smirk at the others as though I couldn't see. They thought I couldn't understand a word but they were wrong. I caught some of it, though I pretended not to. I wished I could speak Welsh like they did, the sounds all up and down and sounding like laughing. I wanted to be part of them, not outside like I was. They had it coming, though, behaving like they did, too stupid to think that I'd have the last laugh.

When I walked into the kitchen later that week, I thought someone had died. Elizabeth was stabbing flowers into the crocus bowl. Sara was snivelling and sniffing. Gwendolyn's face was sour enough to turn the milk. Moses had been dismissed again. Unfair of course – something to do with money: it's always to do with money. Big Duckie was like that, a temper on her like a sudden wild wind, whisking everything upside down and every which way, before blowing itself out.

'He'll be back. We've visitors coming and nothing to give them,' I told them.

Sara didn't believe me, but I was right. A couple of days later, I heard Moses' whistle and there he was, walking across the courtyard with a partridge over his shoulder. I pushed Sara to the window and didn't say anything, but it was Elizabeth, busy sticking myrtle and ivy leaves into a vase at the table, who was nearest the door. She opened it and took the bird from him, wriggling her body like a snake, her laugh giggly, not like a proper laugh at all. Moses always had the smell of blood on him. Those dark eyes looking out from behind that black fringe of hair set those girls flaming, and he knew it.

Sara just stood there, half smiling, half furious with her sister. They'd have fallen out if Elizabeth hadn't got herself a man in the village.

'I'll tell your Gareth about you!' Sara sulked, when Moses had gone.

'Tell him what?' Elizabeth was all innocent outside and no doubt praying hard inside that Sara wouldn't. 'You wouldn't dare,' she said quietly, stabbing a twig into the vase.

A pot what's not stirred just burns on the bottom, but if you take a spoon and stir it about, everything's the better. She thought she was so smart, Gwendolyn, simpering and smiling at me, and all the while speaking words she thought I didn't understand. She was rounded like the cow and fair, keeping herself spotless always. I was sent for the butter one day. I stood watching her from the doorway of the cow byre, her cheek flattened against the cow and her bubby squashed, her clean fingers squeezing those diddies, wrists brushing the full pink udders. Sometimes it felt like I was touching them, and I went all melted inside.

She must have felt me watching 'cos she turned round suddenly.

'Peggin! What you doing?'

She stopped milking to go and get me the butter, wrapped in muslin.

'If you should happen,' she began, red blotches creeping up into her cheeks, 'to see Moses, could you tell him I'm here waiting for the rabbit?'

I left the butter in the kitchen and went to the shed, where I knew Moses was making a cage for his new ferret pups. Jock sat outside, panting.

I tiptoed up behind Moses and said in my best Irish voice, 'Mary, Mother of God! What do you think you're doing there, young man?'

He spun round, dropping his pliers and blinking till he saw it was me. A pair of rabbits were hanging from a nail by the door, eyes all bulging, dark spots on the floor beneath.

'What's the cage for?'

'Ferrets.'

'Ferreting's a job for two, isn't it? Won't you need someone to hold the net?' I said. 'And who will that be, I wonder?'

He shrugged and looked up at me with those dark eyes.

'Not me!' I laughed. 'I was thinking Gwendolyn. Oh, yes. She asked me to tell you they don't want that old rabbit after all. So don't bother taking it to her.'

He dropped his head, concentrating on fastening the door of the cage tight.

He said nothing but hung up the pliers and the hammer on the hooks his father had banged into the wall, unhooked the rabbits and slung them over his shoulder, picked up the cage and set off towards the lane with Jock at his heels.

For a moment I felt good, thinking about Gwendolyn waiting for him in the byre, and then suddenly I didn't. I don't know why I told Moses that. But I didn't want to think about it any more, so I didn't.

Early the next morning I heard shouting in the courtyard. Gwendolyn was in a rage, and Moses was shrugging and walking away. When I was sent to collect the buttermilk later, I said, 'Couldn't Sara go?'

'No!' Mary had that fierce look in her eyes.

Churning is hot work, but Gwendolyn flushed bright red when she saw me.

'Peggin! Why did you tell Moses I didn't want the rabbit? My dad hit me. And we didn't have nothing for our tea. All the kids were crying.'

I felt bad then, 'cos I only meant it for fun.

'I thought you said you didn't want it,' I said. 'That was an honest mistake.'

Such a look she gave me at that, but I didn't let her know how I felt inside.

17

WHEN THE SUN shines fierce in the spring, the light shows up all the winter smears.

'Shocking dirty!' Mary tutted, unfolding the steps and passing me the paper and vinegar. 'It's a wonder those poor dears can see anything beyond them! Might as well be on the moon. Make a good job of it, Peggin.'

There's nothing those Duckies like better when they look up from their books or their writing than to see the sunset behind the hills, turning the sky like a painting.

There I was, cleaning the glass, wondering if side to side was better than round and round for the clearest result, when I heard Jock's yapping, high and excited. Moses came running across the courtyard with something cupped in his hands.

I was down those steps and first to the back door, which I opened as he was shifting whatever was in his hands to just the one, so's to free his knuckles for knocking.

'What you got there?' I asked.

He looked up, grinning. 'Remember?'

He stretched his hand out and there was a little prickly ball not much bigger than a chestnut.

'*Draenog!*' he said.

'It's a hedge-pig,' I said.

'*Tawel!*' Moses ordered Jock, who sat down immediately, panting, drool dropping from his black lips. 'Sit!'

Moses stood there, stroking those prickles with the back of his finger. They were hardly prickles at all, the way they smoothed down. If Moses was bringing this creature to me, I didn't want it at all. I don't like creatures. I pulled back.

He grinned again, rolling it carefully back into both hands.

'Not for you. I found it. Same as I found you. *Draenog.*' His face was as soft as ever I saw, holding it so careful.

'What will you do with it?' I called after him. Jock was up and bouncing and barking again.

'Eat it!' he called out, not looking back.

In summer months, swifts scream over the courtyard and buzzards circle high in the sky 'cos it's cooler up there, like on the tops of the hills. The Cufflyman runs so low you can't even hear it from the back step.

One day Moses came whistling across the courtyard in his shirt sleeves and slapped rabbits, faces all torn and bleeding, down beside me on the stone step where I was shelling the first peas. When the pod is full and hard, it's a great job, driving those peas out with your thumb, sending them rolling and bouncing into the bowl. But there's always the one with the pink maggots and the peas half eaten and I hate that – not knowing by looking at the outside.

He put the ferret cage down by his side: two yellow bodies turning over and over each other. They'd blood on their faces and black beady eyes. Jock didn't look at them either. He sat the other side of Moses with his ears flat on his head, trembling.

It wasn't just rabbit blood on their faces, though, it was Moses' blood too. One hand was wrapped round the first finger on his other hand. When he took it away, it was bleeding and dirty too.

'Don't rub dirt in it!' I said. 'Don't you know nothing? Come here.' He followed me to the water butt. I scooped water in the pail and held his hand under until the water stained muddy red and his finger was clean enough for me to see the line of sharp little teethmarks.

'They don't let go, *y diawliaid*' he said.

'I hate ferrets!' I said, throwing the bloodied water over the stones and dipping the bucket in the butt for more.

'You don't mind eating the rabbits, though, eh?' he said.

'Wait here.' I went and took Mary's ointment pot from the mantelpiece, which I could reach now without standing on a chair, and a strip of cloth from the rag basket.

I don't know exactly what the salve was made from, but the smell made your eyes water.

'What's that?' Moses said, looking as though I was going to poison him.

'Don't you trust me?' I asked. 'It'll sting a bit.'

He never flinched, I'll give him that, but let me smooth it into the bites, not moving till I'd bandaged it round and round and tied it neatly with the two ripped ends.

'All done!' I said, but he didn't move, like he was struck dumb with his finger stuck out, pointing to nowhere. We stood there, looking at each other, his eyes misted with a softness which made me feel strange.

'I've got things to do,' I said, turning away from him. 'Even if you haven't.'

He picked up the cage, whistled to Jock, which he didn't need to do 'cos Jock was always at his heels, and marched off in the direction of the dairy. I never thought much of it.

All that nursing was hot work. I poured myself some water from the ewer in the cold store to drink and sat on the step to watch the birds flitting across the sky. Mary, who I thought had gone to lie down on her bed with a headache, took me by surprise. She thought I'd been doing nothing on account of all the peas not being shelled.

'You're nothing but a shirker, Peggin, and here's me with a headache and Sara setting up for a guest list of four and a cousin who's staying the night.'

'I've been...'

'I've no time for excuses.'

There's nothing makes you crosser than not being listened to. She waved her hand like she was swotting a fly. 'Go to Gwendolyn for all the cheese she can give you. Mr Wordsworth likes the blue cheese the most, so tell her that. Here, put it straight in this basket. We'll serve it on a bed of leaves if you please, Peggin. What in the name of the sweet Lord are those bloody rabbits doing on my table?'

I was off, deaf to the question, walking fast with no humming or sound, keeping all the noise inside. Jock was lying on his side in the sun outside the cow byre and I suppose I should have thought faster than I did. The ferrets' cage was in the shade by the door, but those ferrets were quiet too, one twisted round the other, their faces buried deep in yellow fur.

It was dark inside so it took a minute for the scrabbling and the shapes to make sense. Moses was jumping up, pulling his shirt down, but not before I had seen those buttocks at work. Under him, Gwendolyn's skirt was up over her face and her clean white legs spread in the straw.

'Sorree!' I called. 'So sorree to disturb you – but Mary wants a blue cheese brought over just as soon as you've finished your business. I'll leave the basket here. I'm sure she'll understand when I tell her.'

Moses was fastening his britches and he gave me this look, sly and not in the least abashed, a little smile on his lips. My eyebrows went up as far as I could feel them lift.

Gwendolyn was calling after me. 'No, Peggin! I beg of you. Peggin! Please!'

Off I marched, Jock lifting his head as I passed, wondering what all the noise was about. I was sorry too, 'cos I was left all mixed up so I didn't know whether I thought it funny, or dirty, or what. All I knew was that I couldn't get those pictures out of my head. Moses' smile, that look: what did it mean? And I couldn't answer myself, and that was a new feeling and I didn't like it.

18

A WEEK LATER, Mary's face swelled up with a bad tooth and she could only talk out of the side of her mouth. The Duckies instructed her to tie a cloth round her head and sent me in the late afternoon to the woman who made remedies with laudanum. She lived on the far side of the Llangollen bridge, halfway towards the crossing point up-river, and I wasn't in a walking kind of mood. I was in the mood for a ride on the post-boy's horse, which had just arrived with a delivery.

'As far as the bridge. Please… I don't know your name.'

He cleared his throat. 'Elijah.'

'Oh, Elijah. Mine's Peggin!' I knew how to wheedle. 'My foot is terrible sore.'

Elijah wasn't a boy at all, but a grumpy old dolt, with a face like a half-chewed mangel-wurzel. His eyes were back in his skull like he'd been squinting into the sun too long, his skin was purple and tight over his cheekbones. I don't think he'd ever been asked for any kind of ride before. I was up and sitting on his piebald mare before he'd tucked the Duckies' letters in his leather pouch. What a great feeling, sitting up there with my legs dangling. The tickle of the horse hair felt so good and the warmth of the horse under me. I smiled my sweetest.

'I'm to fetch cloves for Mary's teeth and laudanum.'

That wily man went to mount behind me, but I know men and the way they rub up close and I wasn't having none of that. I wriggled back and told him to ride in front of me. He gave me the angriest look, but I didn't care.

That horse had such a lolloping trot, I was always up when I should have been down and down when I should have been up. My bones were jarred to cracking. If I'd stood up on the horse's back, I'd have had a better ride. I was feeling that maybe I'd done this before when I noticed Jock was running along the road ahead of Moses and his ferrets. I lifted my hand and wiggled my fingers in the air. It made me smile inside, thinking of Moses standing there with his mouth open, watching me.

Near the bridge over the Dee, where the road goes three ways – left to the Mill, right to The Hand, where the coaches arrive, and straight on over the river – the post-boy pulled on the reins and we stopped. When I peered round his body, I saw two men standing by the end of the bridge, talking. The one facing us was a little bent man, stooped over like he'd been carrying heavy loads on his back all his long life and now he was stuck like this forever. He was waving his stick in the air, not like he was about to strike the other man, who had his back to us, but like he was telling him which way to go.

The bent man spotted us mid-wave. 'Plas Newydd?' he called out.

The post-boy nodded and spoke some words in Welsh. The other man half-turned but from behind the post-boy, with his arm in the way, I couldn't see him that well – a short fellow, tall hat, long coat, sleeves over his hands. I never saw his face but there was something about him that reminded me of something I'd forgotten. When you're not sure, the best thing is to turn away.

'Just take me a little further. My foot hurts so,' I begged.

The post-boy shook the reins and we were off again, the horse's big feathered feet slipping on the cobbles.

I was happy to walk back through Llangollen, even in the rain, with the tincture and the cloves in my cloth bag. The river was roaring under the bridge. I stopped in one of the passing places and leant over to watch the white froth curled back in a commotion, splitting round the arches of the bridge, taking my mind away from the black mass of water underneath, slipping past unnoticed.

I went left past The Eagle and The Hand. We weren't supposed to have dealings with The Hand any more, not since the publican brought the Duckies a bill for the hire of their chaises. He came to the back door, where he met Mary. She took one look at the bill and raged at the size and injustice of it, her voice getting higher and higher and louder and louder till the poor man trudged away with his head down and his pockets empty. That weren't the worst of it, either. Those Duckies took all their custom away, and that meant all the custom of their visitors too. It seemed to me, if they owed him, they owed him; but maybe he was too greedy – what did I know?

As I passed the open window of The Hand I heard someone singing. I knew that tune. All the men crowded inside had their backs to the door so they didn't notice me standing there. They only had eyes for the singer, a ragged-looking woman with pink circle cheeks on her white-painted skin. Her lips were scarlet and her eyebrows like two dark arches. Her dress was low and her bubbies pushed up, laced tight underneath so the men could leer at them.

Her voice was not the best but those men didn't care.

My thing is my own, and I'll keep it so still
Other young lasses may do as they will.

When she finished, she forgot to close her mouth, letting her tongue linger on her shiny lips, waggling her bubbies at the men, and putting her hand out for money, which she shamed them into giving. The men were laughing, britches tight.

I stood with that feeling of something long gone rising up and overtaking me. I knew that song. It was pressed right down, but up it came, bringing everything with it.

No one saw me when I turned and ran off up the street. I must have walked or run the length of our lane but I was somewhere else: places and times all mixed up with the words going round and round.

A master of music came with intent
To give me a lesson on my instrument
I thanked him for nothing, and bid him be gone
For my little fiddle must not be played on
My thing is my own, and I'll keep it so still

Mr Gulliver, the organist from St Mary's in Chirk, taught me the song. Every week he took us girls to his house to teach us hymns. I was only small. When I sat on a chair, my feet swung to and fro and weren't on the floor at all. I didn't know what I was singing. Mr Gulliver with the thin mean lips, his tongue flicking over them to keep them wet and shiny; his fingers – even now my shoulders hunched up round my ears, trying to push the thought away – those fingers, so long and pokey. The other girls sang too, but Mr Gulliver said my voice was like a nightingale. I liked that, 'cos it made me better than the others – Lydia and Hannah, who didn't like me and so I didn't like them either, and the quiet one whose name I didn't remember. Several times I had to go on my own, and Mr Gulliver brought his friends and made me sing it for them. I hated them all for handing me round like I was a parcel, hurting me and laughing and making me say, 'My thing is my own and I'll keep it so still,' so they could laugh some more.

Back at the old woman's house, I'd tell Lydia and Hannah what a time I'd had, and show them the sugar comfits and coins and ribbons they gave me, those men who loved me more than their own daughters. I wouldn't share with the other girls because they never shared with me. Those men had daughters, 'cos I'd see them in church. They never looked at me, dressed up in velvet coats and knee britches with hats or silly white wigs. Their wives followed: smaller, broad, grim-faced and bonneted, with the children trailing behind like ducklings.

I took Mary her tincture when I got back and helped her to bed, smoothing the sheets for her and tidying. Her room was on the ground floor now her legs were bad. She had a simple iron bed. Up above it hung a wooden cross with a little Jesus nailed to it, looking down on her. Blood dripped from his hands and feet. I'd be worried it might drip on her pillow. Blood's hard to get rid of, even with soaking in salt. On the table by her bed was a candle and a book.

"You're a good girl, Peggin,' she mumbled out of the corner of her mouth before her eyes drooped. The smell was terrible each time she opened her mouth. I turned away and busied myself folding something or straightening the hook rug with my foot. I wasn't in any hurry to go. There would be plenty of jobs waiting for me.

Music has a way of getting into your mind, entering through your ear and then liking being inside, curling round and round. I must have been singing without knowing I was, while I was folding Mary's clothes.

'My thing is my own and I'll keep it so still...'

'What's that you're singing, Peggin?' Her voice was stronger. That tincture was working fast.

'Oh, it's nothing. A song I remember. Just that line.'

'Hmmm.'

Mary had a strange look on her face, probably the tooth.

And now that tooth must have got into my mind, swilling round with the song. I was falling asleep on my bed that night, thinking about Mary, when a big man, smelling of sweat with his face all painted, was holding me down and forcing my mouth open, pulling my wobbly tooth with his big fat fingers and I was small and crying with the pain while a crowd of people all around me was cheering. Ivor the strongman and tooth puller. Pull a tooth. Draw a crowd.

Then above the cheers, Mary's voice came, loud and clear: 'You can't put spilled wine back in the bottle!'

I sat up, drenched in sweat. It wasn't Mary, just me remembering. Why that? Why then?

Sometimes Mary talks straight and sometimes in a tricky Irish way to make you think about the meaning, but it was true now. The music had broken the seal and forgotten things and feelings spilled about all over the place, making all sorts of things happen which most probably should not have happened.

19

IN THE WINTER when I'm freezing, with chilblains on my hands and feet, I dream of the summer. When summer comes, I long for winter. In summer, the sun is up early and goes to bed late, giving twice as many hours as in the winter to work. The fruit's piled up needing to be hulled, cored, stoned, peeled, halved; the beetroots boiled and sliced; the beans topped and tailed, all to be bottled, pickled and stacked away for the winter. My hands were like a murderer's, red juices to the elbow. Pickling makes the eyes water and the nose run, but the worst is the sweetness from the boiling fruit hanging in the sweltering heat, attracting every wasp in the land.

Mary was supervising us the next day. Sara, Elizabeth, the new girl, Bethan, and I were picking over the soft fruit, white and red currants piled high on the table in front of us.

'Come, Peggin,' Mary said, winking at the others. 'Let's be hearing you singing. It would help us, would it not, girls?'

Their answer was giggling, and I wasn't going to sing for them anyhow. The smell was so sweet with the first breath, but you are soon sick of it, currants being a fiddle, leaving fingertips cracked and sore. Wasps never grow sick of that sweetness.

'Shall I shut the window to keep the waspies out, or shall we die of the heat?' I asked.

'Shut!'

I stood for a moment to watch the wasps banging on the glass and buzzing so angry, still looking for a place to squeeze in – which they did. Sara told us she was stung once as a baby and her arm swelled to the size of a melon, so she was told, though she didn't know what a melon was.

'It's true,' Elizabeth spoke up for her sister, but didn't stop Sara screaming and whimpering, swatting at nothing, running from the table to crouch behind the rocking chair, as though a wasp could never find her there.

When the currants were done, I washed my hands in the bucket at the door. I couldn't bear the way my fingers stuck together with the juice. I was shaking them dry when Mary came out of the pantry with the melons – a fruit none of us, including Mary, knew.

'We can all imagine Sara's arm now,' Mary said, passing one round. It felt like skin, smooth in places and other parts rough and pocked. At the top, where the melons had hung from the stem, it smelt so good.

'What I'm supposed to do with them, I don't know.' Mary was holding one up and frowning at it. 'Lady Fanshawe's cook told me they were delicious with ham.'

Sara, back at the table, sniffed at the melon, passing it to Elizabeth, who passed it to me, simpering in an odd way.

'Did you tell her, Sara?' she said.

'Oh, it slipped my mind,' Sara giggled, as though they were playing with me.

'A man came calling for you yesterday evening when you weren't here,' Elizabeth said.

'A man? What kind of a man?'

'Just the normal kind,' Elizabeth said, eyes still on Sara. 'A bit crazy maybe. He thought there might be a young girl living at Plas Newydd; he said that he'd heard there was. Turned out it weren't us he was looking for, nor Gwendolyn neither. Must have been you!'

Sara's eyes went wide. 'You told me to say there weren't no one else living here!'

Elizabeth looked shocked. 'I did no such thing.'

She smirked, so I couldn't tell who was lying and who truthful, and I didn't like it.

'Oooh! Know anything about this, Peggin?' Mary's voice was teasing. The girls sniggered, even Bethan.

'I don't know nobody!' I said. Unless... the thought flashed into my mind but I didn't tell them. Could it be that man from the paper snooping around again?

The bell tinkled from the library.

'Peggin, you're the only one with clean hands and me with my tooth still plaguing me. You go and see what they want.'

Little Duckie was standing by the open window, a light breeze fluttering the curtain and playing faint moaning notes on the harp.

'Peggin, it's you!' she said, surprised to see me. 'I was expecting Mary.'

'She was up to her ears in the fruit when the bell rang,' I explained.

'What an image! Poor Eleanor is taken badly with the migraine, and we're nearly out of laudanum. Can you ask Mary to send some up, please? It's lucky you went to fetch fresh supplies yesterday. It's a terrible thing to see Eleanor in such pain and so frequently, the poor dear.'

'It's not fair!' I said. She smiled.

'Illness is never fair. Us women get the worst of it, Peggin, but it must be suffered as best we may.'

'Is there anything else I can bring for you?' Those Duckies had taught me well over the years to say helpful things and have them smiling.

'Bless you, no. I'm away to read to her. You could just put this book back on the shelf there, Peggin, where the steps are set. The third shelf – in that gap there.'

And with that she left the room.

The trouble with rugs and fabrics which draped over the chaises and the chairs is that they hold the heat. Even with the windows open, the air was hot enough to give anyone a headache. The wooden steps were sticky and those leather books smelt of the cows they once were. On the top step I still had to reach up with both hands. Like all their books, the letters 'EB' had been pressed into the leather on the front and 'SP' on the back. As I slipped the Duckies' little book back, a card fell from the pages to the floor.

Back down, I folded the steps and picked it up, smoothing the silky tassels at the end. The letters were clear and curly and black so I could read them easily.

'A faithful friend is the medicine of life and immortality.'

As I read the line I felt a sting inside, a sharp jab. A faithful friend... that's what I didn't have, nor never had in my life. Never had I been a faithful friend to anyone. 'Faithful' – that was a word that could never sit with my name. A medicine to life and immortality... that's death, isn't it? A faithful friend must be a powerful thing.

20

IN THE FINAL days of August, after straining the bubbling fruit bottles and washing the muslins, the wheat was ready for harvesting in the fields beyond the cow byre. Twenty hired men and women from the village had to be fed and their thirst washed away with beer. More work for us. When the stooks were dry and taken away for milling, the field was gleaned by Mad Annie and the others from hovels up the lane. That was when the Duckies decided it was time to have the house redecorated. There was not a thing wrong with the house! Those Duckies were always dreaming over their journals and books, wanting to be up-to-date and stylish, to have a change of colour. White now. Everything had to be white with brown for the woodwork; fine for the dreamers, hot hard work for the rest of us.

The rugs had to be rolled up and taken out for a good beating. The furniture had to be pushed into the middle of the rooms and covered with cloths for the painters. All the books must be taken from the shelves in the library and dusted – but the drawing room was the worst, with all the bits and pieces they had: the wooden backgammon set, the little pots and candlesticks and the egg timer, the little pottery figures, the seal's tooth, the walrus tusk and the posies, all to be wrapped in paper and stored in crates. White or brown, that paint stank and made the breath catch in your chest.

Abandoned were the improving Latin or Italian books while the Duckies read poems in whatever room was cleared for them to read in the house or in the garden, so their routine was not interrupted. Tempers grew short because the Duckies had a guest coming and everything must be ready, 'cos the man was a 'poet of great repute'. Poet, soldier, Lord this or Lady that, they were all of some repute to the Duckies and none to me.

When the paint was dry and the empty shelves ready for the books, Mary sent me to beeswax the library floor. Trapped paint fumes mixed with the beeswax and the heat. Sweat from my face dripped down onto the floor in dark spots. When I stood up, my blood stayed in my feet and my head was light as air. Bile came up into my mouth. I thought quickly and leapt for the fireplace – easier to clean. That was the saving of me, 'cos down I came – crash! – on the polished fender, sending the fire irons rolling.

The next thing I knew, I was struggling down the stairs, wedged between Mary and Gwendolyn, with the Duckies in their tall hats and outdoor capes fluttering after us.

'What a piece of luck that we were right outside the door when you fell, Peggin. We heard all the commotion,' Little Duckie said.

I soon felt better, sitting in Mary's rocking chair in the kitchen with the cold water and the fuss, a cloth on my head, and Gwendolyn fiddling with my dress, though it wasn't tight in the first place.

'Fresh air, that's what the girl needs. Why don't we take her with us?' Little Duckie said.

'That's the answer, my beloved. A ride in the trap will have her right as rain.'

They beamed at each other, pleased as pleased, and Mary was beaming too. Not Gwendolyn so much, for she'd a nervousness about her since she knew I had things I could tell if I wanted to.

I'd never been in a pony trap before, just that short ride in the carriage with the man from the papers. Mr Stour had borrowed the cart from his neighbour, who used it on the farm. He'd cushions for the Ladies, who rode up at the front. I was in the back with the Stour boys.

We'd only been jogging along down the lane a few paces, with Gwendolyn standing in the yard watching, when I had the feeling of something inside waking up from long ago, as though it was someone else, but it was me: that jolting and rumbling; that smell of the horse with the leather round his tail; that man sitting close and jangling his reins, and me squashed next to him. Yes! Of course! When I was still Aggie, before I hid under the hedge, rolled up, until I was found by Moses and turned into Peggin. At that moment we turned the sharp corner at the bridge and poles in the bottom of the cart rolled over, knocking me in the ankles.

'Hey!' I shouted, but those dumb Stour boys, three of them, as alike and as wooden as three rungs of a ladder, did nothing. The bottom of the cart was full of old sacks. I tucked my feet under them to be safer.

Wind was teasing the trees, setting the leaves rustling and branches waving. The road was smooth, dry and not rutted at all, with the sky pale and blueish but the sun bright and yellowing everything around it. The mountains made a high purple wall to one side, the Dee rushed down on the other. A low mist hung over the valley.

'Dragon's Breath,' Little Duckie said.

'From the Dragon's back!' Big Duckie said.

I looked where Big Duckie was looking: a line of hills rising up out of the mist.

They smiled at each other.

Eventually, the cart turned right toward the river and bumped over a field, stopping by what looked to me like a giant ruined church, the biggest I'd ever seen. The ladies were handed down by Mr Stour and stood adjusting their hats, ooh-ing and ah-ing and shaking their heads.

'Magnificent! "The ruins of time build mansions in eternity!"' Big Duckie said to Little Duckie.

'"Where there is ruin, there is hope for a treasure,"' the other replied and they laughed and linked arms, their heads touching.

What a place: the walls the tallest I'd ever seen but falling down, with no roof and sad empty spaces in the walls where there was once glass. Long ago, people would have looked out, seeing where we stood now: grass, falling leaves, dark trees, with the hills behind and the sky just the same.

The Duckies strode off with purpose, the boys running after, and Mr Stour driving a peg into the ground, though it was hard as rock and he'd to knock it in with a stone. He looped the reins round, not that the horse was going anywhere. No need, with all this food right under his tired, hot feet.

I wasn't going to stay with Mr Stour, who never said a word, so you felt invisible. I followed the boys and the Duckies.

'There it is,' Big Duckie said. I swallowed a giggle: they looked so funny, one wide grey backside and a smaller one next to it, bending over something.

'Abandoned.'

'Forgotten.'

'We will give it new life,' Big Duckie said, straightening and beaming at Little Duckie.

'We will, and we will treasure it anew. Right boys. Are you up for this now, are you?'

The Duckies moved away toward the river with the breeze trying to take their hats. The sun and the wind had chased the mist away. Everything was clear as clear. I could see then what they'd been looking at: an old lump of stone, half-covered in brambles. The boys, who'd run back to the cart, returned with the sacks. I wasn't sure I should help, faint as I had been. I placed my hand on my chest and followed the Duckies.

Their shoes lay on the bank with their stockings pushed into them, next to their tall hats. Both had their grey hair cut short and square now, not rolled and pinned like when I first saw them. Side by side, arms linked, hooking up their skirts, they stood on the stones in the river with the water over their feet.

'Look at that wee coot now, and the babies behind, see – with their dear little legs, in and out of the reeds.'

I stood behind, feeling like I should have stayed with the boys, but one of the Duckies saw my shadow and came scrambling back up the bank.

'Give us a hand now, Peggin. Good girl. How are you feeling now, Peggin?' Big Duckie asked, fixing her hat.

'A bit better… but still…'

'It was the fumes, you know… overcame you. Take deep breaths, now, Peggin,' said Little Duckie. Their shoes were poking out from their long skirts, but they'd a trail of stocking coming from their pockets.

'Look! A fish jumping for the flies. Did you see that, beloved?'

'I did. Just a flash.'

'A touch of silver and gone. Does it take you back?'

'It does, to the fishing in the lake at Kilkenny…'

'Ah, yes.'

For a moment they looked at each other, then Big Duckie took Little Duckie's hand.

'And now we have it all.'

'We most certainly do.'

'Did you ever in your life see anything as magnificent as this place, Peggin, as Valle Crucis?'

'What were it, before it were ruined?'

'*Was*, Peggin! *Was*. It was a Cistercian abbey, Peggin. Can you not imagine all the little monks rushing about?'

They looked over to the tall walls with the pigeons sitting in the places where the stones were missing, with only the sky above them. At the bottom, the boys were struggling to heave the stone onto the sacks.

'It'll look grand, won't it, though? The font. Down by the little bridge, I'm thinking. Complete the scene, won't it? An old font saved from the brambles.'

The font was on the sacks now and the boys were heaving it, almost lying flat to the ground. If that sack split, they'd have their faces in the mud. A few of the men from the nearby farm came strolling over the fields to help them. It took all of them, with old Stour rolling up his sleeves and pushing with his shoulder, to move that big old stone. How were they to get it into the cart? I followed the Duckies round the corner, walking the whole length of the old ruin. They stood pointing out where the altar would have been, and the places where the monks would have prayed.

'I'm thinking of the music which must have filled this place,' Big Duckie said. 'Do you know any religious songs, Peggin'?

I said I did not.

'Pity. I don't think "The Cruel Mother" is appropriate.'

The two of them laughed and linked arms. I was glad. I did not want to sing here, where the sound would be small and caught by the wind and rushed through the empty spaces.

When we returned to the cart, the men were standing round wiping their faces, and the font was on its side in the bottom of the cart. The red-faced Stour boys were pulling the rolling logs away. Their shirts were sticking to their backs. The cart was low now, with no space between it and the grass. Mr Stour had his cap off and was scratching his head.

'Well done, gentlemen! And thank you from the bottom of our hearts!' Big Duckie said to them all, handing a purse to Mr Stour. 'Get on down to the river now, boys, and cool off. What a great piece of stone, that! We'll all walk, won't we now, for the poor wee horse cannot take more weight. And we've got legs and strength, God be praised.' Big Duckie patted the horse and then moved on to pat the old stone.

'Look at the carving there, those wee faces peering out. Think of the work that went on there. God be praised indeed. What a find! You've earned your wages today for sure,' Little Duckie told the boys, whose shirts were dark front and back now with river water, and their hair black and dripping. Mention of the wages had them smiling and showing their teeth, which were better covered, I thought.

Back at Plas Newydd, Gwendolyn brought out ale, bread and cheese for them, which they ate in the courtyard after the font was in place by the bridge. She was to stand by the food to shoo away the wasps. She looked at me with fear on her face, but I gave her the biggest smile. I could be a faithful friend to her. I could.

21

THE COWS AND everything to do with them was Gwendolyn's business. She brought the milk to the kitchen morning and evening, taking Mary's order for cheese and butter. She walked with the bounce of someone who knows she's nice-looking, her clothes fresh and the bonnet tied under her chin clean and white.

And then one day she didn't appear.

'Gwendolyn's sick, Peggin,' Mary said, waving her quill at me. She was sitting at the table doing her calculations. 'You can milk a cow. There's nothing to it.'

I never had milked a cow, nor knew anything about them. The cow byre was kept clean with fresh straw and hay each day. It was odd to me that the milk was taken so close to the cow's rear end, the part under the tail green and smeared. Mr Stour did the dirty work, wanting the dung for his vegetables; Gwendolyn did the clean work. The buckets were always scrubbed spotless and stood upside down on the shelf in the cow byre. The wooden butter churn too, like a beer barrel, on its cradle with the handle for churning. She'd a stool which Walter had made for her when the first cow arrived all those years before. If I put two wooden legs of the stool at the front and one at the back, I could tip forward to reach the diddies.

Cows are big creatures up close. Those diddies were very long and pink. I sat for a time, looking at the four of them, wondering how to begin, listening to the in-and-out of their breathing and the slow grind of their jaws. My action was sudden, grabbing the two nearest diddies. The cow kicked out, sending the pail clattering.

'Rough, eh? Is that how you want it?' I said to her, grasping those diddies, pulling and pulling.

Nothing came. She was doing it deliberate, turning her head and chewing like that. When she saw it was me, she lifted her tail and the foulness splattered onto my skirt.

A burst of laughter came from the door. Moses! I realised I'd never heard him laugh before, nor had him creep up on me like that.

'Where's Gwendolyn?' he asked, planting his legs wide.

'Sorry to disappoint you!' I said. All I could think about was his bare behind and him tucking his shirt into his britches. I could not stop feeling the heat too, and anger that wasn't only an anger but I don't know what it was: something unsettled.

'Squeeze. Don't pull!' he said, picking up the bucket.

'Oh, you should know!' I said. All I could do was say one thing with a sense behind that was meant to hurt. He batted my meaning away, coming up behind me and leaning over to take the diddy and press it between his fingers. A squirt of milk hit the pail with a loud hiss.

"Go on then!' He pressed the diddy into my hand. Our fingers touched, then he stepped back and stood behind me so I could feel his eyes on me. I leant my head on the cow's warm, round body and squeezed. That was all there was to it! I was soon lost in the good feeling of it, the frothing milk creeping up the pail. I squeezed and squeezed until there was no more.

I went to the other cow, a pretty soft brown one, with big wet eyes. She looked surprised.

'Gwendolyn's sick,' I explained. Taking the second pail, I moved to the far side of her in case the two of them pressed together and squashed me. I squeezed and squeezed but nothing came.

Another laugh came from behind. Moses stood in the doorway with his dark hair falling over his forehead and his sleeves rolled up over his brown forearms.

'She's dry!' he scoffed.

'That's obvious!' I said.

'She's to go to the bull next week.'

I didn't know about cows but it wasn't my job. I walked past him with the heavy pail leaning sideways, my other arm to balance out to the side.

'D'you want a hand?' he asked, slow and staring at me. 'I give Gwendolyn a hand sometimes.'

'I know you do!' I said, light as light.

I expected to start the next day with milking but found Gwendolyn in the cow byre, stroking the cow's neck in a thoughtful way.

'Oh, Peggin!'

She jumped back, pink and flustered, busying herself with pouring the milk into the barrel of the butter churn.

'You could help me if you want, Peggin?' she said, with pleading eyes.

I told her how Moses helped me with the milking. I thought she'd smile. Instead, tears came trickling down her face.

'Promise not to tell,' she said. She stopped turning the handle, bending over to blow snot into the straw. Her bubbies were very full and her face plumper and pinker. I knew, just a breath ahead of her telling me.

'Does Moses know?'

She shook her head.

'He's not married. You can marry him and all will be well.'

She gave me this look. 'I don't know if he likes me.'

'He likes you well enough.'

I stood back and she took the paddle.

'My Da will have my guts for garters!' Tears were running down her face again. 'Father's terrible fierce and he's got high hopes,' she said. 'Me with the Ladies... and the wages... and there's lots of children already at home and all my sisters...'

'You're only having a baby!' I cut in. It might have been reminding me of those crying, hungry children that made the nicer part of me come out.

'I'll speak to the Duckies. They won't throw you out. I'll talk to Moses. You can be wed. You can strap the baby on your back while you milk. It can sleep in the straw and Moses will bring you rabbits to cook.'

All the while I was saying it, I had this feeling underneath that it was not going to be like that. Life never is.

Suddenly, Gwendolyn stopped her churning, ran round and hugged me. No one ever hugged me, 'cos I'm not the sort of person to be hugged. I was like stone and Gwendolyn was like cushions. I was left confused, two people in the same skin: the nice and the nasty, the cruel and the kind. The unkind part was quick; the kinder, thinking part was slow, too slow sometimes. The fight went on inside me and I was in a sort of fear as to which one would win.

I didn't go straight to the Duckies. I went to Mary. She'd say it better than I would. Mary would be the person I'd go to if I needed anything, whatever it might be.

She was sitting in the rocking chair by the fire, mending a tear in one of the library cushions, where the cats had been clawing at the embroidery.

'Mary, if someone was going to have a baby, would that be so bad if she worked here and if she wasn't with a man, and if she could go on working just the same, only with a baby?'

'Peggin!' She dropped the cushion, looking like she'd been taken with terrible indigestion. 'Not you, Peggin! Surely not!'

'Me?' I said. 'Never! How could you think me so foolish?'

Mary picked up her work, sniffing. 'You do not have to be foolish to have a baby, Peggin,' she said quietly.

'I'm not saying Gwendolyn is foolish...'

She dropped her work again. 'Gwendolyn! You astonish me! She's so...'

But she never said what.

'Leave it with me, Peggin.'

Late that afternoon, Jock's barking led me to Moses, who was ferreting in the field the far side of the lane. The cows were waiting at the gate for Mr Stour to take them for milking and would not move for me as I clambered over, pushing them away with my foot. If I opened the gate, they'd be out before I could stop them.

Though it was well into autumn, the field was still lush with grass. No wonder the milk was so good. Moses was over the far side, where the field rises up to the hills. The slope was layered: a drop of bare earth, a grassy shelf, another layer of soil, as though it had slipped. A good place for ferreting, that I knew from the rabbit holes.

Moses was bent over the hole and his cosh up in the air. He brought the net high, froze for a moment, then swooped it down. The two creatures were caught together in one shape in the net: the brown screaming rabbit, the yellow biting ferret. Jock stood stiff-legged and barking in a frenzy, the fur on his back up like prickles, so he never saw me. I was right behind Moses when he pulled the animals apart, dropped the net, put the ferret in the cage at his feet and coshed the rabbit – so savage, with his mouth snarling, and face ugly as sin.

'Moses!'

He whipped round and so did Jock, ready to back off or leap forward, until he saw it was me and his ears flattened and his little stump went mad. Moses' hands were bloody. His face was red and his eyes glittering.

'Peggin! What you doing here?'

I held his stare for a moment.

'It's about Gwendolyn.'

He started to smirk. 'Jealous, are you?' he said, wiping his cosh on his britches.

'She's going to have a baby and it's yours.'

That stopped him. His eyes widened and his mouth gaped. He looked down at the rabbit at his feet, its head a bloodied mess with one eye staring up.

'You should marry her quick,' I carried on. I was enjoying this more than I thought I would. 'Because she's not wed and neither is you. Then her Da won't beat her.'

He turned away, twisting the cosh in his hands.

'It was your fault, Moses. Not hers. You were on top and what could she do? A big strong man like you!' He said nothing. 'Just think: Moses and now Baby Moses… though maybe it'll be a girl… Think of a pretty girl's name.'

I wasn't expecting Moses to leap at me, flinging the cosh away, getting his hands round my throat, shaking and shaking as though I was the rabbit. I was hardly able to claw at his fingers, but then he let go and pushed me hard backward till I was rolling down the bank. When I stopped, I was right by the ferret, which was scrabbling at the cage with its bloody little claws.

And then there was Moses, stretching out his hand to help me up.

'Sorry, Peggin. Sorry.' Then another shock – he pulled me to him, hugging me to his chest before turning away, wiping his nose on the back of his hand. He picked up the cosh and the dead rabbit in one hand, the ferret cage in the other, and whistled for Jock. He left me standing there in the field with drops of rabbit's blood on the hem of my dress.

22

GWENDOLYN AND MOSES were wed in the chapel at the bottom of the lane. The first snow of the year had fallen overnight, making everything pretty. I stood at the back with Sara. Elizabeth and Bethan were with Mary behind us. When Gwendolyn faced Moses, who was pressed into clean britches and a jacket and all uncomfortable, she looked as though she might burst with happiness. She was all smiles and ringlets and pink cheeks. I turned to Sara just as she turned to me and we made our eyes big then small, like a message.

When Gwendolyn turned to face the front I stared at her hair, gold and curling over her shoulders, wondering what it must feel like to brush that in the morning, not wrestle with mine, which is springy as heather. Gwendolyn's father and Walter sat on opposite sides of the chapel. They never said a word to each other, not even afterwards when everyone stood shivering on the steps, wondering when they could go home. Mary said the Duckies were sorry they couldn't be there: Big Duckie had a cold and Little Duckie stayed with her. They sent money, which Mary passed to Gwendolyn. I heard Moses whisper, 'How much?'

This was just another wedding with people saying one thing and thinking another and everyone smiling, being nice, as though life is good, but really knowing it isn't.

Moses never looked at me once.

Gwendolyn had her baby girl. The calf was born soon after, a heifer – allowed to live, though the mother and calf were separated immediately. They bellowed all night long, a sound I hated. I blocked my ears with bits of rag and slept with my head under the cover so I could barely breathe.

The milk was the best, rich and creamy, and made the yellowest butter. I was now the one sent to milk and churn. I knew I should visit but I kept putting it off, until Mary said one morning, 'No duties today, Peggin, apart from visiting Gwendolyn.'

Mary never would give up on trying to make me do the right thing.

'The sweep's to clean the chimneys today, so it's best you're out of the way and ready for cleaning when you're back.'

Snow on daffodils was not right. Flowers came up, shouting, 'Spring! Everything's going to be alright,' and then a late snow falls, saying, 'No it isn't.' I managed to pick a few daffodils from under the hedge, little ones. I did not have anything else to take. Gwendolyn was still living in her father's cottage. Inside, it was dark and smelt of peat and babies. I had never been into a place with so many children in it. There was barely an inch of floor to tread without stepping on a child. I knew Gwendolyn had sisters but didn't know how many. I felt a little bad that I'd never asked her about her family. The girls cleared a path to Gwendolyn, who was sitting on the one chair. She jumped up to show me her baby. Such an ugly creature, more like a boiled piglet: its face squashed up, bald, with spots and flakes on its head.

'She's so pretty!' I said. 'She looks like you!'

'Do you think so?' she said, beaming.

I gave her the daffodils and immediately wished I hadn't, because I had to hold the baby while she searched for a cup for the flowers. I feared I might drop it or it wouldn't like me and would cry. Most girls pick up and cuddle babies as though they were put on earth knowing how to, but I didn't feel like that.

'What are you calling it?' I said, handing it back as soon as I could.

'Her.' Gwendolyn seemed happy enough. 'I thought about Peggin?'

'No! You can't!'

'You've been a real friend to me,' Gwendolyn said, which made me feel bad.

'I've got to go!' I said heading for the door.

'Peggy, maybe. Or just Peg would be nice,' she called after me from the door.

23

A FEW DAYS later I was sent to fetch logs to take up to the new maid, Bethan, who was to lay the fire in the Duckies' chamber. My breath went up the stairs in front of me like some kind of misty fiend, curling and beckoning. The door was open. Bethan was standing by the window holding up a crystal drop to the sun, sending rainbows and gold flecks spinning over the walls.

The moment she saw me, she flushed and placed the crystal back on the table, next to the little black dog the Duckies used for a paperweight.

'Peggin! I was only looking,' Bethan said. She was such a wispy girl, with a pinched face and wrists thin as twigs, her skin yellowy under her white bonnet.

'It's the Ladies' gift for the baby,' she said, taking the log basket and kneeling by the empty grate.

'What would a baby want with that?' I was thinking of Gwendolyn's dark house, those windows thick with dirt. Bethan was looking at me like she was wondering how I dared say something like that. 'You've got to sweep the grate clean before you lay the fire,' I said.

I turned away while she went to work with the little brush. Frost had made crusty ferns over the windows. The velvet curtains were pulled back and held in golden tassels, silky to the touch, like cow's diddies. The Duckies slept in a four-poster bed, dark wood carved deep with flowers and leaves and all kinds of creatures. I found a ladybird cut at the foot of the bed and smoothed my fingers over its shell, then dug my nail into the groove where its legs disappeared. I ran my hand over their smooth grey coverlet and touched the corner of one of the four red bolsters, plumped and set against the headboard. They'd not want those carvings digging in their backs as they sat reading at night.

'Can I start now, Peggin?' Bethan's eyes were still anxious.

I knelt beside her to help lay the fire. I didn't have to. I could have told her what to do and left her to it.

The moment the fire was laid, I told Bethan that Mary wanted her down in the kitchen. As soon as she was gone, I picked up the crystal. It was cut like a teardrop with five sides all narrowing to a point. If you look in a crystal, you can see your future but I could only see myself cut up into parts which did not join up. I curled my fingers round its smooth sides, hiding it completely.

I couldn't stop staring at the bed, thinking of the Duckies sitting side by side in their night caps, propped up on those red bolsters. Little Duckie would read, Big Duckie listen until they were both yawning. Little Duckie would close the poetry book and set it down on the bedside table, snuff out the candle and lie down, two little bonnets sunk into the soft pillows. Maybe one would put her arms round the other.

'Goodnight, beloved.'

'Sleep tight, beloved.'

A friendly squeeze. A kiss on her shoulder. Then what? It could not be like Gwendolyn and Moses, I knew that! An arm might reach round, fondle a bubby, then move on down to pull up the nightgown, stroke what she found underneath, find that place. No! I stopped myself from thinking further. This was ridiculous! I squirmed and laughed at the same time. Two old Duckies, all flab and bony legs!

I didn't even think about it. I walked out of the room with the crystal still in my hand. I wanted rainbows chasing round the walls of my room. The problem was, I never go into my room in the light, only early mornings or late evenings. Then I thought, if I couldn't see them, neither could Gwendolyn, nor her baby, nor Moses neither. I walked straight through the kitchen and out to Mr Stour's shed. Taking a trowel from the hook, I walked down the lane and, making sure there was no one to see me, buried it under a holly bush.

The crystal was missed immediately, of course. Little Duckie went to give it to Gwendolyn when she arrived that afternoon to show them her baby.

Bethan was sent for. She knew nothing. I was sent for. I told the truth, that I had seen Bethan holding it up to the light making rainbows. Bethan was called for again. She cried and said it was so, but she put it back on the table. She did. God strike her down if she didn't.

Mary came to my room that night when Sara and Elizabeth were asleep and I was lying there not thinking at all. In the candlelight, Mary's face above me looked like a gargoyle.

'I know it was you, Peggin. You have a history of petty theft, and a record of lying and deception. I also know if I search for it, I will not find it because you are too clever for that. Some lessons you have learnt through the years from your mistakes, though the wrong lessons. I am disappointed in you, Peggin.'

I sat up, indignant. 'I'm innocent. I'll swear to God, or on the Bible if you'd like me to?'

Mary sniffed. 'That won't be necessary. I don't think it would matter to you at all. You are beyond understanding.'

Beyond understanding, was I? I'd show them what beyond understanding means. I was through with the lot of them anyway. I cared nothing for any of them.

No one would speak to me the next day, not Elizabeth, nor snivelling Bethan, nor even Sara, though she gave me a look, as though she was worried about me. Mary had a frown on her whenever she looked in my direction and was sweet as sweet when she talked to the others.

'Go milk the cow, Peggin. Churn the butter and bring it straight back here. I've a list of jobs as long as my arm for you!' Mary said, with a nasty edge to her voice.

I didn't plan anything. Moses came by just as I was washing out the bucket. He half nodded. Quick as quick, I grabbed his hand and pulled him inside the byre, kicking the half-door shut with my heel to keep Jock out, throwing the bucket down with a clatter. I pushed him back into the straw. We didn't say a thing. With one hand I pulled up my dress, with the other I pulled at his britches and he did not stop me.

I closed my eyes because I did not want to see him naked in his boots, and I did not want to think of him looking at me. He knew what to do. It didn't take long, grunting and heaving, before he rolled off me.

I lay for a minute till I smelt the straw and heard the flick of the cow's tail, the grind of her jaw. I sat up, pulled down my dress and pulled my hair loose. Jock was scrabbling at the door, whining like he knew something was going on.

Neither of us said anything, and we didn't look at each other neither.

'More quinine is needed *tout de suite*,' Mary said, thrusting the bottle at me and a basket, when I took the milk back to the kitchen.

Big Duckie must have been having one of her migraines. I didn't mind going; any reason to leave the house was a good reason. The hedges in the lane were thick with more late snow, so pretty, but as the sun warmed the branches everything started dripping. The rowan tree at the corner was heavy with purple buds. I passed the holly bush where I'd buried the crystal, now covered in snow, but I didn't stop.

I followed my own footsteps back along the lane, looking up when I heard a carriage bowling toward me. Snow was shushing under the wheels and the horses' hooves were muffled and squeaking.

I stood back to let it pass. I heard the 'Whoa!', the horses' fast breathing and the snort and shake of their heads.

As the carriage door opened, I caught a quick glimpse of myself in the black shine of the paint: a young woman with a little waist and full chest, a slim face with mousey hair under a white cap.

'Well, well. Are you not the little maid grown into a fine young woman?'

I walked slowly back to him, planting each foot in a print, carefully. He folded down the step. I smiled and he held out his hand to help me in. It was the man from the paper: same hat; same face, only a bit fatter; and grey in his whiskers. The red cushions inside the carriage were the same red as the bolsters on the Duckies' bed.

This time I had more to tell him.

I did not know when the story was printed. Nor did I need to know, because a couple of weeks later Mary came rushing into the kitchen, where I was measuring the oats for the porridge. Her face was so red, her hair so wild, every muscle hard as iron, I feared she was in danger of bursting.

'Read this!' she said, thrusting the paper into my face. 'Read it!' Spit fell from her mouth onto the paper. She shook the paper until I took it from her. 'Out loud!' She folded her arms as though to stop herself from exploding.

I read the headline in a clear voice.

'Extraordinary Female Affection...'

'Judas. Judas! Twenty pieces of silver, was it? Blood money! What did you do it for? What do you know of love or anything else that is good? I have no words more for you, Peggin.'

I said I'd not said nothing. And I had no words for them neither! But I could stay no longer at Plas Newydd. I placed the cup down on the table, went to my room to collect some clothes, and wages saved with the tips from my singing, safe in a little leather pouch. The purse of money the man in the carriage had given me was still in my pocket. Sara was in the kitchen, chewing the end of a strand of hair. I know she looked at me like she wanted to say something, but I walked past her, out of the door and into the courtyard with my head high.

PART IV
Baby

24

THE STONE STEP of Chirk Poor House was a cold place for Iris to wait. She'd rather be shivering outside than inside, where old Nora would follow her everywhere, muttering, 'Poor wee orphan, I'll 'ave 'ee.' But Iris wouldn't have Nora, not if she was the only person in the world.

'I'm not an orphan!' she shouted at her, but Nora didn't seem to understand.

Her heart jumped when she heard the clip-clop of the horse in the lane, then sank again when the horse passed. She'd been ready since she woke, though Mrs Stebbings had said no one would be collecting her till afternoon.

It wasn't good, sitting like this with her back to the house where Ma had been alive till just a few days before, waiting for a man she never knew about. A father had never been mentioned until her mother took to her bed.

'Your father will come.' The trouble was, Ma was coughing and wheezing louder than her words so Baby Iris never knew if she'd heard right.

Ma coughed and coughed, heaved once for breath, coughed and never breathed in again, though Iris waited and waited. Mrs Stebbings came into the room and pulled her away. Iris didn't want to go 'cos Ma had her eyes open and could see her going, and Ma would not want her to be dragged away from her like that.

Iris wouldn't speak afterwards. She wouldn't let anyone near and then she was so hungry she ate a potato which was too hot. Her mouth was burnt so she cried and screamed; it hurt so bad. Mrs Stebbings was kind until she hit her to stop the noise.

'You're six now, not a baby!' she said, taking her up to sleep in the empty bed where she and her Ma had slept. Iris slept wrapped in Ma's smell. She didn't know where Ma was.

At last a cart drew up at the gate. Iris stood up, not sure what to do. The man got down slowly and tied the reins round the gatepost. He was old with a big nose and a bottom lip which stuck out. He was hunched over, with no neck. He walked right past her into the house. Not her father then. At the gate, the horse breathed out a long low sigh. It was hot and steaming, head low. Sad.

Under the tree lay a few wizened apples, forgotten in the winter grass. Iris picked one up; only half of it was black. The horse was so thin, its ribs showed like hers did. Ma used to say Iris was her own little washboard. And now Ma was dead.

Mrs Stebbings watched Iris from the kitchen window.

Lodo was sitting at the kitchen table, slurping soup noisily from a bowl.

'Poor mite,' she sighed. 'You never get used to it. Death. Not never.'

She'd miss them, Nelly and the little one, who'd been with her since she was a baby: sunny as a toddler, sunny as a child; running, never walking, from dawn to dusk. It would be hard to see her go. Most women had shorter stays but with Nelly's health so up and down, and no help from the outside world, no visitors, she'd stayed on, making herself useful when she could. In truth, the loss of little Iris would be hard. She picked up the pile of coins Lodo had placed on the table.

A shape shifted in the doorway.

'What d'you want, Nora?' Her tone was sudden, sharp. Nora, reminding her how unjust life was; Nora, who must stay because there was nowhere for her to go at her age.

'I'll 'ave 'er. The wee one.' Nora clutched the door frame, smacking her toothless gums. 'Where be she?'

'She's out feeding the horse,' Mrs Stebbings said. 'She loves the horses.'

'She'll be alright then,' Lodo said.

'Who's 'ee then?' Nora said, pointing at Lodo.

He supped noisily, ignoring her.

'Nothing to do with you,' Mrs Stebbings said.

Nora stood frowning as he scraped his bowl, wiping it clean with his finger.

'I'd best be gone,' Lodo said, standing and picking up his hat from the table.

'She doesn't have much,' Mrs Stebbings said, holding out a tiny bundle of clothes as he squeezed past Nora, still standing in the doorway.

'Bought her, did yer?' Nora shouted after him. 'How much?'

'Take no notice,' Mrs Stebbings said, as they hurried down the path. 'God takes the good ones and leaves the rotten behind.'

Iris was standing with her hands either side of the horse's face. It had taken the apple from her flattened palm. Apple juice flicked sideways from its lips, falling onto her skirt like speckles of silver. How she loved its great round feet, feathered white, though the white was muddy. She'd half a mind to kneel down to tease the dirt away and lay each hair separate over the hard hoof but, no, p'raps she'd stand with her hands either side of its face. Its eyes were hidden under those little leather squares: they kept the flies off and it couldn't see anywhere but where it was going. Under its thin, warm skin she felt the plates of bone. Slowly, inch by inch, she leaned forward until her nose rested on the horse's.

'I'll miss you,' Mrs Stebbings said, as Iris stepped away from the horse. 'You'll be no trouble, will you? Be good, like your mother taught you.'

The cart creaked as Lodo hauled himself up on to the seat and took the reins. The horse's head jerked, suddenly alert.

Iris didn't need help: her arms were strong and she could jump and pull herself up. Mrs Stebbings passed her bundle up to her. As she did so, something fell and rolled under the cart.

'My button!' Iris wailed.

'Stay there, I'll get it,' Mrs Stebbings said. The red button was in the mud by the back wheel. She bent to pick it up, but as she did so, Lodo's coins spilled from her pinafore pocket and onto the ground.

She straightened up, red in the face.

'Look what you've made me do!' She passed Iris the button but her voice was sharp. She'd not wanted Iris to see the money. It was a gift, not a payment. She picked the coins up and wiped them on her skirt but when she looked up, the cart was moving off and Iris' head was turned away.

'Bide your time,' that's what Ma always said, though Iris knew she must be brave. As the road started winding down the hill, Iris heard the rush of the river down on her left-hand side. She scrabbled forward and tapped the man's arm.

'Please sir, you're not my father, are you?'

The man flicked the reins and shook his head. 'I'm Lodo, his man. I'm taking you to 'im.'

'Beggin' your pardon, sir,' Iris said. 'Could you take me to my brother, Joe, instead? He's not far away. He makes buttons. Please sir.'

The man's head was shaking before she'd finished. He flicked his whip and the horse's pace increased.

'I'm doing what I've been told. I'll be paid when the task's done. You are the task.'

Lying down in the back of this wooden cart with the wheels rumbling and grating underneath her, there was nothing left to feel. If Iris had had those leather squares over her eyes like the horse, she wouldn't have had to bury her head under her shawl so's not to see. Sounds creep through wool: the creaking, the thumping of hooves, the flicking whip, the man hissing through his teeth like the old black kettle.

25

EVERCREECH SAT ON a stool facing a tin mirror, angled so the light from the oil lamp fell on to the reflection of his face. His moustache lay on the dresser in front of him like a dead creature. It was a humiliation to him that he could not grow his own to such a luxurious length. His upper lip, which he pushed one way then the other, was red from the glue. It was sprouting coarse, irregular hairs which were more like prickles. He had removed the red from his cheeks, and the black from one eye, and was about to start on the other when he heard his man.

'I come for my money.'

'Ah! Lodo! Where is she?'

'Asleep, I reckon, sir.'

'Don't leave her outside, bring her in! Wait, let me fetch her.'

Evercreech, still in his boots and britches and vest after the evening show, stepped out into the night. His man drew the bolt on the cart and eased down the back flap. Iris lay huddled in the dark corner with her shawl over her head, looking no more than a pile of rags.

Evercreech stood back, unsure. He'd pictured himself walking in with the child in his arms. Saved. And he the saviour. On second thoughts, she might wake, terrified. He'd wait for her inside. It might be better to be sitting on the stool, smiling.

'Wake her. Bring her in,' he said to Lodo as he turned.

Everything had been thought of: food put aside, a bed made up by Jenny, one of the tumblers, next to his own so that the child might reach out and touch him if she needed him. Evercreech sprang up. Sitting was wrong. He paced up and down, sat, stood, picked up his red jacket and put it down again. At last the tent flap opened and Baby Iris walked in. She was smaller than he had thought a six year old would be. Tiny in fact, and thin, with more of Nelly in her looks than he had imagined. He'd thought it would be like looking in a tin mirror through the years to his boyish self.

They stood, neither of them knowing what to do.

Iris' face was solemn, her clothes rags. She'd bare feet. He must ask Jenny to find her shoes. She must have shoes.

'Well, well,' he said. Her expression didn't alter. No guessing what was going on in her mind. 'Come here. I won't bite you, you know!'

She stayed where she was.

Lodo coughed. 'Excuse me, sir, but…' He was rubbing his eye, nodding his head.

'What? What?'

'Your make-up, sir – she might be scared.'

'Oh, that!' Evercreech burst into a loud laugh.

'What did you see, eh? A monster, is that it? You caught me in the middle of taking my disguise off. You know who I am, don't you?'

Iris shook her head.

Evercreech, wiping at his eye with grease, frowned.

'I'm your father. Did your mother not talk of me?'

Iris shook her head. The lamp flickered across her dark eyes. Her hair was mousey.

''Scuse me, sir,' Lodo inched forward.

Irritated, Evercreech indicated the coins on the corner of the table.

Lodo jumped forward and scooped them into his hand. 'I'll see to the horse,' he said, backing quickly toward the flap. Iris turned to follow him.

Evercreech caught her arm.

'No, no. You're to stay with me.' Her breathing was fast.

'The horse,' she whispered.

'You want to see the horse, eh? Tomorrow. I've four horses you can see, the stars of the company – or they were till you arrived, my own child! Would you like to ride the horses? Eh? You would, I know it! I could train you up. You and me together. Father and daughter.'

He coaxed her back into the tent, but her face was screwed into a frown.

'Come, come. I've food for you and a bed here, next to mine. We've so much to talk about. Jenny will be here soon and she'll look after you. You'll like Jenny! I don't know much about children and women's things, but she'll be like a mother to you, so now you'll have a mother and father together.'

'My mother's dead,' Iris said.

Evercreech let go of her, rubbing his fingers up and down over his red fingerprints on her arm. He scratched at his sore upper lip.

'She is. I'm sorry. She had someone write to me a few weeks ago and told me to come and take you. Did she tell you that?'

Baby Iris shook her head.

Evercreech pulled his cheeks to and fro. 'She should have prepared you. Come, come,' he said in a heartier tone. 'I don't know what to call you...'

'I choosed Iris.'

'Then I shall call you Iris. And you must call me Pa... but only when we're alone... here in the tent. Don't be shy now. Put down your things: there's your bed, see? Do you want something to eat?' He took a lid from a pot on the table. 'Jenny's cooked you something nice!'

Iris shook her head.

'No, well...' He replaced the lid. Where was that Jenny? Drinking and gossiping with the other girls, no doubt, though she'd promised to look in. Not to stay, not tonight, not yet... oh, there were adjustments to be made.

PART V
Joe

26

A YEAR AND a half after Joe first met Clara on the day he found that his mother was dead, he was riding in Caleb's cart to Chirk to be wed.

For the time being, Clara would remain with her parents at the Trap Inn. Joe would visit as often as he could. Neither of her parents had been keen on the wedding. Gracie, their eldest surviving daughter, had recently died in childbirth, leaving four children for her mother to bring up, the children's father being 'a wastrel and a ne'er-do-well'. Joe was neither a ne'er-do-well nor a wastrel, Clara assured them, running her hand over her swelling belly. Besides, she would be staying at the inn and nothing would be different. She would help her father with the bar, and her mother with Gracie's children – her own baby would hardly be noticed and, honestly, nothing would be any different at all, but they'd all be kept in buttons for life.

Inside the church, Clara, in a pretty dress of primrose yellow, stood by her father's side. He stood tall and frowning, his green eyes angry. Even though Clara's dress was full, the round of her belly was obvious when she turned towards Joe. Just once, they had gone further than either intended. When Clara told him on his visit a couple of months later that she thought she was with child, Joe was aghast, then disbelieving, then, gradually, pleased. Everything had led up to this moment, standing looking up into her grey eyes, about to be wed.

Clara's mother stood a pace behind her husband, dressed in black, still mourning Gracie. Next to her Gracie's four children – the smallest to the tallest, solemn, hair brushed – held posies of wild flowers. For a brief moment, Nelly came into Joe's mind, chased away when the priest cleared his throat. He was ready to begin: his Bible before him.

The shock when the priest turned made Joe flinch. He'd assumed it would be another man. Nine years is a long time. This was the man he remembered: stooped, older, thinner, the nose longer, the cheeks and eyes more sunken. The shoulders of his surplice were still flecked with white skin flakes.

As the priest raced through his words in a shaky voice, Joe thought of Nelly, Baby, Aggie. They should be with him now, and only by thinking their names could he bring them into the room. Gradually he became aware of the silence around him, the priest's glare.

'Speak up. I'm a little hard of hearing!!'

'Oh...' Joe gabbled the words through to 'and thereto I plight thee my troth.'

Another promise to keep.

Looking into his eyes, without wavering, Clara pledged herself to Joe and they were husband and wife. The priest held out his thin hands to take theirs. It was clear he had no idea whose hands he was joining. The priest's hand was cold as a dead thing, but Clara's beneath Joe's was soft and warm.

27

'WHEN AN OPPORTUNITY comes, your duty is to take it,' Joe explained to Clara, his hand on her swollen belly. Eighteen months since they were wed, twelve months since the twins were born, Clara was again so big, she waddled like a duck round the Trap Inn with the ewer, feet splayed out, filling the mugs with beer. Her back hurt her, she'd a constant headache, her feet swelled so her shoes would not fit, and she'd hardly the strength to lift one twin, let alone two. Without Joe there to help her, she did not know what she could do. And now… now… Joe had brought her the news he was moving far away.

'Where?' she said. 'Shrewsbury last time, and now?'

'Llangollen,' he told her. 'I'm to work on the paddles at the mill. Llangollen is not so far away. And at least you've a mother to help you.'

He always ended with this. Usually Clara would close her mouth and let her thoughts sound in her own ears and not his. This time she said, 'And I'm the mother they will miss if I bleed to death and die like my sister.'

Joe could say nothing. That Gracie had died like that, with four young children left behind, was dreadful. But if that had not happened, there would have been no one to look after Clara's twins. God's ways were mysterious. He tightened his jaw. Clara must see it his way. Here was an opportunity to better himself and so better the chances for all of them. It was a rare thing to make such advancement in a world where most people accepted where they were born, lived their lives accordingly and died in the same bed they were birthed in. Not Joe Begg, who had come into this world in the tent of a fortune teller, according to his mother. Her pains had started in the middle of a performance; she had only run as far as the fortune teller's when Joe made his entrance a bare ten minutes later. From button maker to construction worker and now the chance of being assistant to the assistant engineer himself. One lucky event leading to the other.

'It will be better for us all.' He lamely patted her hand.

'Not if I die, it won't,' Clara said.

Joe visited Clara whenever he could, though the refurbishment of the Llangollen Corn Mill took longer than anticipated. That was the way with engineering and construction. Unforeseen problems at every turn, but the result was worth all the setbacks.

Joe was celebrating the turning of the new paddles at the mill, supping a glass of ale with the other men, when news was brought by the driver of a coal cart that Clara had given birth to a baby boy. That's all the driver knew. He thought they were both well. No one had told him any different.

There was no need to rush to see them. What could Joe do anyway? More drinks were called for and the health of Clara, the new baby and the proud father proposed and drunk to.

Travelling back towards Chirk in the coal cart the next day, Joe planned what he would say to Clara. She did not understand the balancing act a man must make. He must be a provider for his family, but also he must fulfil his duty to God, who gave him his abilities and his chances to advance himself. Of course he was anxious to see her, to see his children, but Clara's life was less complicated.

Clara had named the baby Archie before Joe arrived.

An ugly little fellow, this Archie, with purplish skin, but perfect in his mother's eyes: good and placid, so Joe kept his feelings to himself.

'I've to wake him to feed!' Clara told Joe. She was up and sitting on the bed in her room when he arrived. The twins were out feeding the chickens with Gracie's eldest daughter.

'Isn't he beautiful, Joe?' Clara looked down at her baby with a softness in her face that made Joe gulp. She brushed Archie's forehead with her lips then looked up at Joe.

'We need to be together, Joe,' Clara said, the moment she had lain the baby down in her bed.

'Soon, believe me, Clara. I am so very busy. Mr Telford has asked me to help him with his new project, Clara.' Should he go on? Would she be able to share his excitement? 'An aqueduct, Clara. A bridge the likes of which you'd never believe.'

Clara turned away. Perhaps it would be better if Joe were to talk of her situation.

'Think, Clara, my dearest: here you have Gracie's children to assist you, and you are such a help to your father... and the truth is, at the moment, I am so busy, I could not be everything you wish me to be.'

Joe knew that a woman's emotions can run wild when a child has been born. He stayed the night, though understandably – if disappointingly – Clara would not let him near her, the most intimate moment being when he moved her nightshirt to kiss the mole on her neck. She responded with a shudder. Joe lay on his back, staring at the unfamiliar ceiling.

When he left the following afternoon, after entertaining his twins the entire morning, Clara's tears upset him as much as her unspoken words hurt him. He followed her up to her room, though the cart was already waiting for him in front of the inn.

'I must go, Clara. You knew I could not stay long.'

'You cannot wait to be away from your wife and your children, Joe. Everyone's business is more important than ours. I do not believe you ever mean to have us in your life!'

'Clara! How can you say that? I do. I promise you.'

'Promises, Joe Begg, are only words until you make them happen.'

She turned away from him, holding little Archie to her bubby, and would not let him near.

The twins stood solemn in the doorway behind him.

'When did they learn to climb stairs?' he asked.

Clara shook her head and burst into tears once more.

'Just go, Joe.' The twins were crying too, and ran to her for comfort. The last thing Joe saw as he backed away to the stairs was Clara pushing the twins away.

28

THERE WERE MANY reasons why Joe had not visited Clara and the children as soon as he intended. Weeks had passed when he next sprang from a tradesman's cart and walked quickly across the yard of the inn. His heart was beating fast: an odd mixture of excitement at seeing Clara again and an undercurrent of anxiety.

He stood in the doorway to her bedroom, his face halfway between joy and apology. Clara still in her nightgown, her hair straggling round her pinched white face, allowed him to kiss her cheek but would not even hear him out. She thrust the baby into his arms when he was in the middle of explaining about the ledgers: the columns he must rule, the information he must collect and collate.

'Save your breath,' she said. 'Do not spend all the time you can spare me explaining why you could not come before!'

Baby Archie was no more pleased to be in Joe's arms than Joe was to be holding him. His little face was frantic to be with his mother. When Clara turned her back on them to pick up her hairbrush, he began to scream.

'Clara… beloved…' Joe began, struggling to keep the baby from slipping out of his grasp.

'I cannot hear you, Joe,' Clara said, her strokes slow and deliberate. 'I have not had time to attend to my tangles for a week! Take him away!'

A baby is hard to placate when the only thing he wants is unavailable. Joe took Archie downstairs. Clara's father was rolling a beer barrel across the tap room floor, hefting it on to a wooden trestle.

'Fine lungs on him!' Joe said, walking to the back door.

Clara's father said nothing.

Outside there might be more to distract Archie: birds, fluttering leaves – the diversions God provides. Over by the hen coop, the twins were engrossed in some kind of game involving mud, sticks and stones, and chattering.

'What are you up to?' Joe said, over Archie's wailing.

His question silenced them.

Gracie's eldest was spreading laundry on the bushes to dry.

'Give 'im 'ere,' she said, in a weary voice.

To Joe's immediate relief, and then his annoyance, Archie stopped wailing the moment he left his father's arms.

The day was not a success. There were plenty of things awaiting Joe's attention back at the aqueduct. What good was being done on this visit? No one was pleased to see him. On the journey from Llangollen to Chirk, Joe had dared to hope there might be time when he and Clara could be alone, but from mid-afternoon it became clear that was not to be. Archie was unsettled all day, desperately fighting sleep, as though to spite his father. Every time Joe spoke to the twins, their mouths clamped shut. The power of children to deflate a man's feelings was something Joe was unprepared for.

After a long day of being uncomfortable and unappreciated, Joe was eager to be away. Finally, as the tradesman's cart turned into the courtyard, Archie fell asleep and Clara's frostiness began to thaw. She took Joe's arm as she walked with him across the yard.

'I know you are busy with your bridge, Joe, but do not leave it so long before you come again. It would be the better for all of us. The children do not know you! And neither do I.'

'Don't say that, Clara!' Joe said, turning to face her. He lifted her hand to his mouth to kiss her fingertips tenderly. 'My beautiful Clara.'

Clara arched her eyebrows, but her face softened and she smiled, filling Joe brimful with love for her. His eyes misted. Clara pulled him to her, hugged him, then pulled away.

'Sweet words are nice, but not enough, Joe.'

Jogging back down the hill in the cart, Joe felt the good feelings seeping away. He would make good his promise. Everything took the time it took. Clara could not know how hard he worked, that was the problem. She had not the knowledge, neither did she appreciate that her husband was the luckiest of men. Had it not been for his apprenticeship at the Webbers, he would not have met Zachery; without Zachery, he would not have been taken on at the bridge project in Shrewsbury where he met Mr Telford; without Mr Telford, he would never have known about the paddle construction work at the mill in Llangollen; and all this led to Mr Telford asking Joe to help on the aqueduct project.

Back in his attic room, Joe lit a candle and held his shoes up to inspect them. The heels were worn to the uppers, his stockings were wet and black. The leaking shoes caused itching between his toes, hard to bear at night. Should he have them mended again? Or had he time to purchase a new pair? Stout boots were needed for the aqueduct project. A sudden sharp image made him catch his breath: his father, handing his boots to Joe.

'Take 'em Joe. I've no use for 'em. Stuff the toes. Too big now, lad, but you'll grow into 'em.'

Joe sighed, placing the shoes on the window ledge to dry. In the morning he'd buff them until he could see his face in them. Poor father. Though the truth was that his father's bad luck had been the beginning of his own good fortune. As Mr Webber had told him when he first arrived at the button factory, 'Life is predestined according to God's plan.'

God knew how things would work out, though you, down on earth, might not. One thing led to another. That's what Mr Webber believed, before he went blind. Unable to attend chapel, Joe would read to him from the family Bible. When one Sunday he read from Jeremiah, the words spoke directly to him: "Thine eyes are open upon all the ways of the sons of men: to give every one according to his ways, and according to the fruit of his doings."

Joe was smiling to himself when he looked up to see the old man, knees covered in a tartan rug, nodding sadly.

'Not you, sir,' Joe said. 'Me.'

Joe snuffed the candle and knelt for his prayers. Itching toes are not conducive to prayer. The problem might be less in bed where he could push his feet away without scratching them. He should dwell on his good fortune. It was only a matter of time. Clara would see it his way when the baby was bigger, when she thought more of others and less of herself. He should visit her more often. He should and he would.

29

JOE BOUNDED ACROSS the courtyard of the Trap Inn the next time he visited, so eager was he to see Clara. The silence and gloom inside stopped him short.

Neither Clara nor her parents were in sight.

He raced up the stairs. The door to Clara's parents' bedroom was open. Clara's mother lay on the bed, still and white, eyes closed, there and not there at all. Joe stood fighting for breath at the door. His own mother he had not seen dead, but she must have looked like this, marbled and stiff: gone. His gulp escaped into the room. Clara, sitting by the bed, looked up. She came to him.

'My mother is dead,' she said. 'And we are coming to live with you.'

'Soon, Clara. I promise.'

★★★

The next night Joe stood at his window, as he did every night. The house martins were quiet. The sky was dark. No stars – a pity, because he liked to trace lines from one star to the next, drawing the constellations.

He folded his clothes over the arms of the chair, looping the button holes over the cloth buttons – unnecessary but a habit, to leave them visible. Kneeling on the hook rug by the bed, he addressed God directly at first, though found his prayers melding with thoughts and images. Clara. He was speaking to both God and Clara when he said, 'Do not lose faith in me.'

Help came unexpectedly from Mrs Evans, his landlady. Not that she wanted him to leave, she explained, removing his porridge bowl one morning, as his rent was most welcome, but her children were grown now and she needed the room.

'I know it's no business of mine, Mr Joseph, but I can't help thinking of your poor wife.'

Joe opened his mouth to speak, but she hurried on. She knew of a cottage needing a tenant. Two rooms and an attic. The woman who had lived there had been given more than she ever wanted from her rotten husband, and was in the asylum now, poor thing.

Joe's walk to work took him past the empty cottage the next day. It was a mere ten minutes from his office – most convenient. He noted the pretty garden with its hollyhocks and colourful flowers. How the twins would enjoy picking them! He could picture them now, taking them for Clara, who would arrange them in a cup on the table.

His family's arrival at the end of the week took him by surprise. He had sent word to Clara about the cottage to give her hope, but the arrival of her father's cart outside his office the following day was, frankly, unwelcome. It was hardly appropriate for his private life to intrude on his work.

The look in Clara's father's fierce eyes made him excuse himself quickly from Mr Davidson, put on his coat and ride with them back to the new cottage. How he wished now that he had ventured inside, having intended to go back that very evening. Clara took his hand and squeezed it. Her smile banished his unease.

'You are pleased to see us, aren't you, Joe?' she whispered.

'Of course!' Joe said.

Clara's father was unloading the bundles, baskets, trunk and boxes, setting them out on the front path before Joe had located the key – hanging, as Mrs Evans had said, inside the old hen house. Clara was walking down the path with Archie on one arm, her mother's old curtains over the other. The twins were already racing round and round the garden.

'I've got to go. Work to be done!' her father shouted from the cart, picking up the reins and turning the cart round.

'Thank you!' Clara called after him, as he trotted away without a backward glance.

Joe danced ahead of Clara, masking his anxiety in enthusiasm, waving the rusty key in the air.

'It might not be as you want it, Clara, my dear, but I'm sure we can make it so.'

He turned the key in the lock of the front door, pushed it open and ushered Clara forward. She took a pace, then stopped. By her stricken face, Joe realised everything was not as he hoped. Entering himself, he took in the room. Wallpaper hung in tatters from the walls, there was no glass in the windows, the floor crunched as they walked.

'Stay outside!' Clara shouted at the children. What furniture there had been lay in a broken pile in the middle of the room. Joe picked up a chair with three legs, and set it as upright as a three-legged chair can be. He walked on, knowing Clara would not take a step further, and was quickly glad she had not, seeing the pile of shrivelled but obvious foulness in the corner. He turned back to her in haste.

'Clara, my darling,' he said, searching his mind frantically. 'Remember. The woman was a lunatic. They'd to take her away spitting and screaming. She attacked her own husband, I understand.'

Clara rounded on him furiously.

'Hush your mouth now, Joe! I do not want those words in my head.'

She stepped back to the open door stopped and flinched, setting Archie screaming.

'Joe! Do something!' Clara said waving her hand. 'I cannot bear it!'

What? What? He looked down where she had looked and there was a rat on its side, stiff, little legs curled under it. He recoiled in disgust. Arming himself with a piece of wood he advanced, shovelled it up and ran into the garden. The twins were sitting just outside the door on the path with a pile of browning hollyhock trumpets between them.

'Out of my way!' Joe shouted, setting the pair of them running for their mother. They clung to her skirts by the pile of belongings near the road, terrified.

The problem is, Joe thought, hefting the rat over the hedge and stamping on the odd white maggot which had fallen at his feet, the children do not know me. Nor I them.

He stood by the hedge taking deep breaths, hand on his chest, composing himself.

Mrs Evans had not led him to believe the state of the cottage was this bad! He stood tapping his fingers on the piece of wood still in his hand. The seat of a chair perhaps, a piece of floorboard? In truth, Mrs Evans was not at fault, he was. He should have seen inside for himself. He must apologise to Clara, ask if they might all squeeze into his room in Mrs Evans' house until the cottage was habitable, and beg the Evans children to bring brooms and mops, vinegar, ammonia or whatever women used to overcome bad odours, and get busy. The very next day. At the least, he thought to himself as he closed the door and walked to join his family, he had a little money saved. His family could take his bed. He would sleep on the floorboards. Tomorrow was another day. With a little help, all would be well.

He stood at Clara's elbow. The twins peeked at him and buried their heads again.

'I apologise,' he said. 'For all my faults.'

Clara nodded. 'It was only a rat. I've seen plenty of them. I don't know what came over me.'

They smiled at each other. 'All will be well.' Joe said. She nodded her head and shook the twins from her skirt.

30

THREE DAYS LATER, the cottage was ready. Joe stood at the foot of the bed in the attic to undress. The ceiling was higher here. He no longer had to bend to take his shirt off. The side window of the cottage looked out down the river. If he craned his neck out of the window, he could glimpse the place where the bridge would be.

'Think Clara, you will be able to watch the aqueduct grow from your own home!' Joe said, folding his clothes over the foot of the iron bedstead. Soon they would have a chair and a new mattress, Clara having refused to sleep on the old one – and he could not blame her, even though he was eager to make the bed their own. Instead she'd shut the children in their room for safety, before sending the mattress careering down the stairs, instructing Joe to burn it at once. Clara collected together all the soft materials she had brought with her: the thick green curtains which had furnished her mother's room in Chirk, two tablecloths belonging to Gracie, all the rugs and cushions, and piled them onto the bed. Joe, smelling of the fire he had made, spread them over the wooden slats.

'I will get you a mattress tomorrow. They make their own in The Eagle. Stuffed with cotton. No straw for them!' he said to Clara.

Kneeling, in the circumstances, did not seem right. He could say his prayers while lying down.

'Imagine Clara, every night,' he said, as he snuffed the candle and snuggled into her.

Clara turned her face to the wall.

Early the next day, Joe walked into Llangollen to see Jennet at The Eagle. The moon was still up and a few stars visible. He was early enough to hear the late call of the owl and the early call of the blackbird. The Eagle, as Mrs Evans had reminded him, was expanding with all the construction schemes in the area, and the excellent projects for the future. He would ask Jennet. She would know how to proceed.

Business satisfactorily concluded and a mattress to be delivered by cart before the end of the day, Joe must hurry back. The morning sun was only just touching the tops of the hills with yellow light. It would not do to be late.

He was passing The Hand, crossing the cobbles under the arch where the coaches turn into the yard, when a young woman came hurrying out of the courtyard, tossing her head and throwing a shawl round her shoulders. There was something about that action which stopped him in his tracks. The briefest glimpse of her profile – that turned up nose, that jutting chin – stopped his heart.

'Aggie!' he cried, 'Aggie!' but the girl hurried away, leaving him frozen, unable to breathe. She was up the road before he started to run after her. 'Aggie!' But as he called, the girl began to run, disappearing round the corner. He followed to the place where she had disappeared, looked to right and left, but she had gone. Had she not heard him? Or was it not her at all? If she had she heard her name, surely she would have stopped? He must have been mistaken. It was so long now: she must be quite grown, but there was something familiar about the girl he'd seen. His heart was beating so fast he felt faint. He retraced his steps to The Hand. In the courtyard a boy was uncoupling a horse from the empty coach.

'Excuse me… do you know that girl, woman, the one who left just now?'

The boy shrugged and jerked his thumb towards the open door of one of a row of cottages along one side of the yard. Inside a woman stood behind a table sorting the contents of the mail sack. From the doorway, Joe repeated his question. The woman looked at him sharply.

'Who wants to know?' she said.

Joe pressed his hand onto his chest to quieten it.

'Joe Begg. I'm Joe Begg, assistant to Mr Davidson – on the aqueduct.'

'She came up at from Plas Newydd, I believe. Ain't that right, Elijah?' she called.

A bony, whiskery man, tacking up a piebald mare outside, looked up.

'Elijah would know,' she said to Joe.

'Trouble, that one,' Elijah mumbled.

That could be Aggie! Plas Newydd, where those scholarly ladies lived.

Joe checked his fob, wanting to go immediately to Plas Newydd. He was late: the men would be at their work, Mr Davidson already at his desk wondering where Joe was. Joe Begg was never late. Had something happened to him? It had. What? That was the problem – not knowing what to think, his thoughts going one way while his feet sped the other way, along the road to the site.

All day immediate considerations took his full attention, though thoughts held at bay pressed forward with such force he thought he might burst. The blocks from the quarry must be measured once more, numbered and made ready for the men to use in building the next pillar. Precision and exactitude were crucial to the success of the project. He must concentrate. He must.

At the end of the day, he was free of his work responsibilities. Unfortunately for his plans, he had to walk past the cottage before continuing on to Plas Newydd. Clara was whacking a rug in the front garden.

'Joe! Come see!

She pulled him to the front door, where he hesitated before removing his boots.

'The chimney's swept!' Clara said, 'and the grate is new blacked. Look!'

Joe's eyes stung in spite of the windows flung wide. In his stockinged feet, he trod heavily and painfully on a wooden block, stumbled and landed on another. The very blocks he had fashioned for Baby Iris, now discovered by the twins. He was not used to it, that was the trouble: the noise, the confusion, the demands of the children. Clara could accommodate it. This day in particular, he longed for peace. The twins, their faces still smeared with soot, were squabbling over some trifle – the wooden horse, broken now, with only two legs. He'd make another! When time allowed.

'Water butt for you two!' Clara shouted, dumping Archie in Joe's arms. The baby was wailing and smelt unpleasant. She began dragging the twins towards the back door.

'Jiggle him, sing to him, anything!' Clara snapped. 'Put your knuckle in his mouth!'

Joe tried but his knuckle was not to the boy's taste. When Archie squirmed and struggled, he was difficult to hold. The twins came back into the room, water dripping from their faces, hands over their ears, heading straight for the stairs. As Archie's fury grew so did Joe's, and he was on the point of exploding himself when Clara appeared. When she took him, Archie's sobs subsided immediately into spasmodic shudders, as though recalling the horror of being in his father's arms.

Joe stood clenching and unclenching his fists, his agitation replaced by an urge to be gone.

'What's the matter, Joe?' Clara asked in a calmer tone, settling back into the chair and unfastening her bodice for Archie. 'What's on your mind?'

He could have told her, but when he opened his mouth, he couldn't without knowing for certain.

'There's something I have to attend to in town,' he said. 'Urgently.'

'Can't it wait till morning?' Clara asked, but her eyes were on Archie.

'Don't wait up,' Joe said, backing towards the door.

''I won't,' Clara said wearily, rubbing her thumb to and fro over Archie's head.

Following directions obtained after happening across the very post-boy he had spoken to that morning, Joe made his way up the lane towards Plas Newydd. The back door would be the more likely one than the front, he decided.

In the dark, keeping to the hedge helped Joe navigate the obstacles in the garden: a looming shape turned into a stone bird bath, shadowy traps of bare earth became neat flower beds. As he rounded the corner into the courtyard, he removed his hat, smoothed his hair, took a deep breath and knocked on the back door.

A girl opened the door a crack. The light was behind her but she was too small to be Aggie. It would be strange to have a caller after dark.

'I'm sorry to call so late, but I wonder if you could help?'

There must have been something reassuring in his manner, because she opened the door a little wider. Beyond her, he could see the corner of a kitchen table, a flagstone floor, a flicker of light from a fire.

'I'm looking for someone. She might work here. She might not. Perhaps a bit older than you...' The girl glanced behind her. Someone giggled.

'A bit of a character,' he continued. 'I thought I saw her in Llangollen.'

Behind her, someone called out in Welsh, '*Pwy sydd yno, Sara?*' A second girl appeared, holding up a candle: a larger version of the smaller girl, with black hair and freckles.

'And there's no one else but you working here?'

'There's Bethan,' the girl with the candle said, and a third girl appeared and disappeared quickly. Not Aggie. Too small. Too young.

'No one else?' Joe asked.

The two girls spoke in Welsh to each other.

'Just Gwendolyn. She lives in the village with her Da and her sisters.'

No. 'So sorry to trouble you,' Joe gabbled. 'I must be mistaken.'

As he walked back across the dark cobbled courtyard, giggles exploded behind him, silenced by the door shutting.

Disappointment is a weight to bear. Joe had allowed pictures to form in his mind: the door swinging open, Aggie throwing her arms round him, screeching 'Joe, my Joe' into his ear, knocking his hat sideways. He'd laugh at her and she'd take his hand and… well, that was not going to happen. Now the rain had started. His heart sank even further. Would they be able to continue the delicate work of the arch in the morning? The wooden scaffolding would be treacherous and the men difficult, and who could blame them? Fine for him, with a nice, dry office to retire to.

The next day, it was still raining. His office, a temporary wooden structure on wheels, was situated on the far side of the humpback bridge. The existing canal came to a dead end just beyond the office – the very canal which was soon to flow over the new aqueduct. Inside, the office was snug, with a stove ready for the cold months ahead. Through the window, Joe could see the new offices under construction on the other side of the canal, beyond the track used to bring the stones down from the quarry.

Joe shook his coat at the door. Mr Davidson had the bigger desk, the grander chair, the more prominent position, which was as it should be. Joe kept his desk, though smaller, tidy; ledgers and calculations stacked on the right, pens and rules ready on the left. Someone had moved the inkwell and pinned a letter underneath it. He picked it up.

Goodness! Well-travelled. The paper was wrinkled from a recent wetting, the ink smudged.

Joe Begg,
~~Button Factory,~~
~~Oswestry~~
~~Corn Mill,~~
~~Llangollen~~
Try the Aqueduct office

He turned it over, frowned, and tapped his hand with the envelope. The writing on the original address was faint, unrecognisable. He shook it free from its envelope. Not a letter. What was it, now? An advertisement. The kind he used to distribute round the marketplaces when he was a lad. Goodness, he'd not thought he had any memory of that until this moment.

BROWN'S FAIRGROUND
Mr Brown, with the grateful and respectful
acknowledgements...

Joe's eyes scanned the close, dense print to the items in capitals.

Come, thrill to the spectacular feats of
Mr James and Mr Cardona
on the GEOMETRICAL LADDER...

...more small print which Joe raced through...

Witness the Unbelievable Athleticism of
LIGHT AND HEAVY BALANCING...

Joe's eyes strayed to an item at the bottom of the page:

And the breathtaking
EQUESTRIAN EXERCISES of MRS BROWN
In which she will perform with Hoops, Oranges, etc...

Next to 'etc' someone had written in little letters: And me.

PART VI
Peggin

31

I HAD TO LEAVE Plas Newydd. I wanted to. They made me do the things I did. They never thought of that! Fire all the words at me that you like, Mary. Words can't hurt, can they? Just noises in the air and then they're gone.

I took nothing. I'd the clothes I stood up in – boots, dress, shawl and cap – plus six shillings in my purse from the newspaper man with his promise, and the money I'd saved over the years at Plas Newydd: not much, but something. What more did I need? I also took the name they gave me: Peggin. I'd have changed it to Peg if Gwendolyn hadn't stolen the name. I was used to Peggin.

It was raining and the lane was muddy and full of puddles. The quicker I walked, the sooner I'd be in a room at The Eagle, paid for by that newspaper man.

'Give it a week before publication,' he'd told me when he passed me the purse. 'Then add a couple of days and then, if I judge correctly, you'll be out on your ear, dear girl! I'll arrange everything with Thomas at The Eagle. This,' he said handing me a little card, 'is my address, if your plans should go wrong. In any eventuality, dear girl, you have your money!'

I didn't like the way he had patted my behind when I got out of the coach. I had skipped fast down the road to get away from him. Inside I felt light. I had told him nothing that wasn't true.

If you don't know men and how thirsty they are, you wouldn't believe how many places in Llangollen you could get a drink. I passed The Hand as quick as I could. The Eagle was on the far side of town. Inside was crowded, with men on their way home from working on the bridge construction, I supposed, listening to their talk. A chip of stone had flown into this man's eye when he was cutting. He'd washed it out with salt water but he still had a dirty cloth tied round it and tipped up his head to see his ale. I squeezed my way next to a man hunched over a tankard. I'd seen him somewhere before. All bony and whiskery and smelling like horses... the post-boy I rode with that time! Elijah! When I looked at him, he drained his beer, slipped off the chair and walked quickly to the door. I was glad to see him go; I didn't want no one to recognise me. I called out for Mr Williams, like the newspaper man told me to.

The rooms above the bar had beds, but no, I was taken by Alys, the publican's daughter, out into the back yard to an outhouse. The candle she held up flickered in the wind and gave no light at all. When she cupped her hand round it, everything was even darker.

'Privy's there.' She jerked her thumb one way. 'Tap's there,' she jerked it the other. 'Food in the kitchen but he didn't pay for no food.'

In the room, she lit another candle stub before leaving me.

I was hungry. Mean bastard. I'd eaten nothing since the row. Still, I had money. I took the candle for a quick visit to the privy. Plas Newydd had made me forget how privies can be: scurryings and scratchings and stink.

If you feel uneasy, you have to walk as though you've never felt easier in your life. That's what I did. Blowing my candle stub out to save it for the night, I went straight toward food smells coming from the kitchen. Light from the window made the path clear anyway.

The sour-faced kitchen woman gave me a bowl of watery stew, a potato and a glass of ale. I sat in the corner on a chair with the plate on my knees, the beer on the window sill overlooking the yard. Men walked to and from the privy as I ate, though the odd one stopped and relieved himself in the corner against the stone wall. Dirty beasts, men.

I'd the spoon halfway to my mouth when I saw someone standing there in the shadows. I'd know him anywhere, light or dark, by the shape of him. Moses! Had he been sent to fetch me? No. They'd not change their minds about me that quick. Or at all. What then? My stomach turned as I suddenly remembered me on my back in the straw and Moses on top, and opening my eyes and seeing him looking down at me, melting and soft. I didn't like it.

I didn't like it no more now, Moses standing there in the dark outside my room. I weren't going to go out till he was gone, not if I had to sit here all night. I swallowed the last ounce of gristle, washing it down so's not to choke, and peered out again. He was gone.

My heart was beating fast. I sat there, thinking how I was all alone with no one in the whole wide world who knew where

I was, who would look after me. I didn't want to leave that kitchen. Kitchens are safe places.

'Someone to see you,' Mr Thomas, the publican, bellowed at me from the doorway.

I stood but didn't move. Moses? In a public place and in the light, Moses wasn't such a scary thought. I swallowed the last mouthful of ale, belched behind my hand, and walked out to the public bar, head high. Round the counter the men sat drinking and talking, more of them than before. No one seemed to be waiting for me there. Then in the far corner a man got to his feet and stood staring at me. It wasn't Moses.

Running his hand along the back of the settle, he started to move towards me.

'Aggie?' His lips were moving but I didn't quite catch it 'cos it was so noisy in there, and then I knew – like a punch in my gut – who it was.

'Joe?'

Joe. A man, not a boy. But I knew him. I was a woman, not a girl, but he knew me.

We walked towards each other, frozen and moving at the same time, and then stood close, not knowing how to be.

'Aggie?'

'Joe?'

Joe. His name was so full in my mouth like I had wanted to say it and wanted to hear it for so long.

'I can't believe it!'

We stood there nodding, staring at each other, mouths open, not knowing what to do. We didn't hug, nor even touch. We never had. But my body wanted to and he was looking at me like he was thinking the exact same thing. The next moment we were hugging like I never hugged anyone before and he was hugging me so hard I thought my bones would break, and then I felt the corner of the table digging in my legs. I pulled back gasping and he reached out to touch my face just as I reached out to touch his, and then we both sprang back and sat down puffing and laughing, and I don't know what we were doing.

'I thought I saw you one day,' he said. 'Coming out of The Hand's yard.'

'The Hand's yard?' It was so ridiculous just repeating what he said. I had to grip the table to steady myself.

'I called your name,' Joe said. His eyes were just the same, dark, staring straight into mine.

'I didn't hear you, Joe,' I said quickly. 'I'd have stopped. You know I would.'

'You ran away from me!' When his forehead creased, a deep line came down the middle.

'Not deliberate, Joe. I didn't hear you!'

'You ran away from that house in Chirk, too,' he said.

Did he come looking for me? I didn't know that.

'A long time ago, Aggie... Is it really you now, Aggie? Is this happening?' he said, and now the frown was gone and he was shaking his head from side to side.

'It is me, but is it you?'

'It is me!' he said and we were both laughing again. And suddenly we were awkward and silent, sitting there opposite each other, our voices gone and all thinking drowned.

'How did you know I was here?' I said.

'Elijah told me,' he answered.

That was the post-boy sitting at the bar, who saw me when I arrived, when I'd not wanted anyone to recognise me. I was so glad he had.

'Oh my, oh my, I just don't know what to say!' Joe covered his face in his hands and then took them away fast, like curtains whisked back, and there I still was.

The end of the settle cut us off from the rest of the room. I didn't know it, but my hands were flat on the table. Joe reached across and took one. We looked at each other. The feeling was like panic, it was so strong. I pulled my hand away 'cos I didn't know what else to do.

'How...'

'How...' we both started and stopped at the same moment.

'You...'

'No, you...'

I didn't know if I was asking or answering.

He told me about buttons and Oswestry and paddles at the mill, and I couldn't believe that! The mill! I'd passed it for years and never even thought of Joe once. Our paths must have crossed a hundred times, my feet treading where his had trodden and never knowing it.

'The miracle is that we didn't meet before! Not that we have now!' Joe said.

'I was at Plas Newydd,' I told him. 'The Ladies, you know?'

'I visited once. The girls who answered the door said there was no one else working there.'

I didn't have time to even think badly of them because Joe was talking again, telling me about the aqueduct. I must know about it.

No, I didn't.

'The bridge?'

Oh, yes. I'd heard talk.

Then he told me of Clara, his wife, and his children: twins and a boy. 'You haven't...?'

I laughed and shook my head. 'Married? Not me! Never!'

Joe acted surprised by the way I scoffed. I thought then that Joe didn't know me at all.

He reached for my hand again, face serious.

'I met Clara the day I went to Chirk to see our mother. Nelly.' He swallowed. 'She wasn't there.' He paused, biting his lower lip. 'She'd died a few days before.' He waited, as though expecting me to say something, but I didn't have anything to say. 'And Baby Iris was gone too,' he said.

'Iris?'

'She chose her own name,' Joe said. 'But I still think of her as Baby.'

And I never think of her, I thought, but didn't say.

'Mr Evercreech came for her. Remember him?'

I did: purple coat, long nose, that hat with three corners.

'He was her father.'

Joe looked at me, worried about the shock he'd given me, but it was just like a thing that had happened to someone else a long time ago, that was all.

At that moment, Jennet came to our table to collect our mugs.

'It's late!' she said. 'You're the last ones here. You going to your room or what?'

I hadn't noticed the room emptying and I don't believe Joe had either.

'No, no. She's coming with me,' Joe said, getting to his feet. 'She's my sister, Jennet! We haven't seen each other since we were children!' She smiled and nodded at me, Joe beaming.

'Sorry,' he said, when she had gone.

I don't know what he was sorry for, but I followed him to the door.

'I'd better get my things,' I said. In spite of a full moon, the courtyard would be dark, shaded by the inn. I hesitated and then I asked, 'Joe, could you come with me? You know, just in case.'

There wasn't another person in the world I would have asked that favour.

32

WE WALKED BACK in the moonlight along the river from the inn to Joe's cottage. The water raced faster than we were walking and yet the white light on the surface stayed flickering but not moving. The night was quiet and so full of noise. I could not decide if Joe was unreal, or whether it was me and I'd walked like a ghost into someone else's life.

The cottage was dark, apart from an orange light in the downstairs window. Two storeys, and a roof hanging over, making it squashed-looking. We walked up a path, Joe in front, me behind. He opened the door and I had this feeling like I had no business here. He scraped his shoes carefully while he took his coat off and hooked it up, leaving his boots under a little settle. He waited for me to do the same. Our shoes were dark shapes, side by side, and I shared his peg. He rubbed his hands and turned up the light on the lamp in the window. Everything was neat and tidy and clean. Joe called in a loud whisper up the wooden stairs.

'Clara!'

He waited, head on one side. No answer. He shrugged.

'Don't want to wake the children,' he said. 'Oh, there's so much to tell you!'

He clenched his fist, excited. And I was standing, awkward in someone else's life. I could talk in the noise of The Eagle but not here. If he'd asked me a question, then I might have been able to speak. All I could do now was note the items in the room one by one: the low beams across the room, a table, a rocking chair, the smothered fire in the grate.

'I'd have asked Clara to keep the fire going if I'd known how the day would end!' Joe said, pulling two chairs to the fender. 'Sit!' he said.

I had just settled when the flicker of a candle from the bottom stair lit up a figure in a white nightgown, a plait hanging over her shoulder. Her face was still caught in sleep.

'Clara,' Joe said, leaping from his chair. 'I found her. Aggie! My sister. A miracle.'

Joe bounced from foot to foot, bursting to talk to me, but not when Clara was standing there. We stood in silence till Clara said to me, 'Don't keep him up too late! He's to be up early in the morning. Joe, take the rugs from the chest and make a bed for your sister down here.'

Immediately, Joe started collecting the cushions and rugs and setting them down by the empty hearth, happy with something to do. Clara shielded her flickering flame as he shook the rugs.

'I told Aggie about the children,' Joe said, nudging the pillow with his foot. 'What a surprise, waking to find an aunt they never knew they had.'

He rubbed his hands together. Clara yawned and turned to leave, giving him a dark look.

'I'll leave you to it then, Joe.'

'I'll not be long,' he said, making a face when she'd disappeared. Like he used to do. It had always made me laugh.

'Big eyes, Joe. Remember?' I said.

'"Do big eyes, Joe",' He mimicked a childish voice as he sat down by the hearth.

'I never was like that!'

He grinned. 'Worse.'

'And you were the good one.'

'Always rescuing you,' he said.

'You looked after me, Joe,' I said.

'I did.'

Joe sat leaning forward with his elbows on his knees, looking up at me from under a wave of hair.

'Your eyebrows are bigger.'

He ran his finger across them.

His teeth were different too – browner, more horse-like – but I didn't say that.

He loosened his waistcoat and shirt, and tugged the kerchief from his neck.

'Look at you, in a waistcoat!' I said, mocking, but Joe didn't sense that.

'See the buttons – I started in buttons, but you know that.'

All I knew before tonight was that Joe never came looking for me. If he didn't think of me, I wasn't going to think of him. I was out of his life and on my own.

'And now I'm the assistant to the assistant engineer on the aqueduct,' he said. 'You see, Aggie, you can make something of your life.'

This was the Joe I'd forgotten and now remembered – annoying Joe. He never asked me one question. His life was the one he was interested in. I didn't say anything, just waited in the silence. He yawned and stretched out his legs, wriggling his toes in his stockings.

'It's been a time, Aggie.'

I hadn't thought much about things that were behind me until now. It was a long time.

He slapped his knees and stood up.

'If I don't go to sleep now, it won't be worth going to bed!' he said.

'And Clara's waiting for you.'

I could not sleep. The silence was too full. I stared up at the ceiling, thinking of Joe above me, Clara next to him. She seemed nice enough. Tall. Joe, my big brother, was small beside her.

So Ma was dead. I'd thought she must be. Years ago, Joe said, when he was making buttons in Oswestry. I must have been at Plas Newydd. About the time the harp came. The wind played those strange, sad notes like a ghost. Ma's life had stopped, like I had stopped thinking of her after she chose the new baby and left me behind.

33

FOUR BROWN EYES were looking down at me when I woke, from two faces that both looked like Joe's: round, solemn, one with longer hair – that was the main difference.

I sat up as Joe appeared, hopping on one foot while he stepped into a long black boot. His waistcoat was undone, his shirt unbuttoned, his hair standing up on end.

'This is your Aunt Aggie. My sister. Lost but now found! This is Joseph and this is Josephina.' He beamed but their expressions remained the same. 'I wish I could stay but I'm late for work.'

Picking up his leather satchel, he sped to the door. Clara came out of the kitchen, baby on her bubby, holding two apples, which she tossed to the children.

'Run after him and straight back.'

Without releasing her nipple, the baby turned and stared at me. Not a friendly stare at all, so I stared back in the same way. He wasn't a new baby, big enough to know who he liked and who he didn't. He opened his mouth so milk spurted into the air, and his whole face turned into the widest mouth you ever saw. He screamed fit to burst glass.

I didn't care for children much. The twins were wary of me and I was of them. I'd never known twins before. In front of the house was a grassy garden, bright in the spring sunlight, new leaves unfurling on branches. Last year's dry leaves were still piled up under the hedge where the wind had blown them. Chickens clucked around the mud patches, scraping at the soil with their scaly feet.

Joseph was the better with the baby, sitting him in his little wooden walker, throwing dead leaves into the air for him to watch. Josephina sat poking in the mud in the corner by the hedge. Every few moments she would stop and lean forward. I crouched down too but she didn't look at me. There was nothing to see but a hole and a pile of earth.

'What have you found?'

Her shoulders moved to her ears.

'What are you looking for?'

'Nothing.'

A day is short when you're working every second, but stretched out and uncomfortable when you couldn't be yourself and you didn't know who you were, and neither did anyone else.

As the sun sank behind the hill, taking the spring warmth with it, I pulled my shawl round my shoulders. Joseph and Josephina were snapping twigs for kindling outside the back door. Inside, the cottage smelt of boiled laundry. In the kitchen Clara was jiggling the baby over her shoulder while she chopped at a turnip. I could have asked if there was anything I could do but I didn't.

'I thought I'd go and meet Joe,' I said.

Clara's mouth went down at the corners and she looked away, sniffing.

'He's my brother, you need not worry about me,' I said, and then wished I hadn't. She might not have meant anything and now she would know me for a vex and here I was with a chance to be someone different.

'It must be nice to do what you want when you want. That's all,' she said.

I walked along the lane past where builders were roofing a new house with slates. The walls were lime washed and bright.

Clara had told me to go to the place where the canal ended, where a steep bank led down to the River Dee. A man was mixing a mud of rank-smelling mortar. He saw my face and grinned broadly.

'That's the ox blood, that is!' he said cheerfully. 'Get used to it. Need a strong mortar to hold the stones. The lime's a stinger in the eyes though.'

My eyes were beginning to smart too so I hurried on, up and over the humpback bridge and down the other side to the office, which was only a hut with a shoe scraper by the step. I walked on past the hut to a platform which jutted out over the bank. I went to the edge and stepped back, panicked. The drop was further than I thought, but the biggest shock was the size of the giant blocks rising up into the sky, ending in a half arch overhead, leaning into nothing. All the columns were joined by wooden platforms. I had not realised until now that Joe was working on such a project. How could such a monstrous bridge be built over a river so wide and fast-flowing? The thought that it would carry barges and water overhead made no sense at all.

Suddenly I felt someone behind me. I jumped in shock, turned and saw it was Moses.

He stepped towards me, but I dodged him and started back towards the hut.

'Go away, Moses!'

'Wait, Peggin! Let me speak to you.'

'I don't want to talk to you, Moses. Don't follow me no more! Go home. Go back to Gwendolyn and your baby.'

I pushed open the door of Joe's office and closed it behind me, trying to make my breathing quieten down.

'I've been running!' I explained, hand on my chest.

Joe looked up and blinked like he hadn't remembered who I was, and then he did.

'Spectacles, Joe?' I said.

He pulled them off, smiling.

'For close work, Aggie. I have to keep the figures neat.'

'Have you not a headache?' I asked, taking off my shawl and dropping it on the bigger desk.

'Don't leave it there,' Joe said. 'That's Mr Davidson's desk. Hook it on the door. What a surprise!' he said, rubbing his hands. His fingers were stained with ink.

The smell of the lamp made the air difficult to breathe. The room had only the two desks and bare boards, wooden walls too with two little windows, one at each side. I glanced out of one window, shrinking back quickly. Moses was standing outside.

'What's the matter?'

'Someone following me I don't want to see. It's nothing.'

'Trouble?' Joe asked.

'More a nuisance. He'll be gone soon.'

Two browning apple cores lay on the desk in front of him.

'I throw these into the hedge for the birds.' Joe blotted his work with a rolling iron and shut his ledger. 'I'm so glad you came!' he beamed at me, changing from the Joe I didn't know to the Joe I did.

'I want to show you something. Do you believe in coincidences? I don't know what to think about this. It only came yesterday, all the way from Manchester, the very day that I saw you again, Aggie. Makes you wonder, doesn't it?'

'About what?'

He hurried on. 'I haven't told Clara about this… She might… well, let's see what you think.'

He reached under his books for a letter, which he took out of the envelope.

'Can you read? Or should I read it…'

'Course I can read!' I said.

I went round to his side of the desk and leant over the document. 'Manchester Free Press. What is it? Not what's-his-name, is it?'

'Evercreech?' Joe shook his head. 'Browns.'

'I said I can read.'

'But look here.' Joe pointed with his inky finger to the end of the advertisement.

'"Mrs Brown… hoops, oranges… and me".'

It took me a minute from reading, hearing, repeating and then to understanding.

'Baby? Is that what you're thinking? Our Baby?'

34

I SLEPT THAT NIGHT with the twins in their bed upstairs. It wasn't a big bed. Their faces, lit by moonlight, so sweet, their skin so smooth. Joe didn't know me. And I didn't know him either. Nor Clara. Nor his children. He would not want me here if he knew the things I'd done.

I must have slept 'cos I woke with arms round me, legs tangled with mine. I felt them pulling away from me, getting out of the bed, leaving me to roll back into sleep. What a thought! No duties to rise for, no fire to lay, no breakfast trays to arrange, no floors to sweep, no one ready to fill my day for me. I dressed under the bed clothes and went down the stairs. Dirty linen was piled by the half-open back door. Clara, with baby Archie on her back, was turning the mangle.

'Scrub, rinse or wring?' Clara said.

The children looked up at me, pleading.

'You're doing a fine job!' I said. Their little fingers were pitiful, stretched over those big lye blocks of soap.

'I'll wring.' At least the clothes would be clean. I squeezed the smaller garments and flung them over the bushes. Clara took one end of the first sheet, I took the other. She twisted one way, I twisted the other until the water squeezed from the middle on to the ground. She picked up a second sheet and started to twist as fast as she could. I had hardly started before

I was showered with water and Clara was laughing, and I was too. She weren't as bad as I judged at first.

Of course, the rain started when we were nearly finished. The twins grabbed the clothes from the bushes and we raced inside to drop them over the pulley in the parlour. The cottage was dank and miserable with sheets hanging low from the ceiling and taking all the warmth from the fire.

Lunch was bread and cheese. Afterwards, Clara fed the baby while the twins were playing knuckle bones in the corner of the parlour, under the damp sheets. I thought I might play with them. When they looked up and saw me by them, watching, their chatter faltered and only started again when I walked away. I couldn't get on with children. I didn't know how to be with them.

The next day when I went out, a horse was pulling a trolley along the canal towpath underneath the bridge. I leaned over to see: a broad-backed, strong shire, black and tan with white feather feet and a blaze down his nose. That block of stone was enormous. Two men in shirt sleeves waited, holding long iron poles. When the horse stopped, they stepped forward, unfastened the straps round the stone and began to lever it down to the ground. It was a mighty weight; the men were struggling and straining every muscle. Once down, they stood back, wiping their heads and necks.

Another man in a bowler hat bent down to inspect it. He placed his chisel on the stone, struck it three times with his hammer, blew the dust away, stroked the stone, bent down again and nodded. The men levered the block onto a wooden ramp behind them, pushed the stone to the edge of the bank, where they stopped to fasten the ropes round their middles and three times round their wrists and together they tipped the stone over the edge, sliding it down out of sight, leaning back to take the weight on the ropes. The horse stood patiently, steaming in the April air.

That horse started me thinking. Seeing that shire, hearing the thump of its hooves, took me back to when I was small, watching those horses cantering round and round the ring. A man in little black shoes leapt up onto their backs and I wanted so to copy him, to feel the thud of the hooves.

'The breathtaking equestrian exercises of Mrs Brown...', that's what the poster said. 'And me.'

The idea came like a stuck door flying open. I ran the rest of the way to the office and burst in. Joe was alone, working at his desk.

'I'm going to get her, Joe.'

He looked up.

'Who?'

'Baby Iris.'

He blinked as though he couldn't quite understand, and then suddenly he did. He put his quill down and jumped up.

'I'll find her, Joe. I'll bring her back!'

I saw that flicker in his eyes.

'You don't believe I can, do you? You don't trust me.'

'Of course I do, Aggie,' Joe said, all hurt and earnest.

I knew he didn't. Why should he? But I'd show him the person I really was.

35

THREE LONG DAYS on the road from Llangollen to Manchester shook me stupid, sitting up on top of the coach in the wind, rain and more rain. I must have been dozing from the tiredness, 'cos when I heard 'Manchester' – that word I'd been waiting for for so long – I didn't hear it till everyone was pushing past, jumping down on to the cobbles. I was the last one left sitting there. I couldn't move. I'd never seen such a confusion. I could hardly see the cobbles for the people: men, women, children, dogs everywhere. Cases, trunks, bundles, parcels, baskets – wooden crates of chickens piled up in the middle of everything, feathered heads sticking out of the slats. Manchester was a town, I knew that, but I hadn't thought what it would be like. How could I, 'cos I'd never been to a place bigger than Llangollen.

'You staying there all day, missy?' a man shouted up at me.

I took a deep breath and jumped down. I could do this. I could. I had my bundle in my hand, and my money tucked safely down my dress. An archway ahead must lead out to the town. All I had to do was walk through. A dog was sniffing round in front of me, a scruffy creature with a sore on his back to make you wish you hadn't seen it. A man passing by kicked that dog hard, making the poor creature leap away squealing – the exact sound I wanted to make. Panic was growing inside. I tried to swallow but my mouth was sand. I'd half a mind to go straight to the ticket office and ask when the next coach south to Hereford was, but I was here for a reason and that reason was Baby Iris. I had come to fetch her and take her back to Joe. And that's what I was going to do.

Clutching my bag, I was about to turn to walk out of the yard when a coach swung in under the arch and almost flattened me. I leapt backward as the coachman screamed: 'Out the bloody way!' I felt the heat as the horses clattered past me.

'Look out!' another voice shouted closer behind me. A barefooted boy with a sack in one hand had his shovel raised ready to strike me. I'd missed stepping into a pile of steaming dung by a whisker. If I didn't keep my wits about me, I'd be squashed or beaten senseless before I ever got to see Iris.

Keeping tucked in close to the wall, I walked away under the arch. Left? Right? Or straight on? I crossed over the road. An old man was leaning against the brick wall of a house on the corner where three streets met. His coat was tight, the collar turned up, a battered hat on his head.

''Scuse me... could you help me, please?' He stood up straight and looked at me as though I'd fallen from the sky. 'I'm in need of lodgings.'

He turned away shaking his head, pulling his hat down low. On the opposite corner a woman was dallying, looking this way and that. Her bodice was low-cut and tight-laced and she held her skirt hitched up in one hand to show her white leg. I crossed over but before I'd even asked, she shouted at me, 'Find y'own corner!'

My throat tightened. I breathed sense into myself and marched firmly forward along the street in front of me, which was the easiest thing to do. The houses either side of the street were tall and made of dark brick. When I looked ahead, they seem to be leaning in. It was better to look down. The cobbles were grey as the strip of sky above. The only thing I could do was keep on walking, one foot in front of the other.

I came to an inn. A sign hung above my head: a dingy red lion standing on his hind legs, with a faded crown on his head. Inside, the walls of the long, low room were the same smoky yellows as the inns in Llangollen, with beams criss-crossing the ceiling. The wooden rail round the room with pegs sticking out of it was something I'd not seen before. At one of the trestle tables, two men were supping with their hats on the pegs above them. Another group of men stood at the end of the bar. Two dogs were sniffing round the tables but no one was taking any notice of them.

'Can I help you, pet?' A woman with big meaty arms like a man's stood behind the counter. Her cheeks were rouged and she'd a tall white bonnet on her head, a black spot as big as a halfpenny piece on her cheek. She glanced up at me and lifted her eyebrows: two furred arches.

'Like 'em?' She touched one eyebrow with a finger. 'Mouse skins. I made them myself. Good, eh?' She winked.

'I'm looking for lodgings…'

She started talking before I'd finished.

'You want to be careful, pet. There's lodgings round here I wouldn't send me worst enemy to. Fevers and mucky characters. You want to watch your money, girl. Some would take your head from your shoulders to get a purse.'

They'd have to rip my clothes off first, but I wasn't going to tell her that.

The Manchester way of talking was new, not up and down like Welsh but thick and quick.

'Hey, Nance. Someone looking for a room. Decent, mind.'

A woman in a bonnet and black dress sat alone at the far end of the room near the peaty fire, smoking a clay pipe.

'She got money?' she asked.

The woman behind the bar raised a furry eyebrow at me like a question.

'Mrs Walker just put one out on t'street.' Nance's voice was husky and low. 'If this one can pay, I'll tek her. If not, I won't.'

'I do have money,' I said.

Nance nodded, tapped out her pipe and slipped it inside her coat, rose and signalled for me to follow her. Out in the street, she walked fast, not wanting to talk, ignoring the ragged women and children standing every few paces with cupped hands stretched out towards us. I couldn't look at them, nor up at the tall buildings either side, without feeling they were squeezing in on me like blinkers.

There's not so much air to breathe in a town thick with smells. I was like an old woman gasping to keep up with her. It didn't seem right, passing the beggars when I had that purse pressed against my chest. I had to be careful, though, 'cos even 30 pieces of silver wouldn't last forever. I had thought to purchase the tickets for the return to Llangollen; costly they were too. Spending that money on something good – taking Iris back to Joe – might get rid of Mary's words: 'Judas... blood money.' I shouldn't care like I did. I'd never see Mary again. When I was sold to that woman, that was blood money. I saw those coins counted into her hand. Selling a child is a whole lot worse than selling a story to a paper which no one reads and no one cares about, and is true, every word of it.

The house Nance left me outside was just like the others in the street, with no gaps between them, all one solid line of bricks.

'Tell Mrs Walker Nance brought you,' she said, knocking on the door. 'She can pay me when she sees me,' she added before she turned, marching back the way we'd come.

The house went up straight from the road, up and up into the gloomy sky. Four windows one on top of the other.

The door opened.

'Mrs Walker?' I said.

'Don't let the warm out!' she said, pulling me inside. There wasn't any warm in that house, then or later. She stood in the gloom with her sagging face and white hair under her cap, holding a candle up to stare at me, up and down and up again, before she beckoned me to follow her. She walked rolling side to side. Yes, she had a room. Just that morning she'd thrown out a man with no money to pay her.

'Bastard,' she muttered, heaving herself up by the banister rail. 'Got to have your wits sharp round here. Cheats and ne'er-do-wells and all sorts.'

I never thought she'd make it up those four flights, pausing on every landing, hand on her heart, wiping her brow. Each landing had a stronger smell of old air and rottenness than the last.

Right at the top, she pushed the door open to an attic room with no room for a person to stand upright. Still, a roof, four walls, a bed and a door was all I needed. On the bed was a pile of covers.

'Six pence a week.' She stood at the door, with her eyes drilling into me.

I turned so my back was to her and put my bundle on the bed, unfastening it with big, obvious gestures though all the time I was slipping the purse out from my bodice. I counted six pennies from my hand into hers.

She nodded, smiled a gappy smile and went, leaving me wondering if I should have said four and no more. I didn't know as much about the world as I'd thought. It wasn't good being all alone in that cheerless room right at the top of that house, in that dark place called Manchester, so far away from anything I knew.

At least I still had the sense to split my money. 'Cheats and ne'er-do-wells', people with nothing and hunger in their eyes. If I'd not much money on me, I had no fear of losing everything. I hid the pouch from Plas Newydd under my mattress, tucking in the corner when Mrs Walker came back without knocking.

'I've a kettle on downstairs, 'I've some soup. Just an extra half penny. I'll leave you then.'

This time I waited till I heard the latch and her footsteps on the stairs before slipping the purse back in my bodice. I'd carry it next to the handbill. I shook it out.

BROWN'S FAIRGROUND
Mr Brown with the grateful and respectful…

And there at the bottom:

The breathtaking
EQUESTRIAN EXERCISES OF MRS BROWN
In which she will perform with Hoops, Oranges, etc…
And me.

I sat on the hard bed to think. I couldn't say how it would be if a person Iris didn't know existed appeared and told her she'd come to save her. I'd bring her back to this room, and we'd share this bed, which was narrow, but we'd be sisters fitting together like we were one person.

'Do you remember me when I was a baby, Aggie?' she'd ask.

I'd tell her that I saw her last when I was six and she was a baby. Ma was carrying her. I met them on the stairs by the window… and a big black bird was outside laughing at me and saying: 'She chose her, not you.'

I folded the letter carefully and tucked it back into my bodice. The attic smelt of mice. Somewhere down below, a door opened and slammed. I'd never lived like this, stacked on top of other people, and I didn't like it. Nearby a man was whistling. Someone shouted and a woman screamed, 'Hush your noise.' Just the thickness of the wall away was a person with a cough, the kind that hurts to listen to.

The way not to hear outside noises was to listen to what I was thinking. That's what I'd learnt on that wet, bone-shaking journey to Manchester. Those long nights in the coaching inns, crazy for sleep, trying not to hear the snores and mutterings and worse. Six of us to a bed!

It must have been that shaking on the coach. Suddenly I was thinking of the things I shouldn't have done; spying on Moses and Gwendolyn; and later taking and burying that crystal so no one could see it at all. And those Duckies had taken me in when they didn't have to, taught me to read and write and how to be. Mary, who'd been good to me: angry sometimes, kind sometimes, fair always; trying to teach me right from wrong. Mary knew me, all of me, like no one else did. I'd let her down. I shouldn't have told anything to that newspaper man. Nothing was any business to anybody but themselves. They were good, kind people. I wished I could go back and say I was wrong, they were right, and I was sorry.

Then there was Joe, taking me in when he didn't know nothing about me. I was his sister and that was enough. Whatever he heard later, he'd know I had done this one thing: brought Baby Iris back to him, 'cos that's what he wanted more than anything.

I left the blanket and ran down the four flights of stairs to the kitchen. Mrs Walker had promised me food and I was hungry. She might know where the fairground was. No need to show her the paper, nor tell her anything more.

Her kitchen was warm from the fire and the smells, old and new, were all mingled up like the soup. The pewter spoon was bent and old with snagged edges to catch your lips if you hadn't noticed. That soup wasn't as good as Mary's, more like water with grease and strange green streaks floating.

Mrs Walker was up on a chair wiping grime off the windows with brown paper. Her bare ankles were purple and bulged over her cracked shoes. She eased herself down, standing back to admire her work. Outside was a brick yard and the tall backs of more brick buildings and not much space between; the glass rippled like water.

'We had a pig there once,' Mrs Walker said, her eyes still on the yard. 'How's the soup?'

I nodded.

'Finish it off!' She gave me a little flick of her eyes as she was tipping the ladle into my bowl. 'And then you can tell me what brings you up here.'

She wanted so much to know my business but I wasn't going to tell her nothing.

'Do you know Brown's Fairground?' I asked.

36

I HAD A map in my mind: two streets, four ginnels, another street and five more ginnels.

'Count each one of them, mind,' Mrs Walker said. 'Don't want you turning off into... well... don't. Turn too early and you'll be in the canal and the factories... All those little streets with rascals and thievery, packed together like rats!' She shuddered. 'When my husband was alive, this was a respectable part of town – before they built the canal and the mills.' She shook her head. 'Keep going straight and turn right past the tannery.'

The first street I crossed was where I first noticed the smoke: great clouds of it. I thought there must be something on fire, but I couldn't see where it was coming from. At the second street, I stopped. Down at the bottom was a giant building which filled the sky. Smoke was belching out of two chimneys on the top.

I was standing halfway across the street, gaping like a fool, when a cart swung round the corner.

'Whoa!' the driver shouted, pulling up hard, jerking the horse's head right up in the air as I leapt to the side.

'You goin' down to Alvesters'? Cotton mill?' He shook his reins and the cart rumbled on over the cobbles.

Not knowing what people were saying, not knowing how to be – it wasn't a good feeling. I didn't like Manchester. Too big. Too many people. I liked it back home where the clouds were white and only smelt of rain. I'd never thought of what we had back in Llangollen like I did now.

One street, four ginnels and then another street. I wasn't going to stop for anything. I hurried across the cobbles, head down, which was lucky 'cos of the filthy gutter I had to jump over right in the middle. There was nothing this bad back home. I only glanced up for a moment, but by the time I looked down I'd seen a street of mean, black brick houses all crushed together, with children – so many of them – on the doorsteps. There were women and men too, standing about, but I didn't really notice them – it was those little children, all staring at me. It was quiet, too, which wasn't right, not when there were so many of them in such a small space.

By now there was a swell of people, all going in the same direction as the sun went down. The front doors of the houses opened right on to the street, so we had to walk in the road, being careful with the puddles and the horse dung. Children too, with shoes, darting ahead, then running back. All kinds of people were in that crowd, some smart, some not. The man in front of me had a tall, shiny hat like the Duckies wore. But every kind of hat was going to Browns': bowlers, peaked hats on the men, the women in bonnets – flat straw ones on the tops of their head, or bonnets and caps like Mary wore.

We were marching along when two barefoot boys in britches with more holes than cloth and big caps down over their eyes came out of one ginnel and walked up to a family of four. The woman screamed and her two children rushed to her side, while the man whacked at them with his stick as though it was a sword. They hadn't done anything. I suppose it was not what they had done, but what they might have done.

I knew we were near the tannery 'cos of the stink. Round the corner, head down, I nearly bumped into the back of a queue. Up ahead, a painted sign saying BROWNS arched over the road, making my heart thud harder.

Slowly we all shuffled forward until there were people behind me and I could hardly notice the stink of the tannery. A little girl in rags came up to the man standing ahead of me and held out her hand. He looked away but she just stood there until he puffed out his cheeks and took something out of his waistcoat pocket to give her. He looked left and right to see if anyone was watching, though I couldn't say whether he was ashamed or proud of his charity.

I tried hard to look away when the little girl moved on to me because I didn't want to be seen fiddling for my purse. She was wily, though, and tugged at my dress till I looked at her. Her scalp was all tufts with bare patches, and her eyes big with needing. It was like I was looking at myself, long ago. I knew what it was like for people to act like you're not even there when you are. You want so badly to kick out and scream and bite and claw at them, take their money and run 'cos it's not fair that they have some and you don't, but you can't. I gave her the penny that was in my hand ready for my ticket and fumbled for another under my shawl.

Being in a crowd of people talking and laughing, or even squabbling and shouting, makes a person feel very alone. Inside the huge tent there wasn't anyone else standing by themselves. To one side of me was a wooden barrier, keeping the cheap standing section from the seats. On my side, we stood in darkness, just the place for a thief to slip a hand into your pocket. In front of us the performance ring was lit yellow, but the smell of burning fish oil was nasty.

The show began with a crash of cymbals and a fanfare, and an announcement which I couldn't hear. I couldn't see; only the backs of people's heads. Once, when someone moved, I had a glimpse of a man in tights and a vest standing on the shoulders of two other men, his hands out as though he was about to fly. It gave me the strangest feeling, like I'd seen this before. I stood puzzling until I felt the air change and I knew the horses were coming.

That's when I moved forward: barging through, not caring about the jabs and the tut-tutting I received in return, nor even the poke of someone's walking stick in my back. I wasn't stopping till I could see, and then there they were: tall plumes on the horses' heads, faces straight down, eyes blinkered as they cantered in that slow, steady way. I felt their feet hitting the sawdust in my bones.

A woman in spangles vaulted up on one of the horses. She crouched, she stood, she tipped upside down in a handstand, but all I could see were her two feet in soft pink shoes. The shoes disappeared, and the crowd cheered and clapped. My heart pounded and my head bobbed from side to side. I caught just a glimpse of a girl running through the tent flaps: pantaloons, a green shiny top, hair up like the horses' plumes, a thin face, upturned nose. Then she turned away and all I could see were the hoops, decorated with coloured ribbons and flying through the air, one after another.

Two heads in front of me nodded together, then moved apart like curtains, unveiling Mrs Brown on the horse's back, juggling with the hoops. I didn't care about her, just Baby Iris. So small: a child with thin arms and hair scraped back from her face, and so far away. The heads leaned together again and I could see nothing. I squirmed forward. I was near the front, just two people in hats in front of me. All round me the crowd burst into cheers, wild clapping and whistling, and the two people in front of me started to move away so I could see. Mrs Brown was bowing, her heels together and splayed like clock hands. She stood up and held her arm out to Iris, who bowed low. When she straightened up, for a moment it was as though I was looking into my mother's eyes.

Before I knew what was happening, I was part of the flow of people streaming out, meeting another stream of people ready for the next performance. Those poor horses would hardly have time for a drink. I had to see her. I had to. Tapers stuck into metal rings round long poles lit my way round to the back of the performance tent: orange tongues of fire tipped with thin curls of black smoke lit up the lines of shelters reaching out into the dark.

I followed the smell of the horses into a tent. Inside it was dim and full of smoky shadows and yellow flickering light. I slipped in and stood back against the burlap wall. A boy was rubbing down the two horses I'd been watching with straw.

Horses skitter about when they know something is going to happen, nervous and excited, all jumbled up. After a few minutes, the boy was flinging the saddles on their backs while they danced from side to side, heads tossing up and down.

While he was bent down tightening the girth straps, Mrs Brown appeared in the entrance to the tent, the spangles on her skirt and the band round her head catching the light. She scuffed her pink slippers in a tray of chalk. Suddenly, Baby Iris stepped forward from the shadows. I had to slap my hand over my mouth to stop myself from calling out. She unhooked a bag from the wooden pole in the corner, and began tossing oranges up into the light. She caught the last orange and off they went, following the boy leading the horses, leaving me alone in the tent.

This wasn't the right moment. Not just before a performance! Tomorrow. In daylight. That would be better. She might see Ma in me just like I'd seen Ma in Iris; she'd see that I was Aggie, her sister, come to take her home to Joe. Tomorrow.

When I was walking back to Mrs Walker's through the busy streets, I was full of hope. Everything was going to be good. We would all be together.

But when I got into bed and I was alone and all around was black, everything was different. Lying in my narrow bed at the top of Mrs Walker's house, demons came from inside me, escaped from where I'd kept them far away in the dark, without air to breathe, without voices. Now they were out, they were screaming.

Why would Iris want to come with you? How could you think such a thing? Only a fool would trust you. No wonder your mother picked Baby Iris. She made the right choice, didn't she? On and on, worse and louder when I lay down, and worse still when I had my eyes closed and the inside was all I could see or hear.

I must have gone to sleep, because I woke up and the sky was light and the demons had vanished.

37

THE PLACES WHICH had looked exciting in the dark looked shabby and tired in daylight: the painted arch was drab and the metal letters rusting, the stripes on the booth cracked and peeling.

'I've come to see Mrs Brown's assistant. I'm her sister,' I said to the man at the entrance, who narrowed his eyes, before nodding me through.

I'd planned to ask the stable boy where Iris was. Inside, the tent smelt the same and the horses were feeding quietly, tails free and swishing as the boy forked dung into a sack.

'Excuse me. I'm looking for Mrs Brown's assistant,' I said. He looked up. 'Could you tell her there's someone to see her.'

Holding coins out like a rich person felt wrong, but when the boy propped his fork against the side, snatched the money, and ran off, it didn't feel much of a price to pay. Now it was me dancing and restless inside, like the horses. My mouth was dry as baked earth. If Iris came, I'd have no voice to speak to her. Should I put my shawl over my head, or round my shoulders – be clear to her right away, or a mystery? I didn't have time to decide, 'cos there she was, right there in front of me, not in her pantaloons but a scrappy skirt and a dirty brown shawl. Her face was so small, her eyes so big.

'Iris?'

'Who wants to know?'

'Me. Aggie. Your sister.'

We stood staring at each other while the world went on around us: sparrows flitted to and fro and the horses chomped their hay. There was so much to say but I couldn't speak.

Iris was the first to look away, hugging herself inside her frayed shawl.

Her eyes said something, but I didn't know what it was.

'Ah, there you are, Iris!' Mrs Brown came striding into the tent. She'd a short skirt over her blue and red pantaloons. A man in long boots walked a pace behind her. He'd a tall hat on his head, a loose frock coat, a red scarf at his throat. He stood fingering the long whip he held in his hand. The boy, who'd been lazily shovelling the dirty straw nearby, stopped his work and stepped forward, standing to attention, holding his shovel like a musket. When he realised the man wasn't paying him any attention, he went back to shovelling, but twice as fast and with much scraping and grunting. The man – Mr Brown, I assumed – stood back in the entrance, looking me up and down in a way that made me pull myself taller and breathe firmness inside me. He'd a glaring fierce look in his eyes. He tipped his hat with the end of his crop and left. He might be the man in charge of all this showground, but I didn't like him.

'Don't you keep me waiting, Charlotte,' he called. 'You be ready and waiting for me this time, d'you hear?'

Mrs Brown tossed her head as if she didn't want to hear him. She didn't look so fancy without her spangles and make-up.

'You ready, Iris? Warmed up?' She walked straight between Iris and me as though I was invisible and started her exercises, stretching her thin body, lifting her arms above her head, pulling back her elbows so her chest stuck out, bending her legs, picking up one foot after the other behind her back, grasping her ankles.

I cleared my throat loudly. She stopped stretching and looked round at me, surprised.

'Can I help you?' she asked, forcing a smile that wasn't a smile at all.

She was young, not much older than me, with a sour expression and a mouth that went down at the corners.

'I'm Iris' sister.'

Mrs Brown stopped still. 'You never said nothing about a sister!' She spoke as though she was cross before the words turned into a laugh.

'Iris didn't know about me,' I said. If that was true, and Iris didn't say it wasn't, I felt suddenly sorry for myself, 'cos that meant Ma had never talked about me, nor even mentioned my name.

Mrs Brown stood looking at me suspiciously.

'She was only a baby when I last saw her,' I said. 'And I was only six.'

Mrs Brown took hold of Iris' arm, pulling her towards her as though she was hers.

'We lived in Chirk, and before that with Mr Evercreech,' I said, annoyed that I had to keep on explaining myself.

At the name Evercreech, she let go of Iris' arm.

'Well, well,' she repeated. 'Iris is a busy girl, aren't you, Iris? My assistant!'

Iris looked up at Mrs Brown as though she was her big sister, not me.

'We've acts to rehearse for. You could stay for the show if you like?' Mrs Brown said.

'I've seen it – yesterday.'

Mrs Brown shrugged and started exercising again, reaching her hands behind her neck, pulling her head to her chest.

Iris looked up at me, waiting for me to say something.

'The show was what the posters said... spectacular... especially the horses... breathtaking... your act was the best,' I said. 'The hoops and oranges thrown just right and...' Mrs Brown was also looking at me. 'And you are such a horsewoman... took my breath for sure!' They beamed at each other.

'I like your sister,' Mrs Brown said to Iris. 'If you want tea, I think we've got time before rehearsal.'

I don't know if Iris was that keen, but, I said, 'Please,' and then 'Thank you,' like Mary had taught me.

'Saddle up! Take the horses to the ring!' Mrs Brown shouted to the boy.

All I wanted was for her to leave Iris and me alone, but Mrs Brown was not the sort of woman who thinks that anyone might want her to go away. We walked three in a line up a muddy, rutted path between lines of canvas tents.

Even when we reached Mrs Brown's tent, she did not leave us but told Iris to fetch stools so we could sit outside, the three of us together, and then she told Iris to fetch me tea, telling her the water in the kettle was hot enough. She placed the stools, one over the far side for Iris and one next to mine for herself.

'We don't drink before rehearsing,' she said, handing me the tin mug. The water was barely warm.

'Tell me, how did you know where to find Iris?' Mrs Brown leant forward, seeming friendly enough but her words still testing me out.

'I told you,' Iris said quickly.

'Oh, yes. Your brother. Where was he now? At a button factory somewhere,' Mrs Brown said lightly. 'I forgot.'

She was lying, of course. She'd not forgotten.

I sipped my tea and said nothing. Iris was taking something from her pocket. She stretched out her hand to show me.

'Joe made this,' she said. In her palm was a little red button. I was about to take it, when Iris snatched her hand back.

'So, you two must have a lot to talk about,' Mrs Brown said, standing up at last. 'Ten minutes, Iris.'

At first her absence made no difference to the awkwardness, the silence. Ten minutes. My heart was racing.

'Why did my father never say nothing about you?' Iris said suddenly.

'Because Mr Evercreech wasn't my father,' I said. 'But Nelly was my mother like she was your mother.'

Iris frowned and chewed at her lip.

I hardly knew many more details to tell her.

'My father was called Luca, 'cos he was Italian. He was one of Evercreech's entertainers – a slack rope walker,' I told her. 'He died.'

'My father died too,' Iris said and looked up at me. This was the first time we had really seen each other. 'He got the pox so he sold me to Mrs Brown 'cos he couldn't look after me no more. And then he died.' Her little shoulders rose up to her ears in a half shrug. 'So, we's both orphans.'

I took her hand and squeezed it.

'I was sold too!' I said, glad 'cos we shared something more than blood.

I'd told my story over and over, how I was sold like a sack of coal, but the moment I took Iris' hand something shifted inside, and I knew it wasn't quite like that. I saw someone counting coins into Mrs Price's hand before she took me. But I knew she didn't buy me. She was the one who took the money and me. With Iris' hand in my own, I had to say the words out loud for the first time, make them true.

'Not sold, exactly. The priest gave money to a woman to look after me 'cos I couldn't go with you and our mother.' It was hard, telling it like that. 'A kind of selling,' I added.

'Being sold ain't a bad thing,' Iris said hastily. 'I didn't say that. I was good with the horses. My father trained me. I was worth the money.'

By the way Iris lifted her head and the strength in her voice, I knew this was the way she said things to herself. She might look like a little girl but she was tough. Like me.

'You're worth something until suddenly you're worth nothing,' she said.

'Iris!' Mrs Brown called from inside the tent. 'Rehearsal time – come along!'

Iris jumped to her feet.

'Walk with me to the arch,' I said.

'Iris!' The flap opened. 'Oh. Still here?'

Mrs Brown had changed into faded pantaloons and a tight green bodice.

'Iris is going to show me the way,' I said. We stood there, Charlotte and I, eyes level. She'd scraped her hair back from her face, making her mouth a pale, hard line.

'Come back quick,' she said to Iris, who set off, leading me back down the muddy path. 'We don't want him angry again, do we?'

Iris stopped under the arch. 'Tell Joe you saw my act. Tell him like you said it just now... throwing just right... how I was good... say what a show it was.'

Her eyes were urgent. It was now or never. I took her hand in mine.

'Iris. Wait. Listen. I've come to take you home. I've got a ticket for the coach. Back to Joe. We'll all be together like we were, like we should be. A family.'

'But I ain't coming nowhere,' she said, quick as quick. This is my family now.'

She tried to pull her hand away, but I had it held tightly.

'I could come back tomorrow, when you've had time to think about it.'

'I don't need to think about it. Leave me alone.' Her eyes were full of tears as she pulled her hand back and I let go. She staggered back two paces and as she did so, her shawl slipped, showing dark purple bruising on her arms.

'I fell,' she said, racing away from me. 'I fell…'

38

I DON'T KNOW why I paid money for a room I couldn't sleep in. That night I got up and paced that attic at least ten times thinking up a new plan. By the time the first cart rumbled down the street below, I knew what I was going to do.

I wasn't going to go back to Joe until I'd tried one more time. Iris might have been testing me... or maybe she wanted to come with me but didn't think it right, or didn't have the pluck. Everyone should be given a second chance. I could tell Joe I tried and tried again and that would be the truth. Iris might turn away or refuse to see me, or Mr Brown might chase me with his whip, but I'd put up a fight this time, I would. Iris didn't know nothing about me. What kind of a sister accepts the first refusal, nods her head, turns and walks out of her life? A coward and a weakling, that's what. Iris didn't know what I was really like at all. How could she?

No one was going to Browns' Showground early in the morning. The street was empty, just a few men walking quickly towards the factory, collars up and heads down. A boy came running along the road toward me with a wooden tray on his head, leaving a smell of fresh baking on the air as he passed by.

'Wait!' I called. I bought two sweet buns for a halfpenny, thinking I might have more chance if I had one to give Iris.

This time there was no one in the booth by the arch, and no one stopped me as I walked past other tents, following two children on tall wooden stilts – a good way to walk in the mire. It must have rained in the night. I could only pick my way, holding my skirts out of the worst of the mud.

Iris was sitting outside the Browns' tent, hunched over on a stool, her knees up to her chin, with an old sack round her shoulders. I stopped and stood there, not knowing how this would be. She looked up, sharp. I held my breath until she jumped up, smiling, and I breathed again.

'You came back!' she said. 'I never thought you would, and thought you weren't my sister at all but an imposter.'

She said that word as though she liked to say it, all pleased with herself.

'My father said I must watch out for imposters. Most particular. You ain't no imposter, are you? I knew you wasn't.'

She lifted the flap behind her and called out, 'My sister is come and we're going to go down to the field before she gets the coach.'

She didn't sneak away like I would have done, nor ask permission, which I thought she was going to, nor wait for a reply, but glanced up at me as she ran off down the path. I was fair bursting with pride. I never thought it would be like this.

'Come!' she called from halfway down the path, still with that sack round her shoulders.

The day was sunny and warm for this time of the year. Iris wore her ragged green pantaloons, a jerkin and as well as the sack, a shawl tied at the side over her pantaloons. At the end of the path we jumped over a barrier of fallen tree trunks to the scrubland beyond. The horses were over the far side of the field. They looked up, maybe wondering if she'd come to fetch them or feed them, but when they saw she was heading away, they went back to eating. The field was wet after the rain, and the hem of my skirt was sodden and heavy by the time we reached the mass of brambles at the edge.

'Come on!' Iris said, untying her shawl and fastening it round her head. She ducked down onto her knees and started to weave her way through. Crawling in a dress is not easy. I was almost through when a thick bramble sliced at my cheek, catching the skin under my eye. When I heaved through on my elbows, Iris was standing right on the edge of a canal.

'I come here when I can,' she said, spreading the sack over the stone to sit on, dangling her feet over the edge. I was anxious for my shoes, so took them off before sitting next to her. My dress hung down, wet and muddy from the crawl.

'You're bleedin',' Iris said, reaching over to wipe my cheek.

'Joe's working on a bridge in Llangollen which is to take the canal right over the river.'

When I said the words like that, the whole idea sounded mad, but Iris just nodded.

'Don't he make buttons no more?'

I shook my head. 'He's more important now.'

'Buttons is important,' Iris said.

We sat there, not saying much, but it was good: the two of us, strangers and sisters, but it didn't feel to me as though we were strangers. I patted my cheek with my fingers but the scratch was nothing much. It was so quiet, just coots calling and birds in the brambles behind us. Rivers roar and streams make a deal of noise. Canals are silent. Here, if we'd whispered, we'd still have heard each other. A horse whinnied from the field.

'I comes out to see the horses,' Iris said, ''cos I like them best of all things.'

'I used to watch the horses when I was little,' I said. 'I liked their eyes, 'cos they knew everything.'

Iris understood. 'So we're sisters and we both like horses.'

I nodded.

'But we don't look nothing like each other.'

'But we are sisters.'

It wasn't easy to think what to say next, sitting there on the canal bank – and then I remembered the buns. I handed one to her, the one which wasn't so squashed-looking. They were sticky and so sweet.

Iris kicked her feet against the stone wall of the canal as she ate. Seeing her feet so small made my throat swell so I could hardly swallow, but I mashed the bun round in my mouth. Iris looked up at me, swallowed and licked her fingers carefully.

'I ain't coming back with you. I can't.' She looked away and pulled her shawl up over her arms.

'Do they treat you right, Iris? Do they...?'

'I fell,' Iris said quickly, with that set of her jaw. 'I told you. Horse work is dangerous. If the horses get whipped to make the act good, why should I be different? Bruises go, anyway.'

I knew then that there wasn't going to be anything I could say to make it different. She was like me, my sister. She had a will on her, she knew her mind, and she would be alright.

I stood up, stamping the blood back into my feet before stepping into my shoes.

'I've got a coach to catch.'

I put out my hand to pull Iris up, but she didn't take it.

'And I got a show to do.'

I took one last breath. 'Iris. If ever, ever...'

'I know.' She cut me off, picked up the sack and went towards the gap in the hedge, dived under it and disappeared.

39

ON THE WAY back to Mrs Walker's, I felt as though my shoes were weighing me to the ground. The cobbles turned my ankles. The houses either side were tall and grim. Clouds had smothered the sun and the blue sky and it was nothing but browns and blacks and greys. I couldn't wait to be gone. The rain started, a few drops one minute and a torrent the next, twisting through the cobbles, turning my hair to dripping rat's tails. My clothes smelt of wet smoke. By the time I reached Mrs Walker's, I vowed I wasn't going to spend another night in this place.

Up in my room, I collected my few possessions and stood for a moment, shifting from being here to being gone. Rain dribbled down the window. It could not have been past noon, but there was barely enough light to see down to the street. The drip-drip-drip on the floor from the leak in the ceiling drove me to leave so early. I turned, quick as quick, snatched up my bag and tipped up the mattress to take the money.

It wasn't there.

At first, I couldn't believe it, then I did. Anger swept over me like heat. I knew who'd taken it: Mrs Walker with her bad legs, the only person who knew when I left the house, who'd watched me as I paid her sixpence that first day, turning her all sweet. I didn't even care. Judas money anyway. I should never have had it. Mary was right.

At least I still had the tickets.

I ran right down those four flights of stairs, straight past Mrs Walker's door. I didn't shout out bad words or nothing; all the bad was gone from me. This was what I deserved.

PART VII
Joe

40

JOE ROSE FROM his bed before dawn. For one moment he could not think why the faint light came from the far side of the room, before remembering: he was in the limewashed house up at the top of the riverbank, at the side of the new canal. If this wasn't a moment of pride, he didn't know what would be: a dwelling place, newly built, adjacent to Mr Telford's own accommodation! No one had breathed in the smell of damp plaster, watched the dawn through those panes of glass, tiptoed over those new floorboards – with no danger at all of his head touching the ceiling, nor Clara's either.

It all happened so fast. The very day Aggie left, Davidson handed him the key to the new front door. Clara would not wait a day, packaging up her possessions and piling them onto the cart Davidson arranged for them.

A question flashed across Joe's mind as he pulled on his undergarments and stockings, and whipped his nightshirt off: how would Aggie and Iris find them? The new tenants would surely redirect them. Everyone knew Joe Begg. He picked up the clean shirt Clara had left on the chair. He slipped his arms into his jacket and patted the pockets. Everything in place.

'Don't wake 'em,' Clara begged, turning over, pulling the blanket over her shoulders giving Joe just a glimpse of that roundness under her nightgown, that mole on her white neck. He cleared his throat, picked up his boots and tiptoed downstairs to the porch. A grand idea, a porch. You could close the family world behind you, step into a space, and open the outer door on to the world of work.

On one leg, Joe stood at the door, lacing his boot. Next to his second boot lay his old belt, which he had flung there the previous evening. He picked it up. The recollection of threatening his children with it if they were not quiet was uncomfortable. The twins' excitement at the upheaval had resulted in an evening of frayed tempers and tears, putting him into a vexed mood. Clara's anxieties had tipped him into anger: all that madness about the dangerous canal and the little ones falling in and drowning.

Why could they not appreciate their luck in being invited into this new house by Mr Davidson himself? Convenient for him, certainly, having Joe on the site, as Clara pointed out; but convenient for Joe too. The main house, designed for Mr Telford's use when he visited, was sufficient for their new offices and Mr Davidson's needs, which were few, his wife being dead and no children to consider. Joe had not liked to pry further, though Clara had said that his lack of curiosity proved his unfeeling nature.

'If you're not chiselled out of rock you've no place in Joe Begg's life!' she said loudly as she shooed the children up the new stairs to bed.

How quickly Clara forgot where they had come from, he thought, closing the door behind him and walking down the short path to the iron gate. Years, they had lived apart. Then, when they had cleaned the cottage Mrs Evans had found for them from top to bottom, she did nothing but complain: the fire would not draw properly, the fox had easy access to the hens over the broken back wall; the beams on the ceiling in their bedroom were so low she was forever crowning her head on them.

Joe stopped by the edge of the canal. The lifting materials – the wooden platforms for the construction, the tools, the tarred ropes, the fixings – lay heaped up in piles on the far side, outside the old office. Today, the new blocks would be coming down from Cefn Mawr. He must consult with the stonemasons to make absolutely certain every stone was remeasured and marked according to Mr Telford's exacting standards.

A lone star shone high above him, reflected in rippling light in the canal water. True, the canal was near the new house, but if Clara kept the children back behind the iron railings, they'd be safe. And now she was talking about needing a girl to help her with the children! It had occurred to Joe that Iris might be able to help. She'd need employment. Or Aggie? Though two women of equally firm opinions might not be best suited for one being in the employment of the other.

Having no news was agitating. He must be patient. Joe looked up to the distant pale, rosy-blue heavens. Look up, Aggie, he thought. Look up, Iris. The sky above joined things up that were far apart.

The first men – the navvies – loomed out of the mist, shoulders hunched, having walked from Llangollen or the neighbouring villages carrying their tools on their backs:

shovels, picks, mallets, hammers, everything they might need. Over a hundred men were already employed and soon he'd be employing many more. Mr Telford himself had been diverted to his new project, a road on the opposite side of the valley, the final part of his plan to bring the communication systems together. A genius, that man, creating a pivot point where everything met and parted.

'Morning, sir.' One of the men touched his cap as he passed.

'Morning.'

That 'sir' made Joe's chest swell, though at the same time it did not sit comfortably.

Churned mud paths led down the steep banks to the Dee. Even in his new boots, Joe slipped as he descended. He must get stone steps laid without delay. Mist lay like a fleece a foot above the surface of the river, still and white and thick. He looked up to the arch, half-built above his head. Hard to think there would be a way soon to get to the far side of the Dee with your feet dry. Believing that didn't come easy; and Joe had sympathy for the men who preferred to keep their heads down, thinking only of their small part, unconcerned with the bigger project.

A sudden breath pulled the blossoms from the trees, scattering them over the water, whirling them away downstream, stirring the mist coverlet over the river. Briefly, he thought of Clara pulling the blanket over her shoulder. The surface rippled and swirled then settled, glassy smooth. One day, Clara, I will be the husband you deserve. And you will be my Clara again.

Later that morning when Joe walked down the newly laid steps back to the river, the mist had lifted. Not a cloud was in sight, the sky a deep blue. On the far side, little figures moved on the bank by the old tree stump. People said that an old oak had been there for hundreds of years before it was struck by lightning the day old King George died. At first, Joe presumed the figures were curious visitors, the coach making regular stops now for passengers to marvel at the construction. But no, someone was in the water. Baptisms were often held there, he'd been told, the minister up to his waist in the river, dipping a new believer clean in the mighty rush of the Dee. Faint cries drifted over from the far bank – not singing, more frantic.

One of the men knocking the wood into place for the new platform came and stood by Joe, shielding his eyes and squinting over the river.

'What d'you make of it?' Joe asked.

'Found something they didn't want to find, is what I'd say,' the man said, spitting into the mud.

41

Peggin

I WAS NOT IN a hurry to disappoint Joe. I left the coach in Chester, spent the last of my money on lodging for two nights in Wrexham and walked slowly the rest of the way to Llangollen. My pace along the Dee from the bridge to the cottage was even slower. A woman I did not know, feeding hens in the front garden, redirected me to Joe's new house, which I'd passed before and seen the men up on the roof attaching slates to the raw beams. The main house was grand, with big windows either side of the front door and two the same above. A smaller house was attached to one wall; both were bright white with new limewash. I'd thought before that the grander front door was ready for a man of importance, and the narrower one, which I was approaching, would fit a man of lesser standing. I'd never thought of Joe.

I stood knocking with a sinking feeling. Clara opened it, glancing over my shoulder.

'Just me,' I said. She nodded and her face went softer than I'd ever seen it.

'Fire's burning nice. I'll make some tea,' she said. 'You must be ready to drop.'

I wasn't used to kind words. I hooked my cloak up on an empty peg in the porch.

'That's Joe's peg,' she said.

The twins were playing in the corner of the parlour. They'd built a tower out of wooden blocks and had sticks and pegs for some army of men they were moving behind the table legs. They didn't notice me until Clara said, 'Look who's back!'

Archie was asleep in his basket, grown now so his head was touching one end, his feet the other.

'Peace!' Clara smiled, handing me a cup of tea. 'Come sit, tell me what happened.'

We sat face to face as I told her, trying to keep the facts distant, not like I was living it all again.

'She didn't want to come,' I ended. 'She said the entertainers were her family.'

'Don't tell Joe that,' Clara said quickly.

'I wasn't going to,' I said, a little sharp. I wasn't going to tell him about Charlotte Brown nor Iris' bruises, nor my mind racing away, making a story which probably wasn't true.

Clara sat forward and touched my knee. 'Don't blame yourself.'

'I wasn't,' I said. But we both knew I was.

'My eldest sister went away to work for a cousin in London, the day after I tore pages from her Bible in a rage,' Clara said, rearranging her apron over her knees. 'I never saw her again 'cos she died. I thought it was my fault.'

I should have touched her knee like she did mine but we just sat quiet. Her face was more lined and tired-looking than I'd noticed before.

'What did Iris look like?' she asked.

'Small, hair fairer than mine, and straight. When I saw her first, I thought I was looking at my mother, and I didn't think I remembered what my mother looked like!'

Archie's basket creaked as he stirred.

Clara peeped at him. 'You wonder, don't you, what they're going to turn out like?"

'I wouldn't know,' I said.

'Oh, you will – one day,' Clara said, lifting Archie out of the basket, hot and red from sleep.

'Never,' I said.

Joe still wasn't home when the twins went to bed. I'd washed, rank from four days of travelling, and was changing into fresh clothes Clara had lent me while they were pulling on their nightshirts, pretending not to look at me, though I knew they were from their giggling.

Downstairs, Clara sat in the rocking chair with Archie at her bubby. I collected the wooden blocks from round the table.

'They should have done that!' Clara said.

When Archie was fed, he sat contentedly on Clara's hip as if riding a horse as she brushed the crumbs from the children's tea into her apron and laid out three pewter spoons.

'We'll have the best dishes,' Clara said. 'I've never had an occasion to use them till now.'

'But I came back alone!"

'But you came back safe!' Clara smiled at me.

The plates were pretty, faded violets and ivy twined round the rims and bowls.

'They're the finest I've ever had,' Clara said. 'The blacksmith who made the railings and the gate rescued them from a big house where he shod their hunting horses. My mother would have loved them. She never had such fine things. Don't use the chipped one. Do you like them?'

I did. As I lay them, placing the flowers just so, I thought of Mary and the way she adjusted the china on the table at

Plas Newydd, making sure the letters EB and SP, the Duckies' letters, were at the top.

Clara was standing quiet, just watching me.

'Do you miss your mother?' she said.

I shook my head. 'She gave me away!' I looked up and saw Clara's face all soft, so I added, 'Mary Caryll up at Plas Newydd was more like a mother to me.'

The house gave a shiver as a door slammed shut next door.

'Ah,' Clara said, passing me Archie. 'That'll be Joe. His office is just the other side of this wall. I'll heat the soup. He'll get over it,' she said, going through to the kitchen.

The door opened. Joe stood there raising his eyebrows, questioning. I shook my head.

'Ah, well.'

You can see in someone's face when their words don't match their feelings. He walked quickly through to Clara in the kitchen, squeezing my shoulder as he passed.

I couldn't see round the corner so didn't know how Clara was with him until he came back out carrying a bowl of soup and she followed with two more, setting them down on the table. He sat one side. Clara motioned me to sit opposite him.

'Give me Archie – I'll take him up. You tell Joe everything.'

She straightened Joe's collar, smoothed the back of his head, then turned toward the stairs, her face still that soft way.

I was hungry so I told him the story while supping the soup. The second time of telling made it easier, further away. Joe sat there with his hands either side of his bowl and didn't touch his soup once, breathing deeply. I began to think Iris had done the right thing.

'The truth is, Joe,' I said, trying to hide my irritation, 'she's happy where she is. You should have seen her, Joe, the way she threw those hoops, the way she danced round that ring, her bow. She's got prospects in Manchester, Joe. She's got her horses. She loves them, like I used to.'

As I said it, that was the way I saw it and felt it.

Clara came downstairs and sat, looking from me to Joe, who was picking at the bread.

'Eat your soup, Joe.'

The way he sat – eyes down, saying nothing – had me more and more vexed. I nearly told him straight, 'She said the entertainers were her family, Joe. She didn't want to come.' Time was I would have done.

'So. Now I'm back.'

At least Joe could have said, 'Thank you for trying, Aggie. Thank you for going all that way, spending your own money, and I'm sure it was disappointing for you too.'

'Don't worry, Joe!' I said. 'I'll get a job. Somewhere else. Soon as I can.'

Joe looked up. 'No, no. You must stay here. Aggie could help you with the children, couldn't she Clara?'

'I'm not good with children,' I said, sharper than I meant. 'I don't want to stay here, getting in your way.'

'I'll ask Mr Telford…' Joe said.

'I've no construction skills!' I said with a laugh.

'Mr Telford knows Sir John at Chirk Castle,' Joe said.

'Not Chirk,' I said quickly. 'Not Llangollen either. Some place where nobody knows me and I don't know nobody.'

'There's no hurry, though,' Joe said to Clara. 'Is there?'

'The sooner, the better, that's what Clara's thinking,' I said.

'You can stay and make yourself useful till Joe finds you something better,' Clara said quietly. She and I looked at each other, both of us searching for the intention behind the words.

42

SUNDAY BEGAN WITH chapel. Though it was an age since I had been to any kind of church, it was the same as it always was: a preacher who liked the sound of his own voice, a heaviness in the air, and me fighting sleep. The day ended with Clara and me stitching and mending by the fire in easy silence. I liked stitching no more than I ever did, but kept my thoughts to myself.

Monday was washday, in spite of low clouds threatening rain. I scrubbed, I rinsed, I squeezed till my arms were sore and my hands swollen. The twins rubbed the collars and cuffs with lye soap up and down the washboards until they were tetchy and squabbling and sent to bed in the middle of the day. I wished Clara would send me to bed.

Later, while she prepared the evening meal, the twins set up skittles in the parlour, which was a good game until Clara shouted at them for playing an outdoor game indoors. Drawing in the condensation on the windows seemed harmless to me, but Clara scolded them for smearing, giving them paper and vinegar to wipe the glass clean.

That evening Joe had a meeting in town for the men who'd put money into the bridge.

'Men thinking how much money they could make, when they've a fortune in the first place!' Clara said, helping him tie his kerchief.

'That's the way it is!' Joe told her, buffing his buckled shoes on a rag to bring up a shine. Clara shrugged as though she knew little and cared less about the aqueduct project.

Not long after the children had gone to bed, Clara yawned and stretched. 'I'm to bed... She stood up. 'The dishes need doing. The fire's near burnt out. No need to feed it at this hour. Joe'll not need it warm when he returns.'

Gone was her soft look and back came the Clara I had first met, but I liked her better, knowing her better. Now she was more herself, I could be more myself too, with no risk in that.

There was only enough cold water to cover the bottom of the bucket. I wasn't going out to the well to fill it with the rain beating down. I sluiced the worst from the plates and stood them to dry, thinking if I'd brought Iris back with me, things would have been different. She'd be talking about life back with Evercreech. I could tell her what I remembered – which wasn't much, but we'd make a story of it. Thinking about what might have been made me heavy. The best way not to feel low is to feel angry. Curse Iris for not coming with me!

As it was only April and still quite chilly, there was a fire in the parlour to help dry the damp laundry, but Clara left it to die down when she went to bed. I was left alone in the cold, not ready for bed. Why should I sit and shiver? I picked up the log from the hearth and threw it over the ash, and was on my hands and knees blowing to set the sparks leaping when Joe came back. He stood shaking the drips from his hair, his nose red from the cold outside. I read the message in his face clear as if he'd spoken it: 'I should have gone myself. Iris would have come with me.'

'You couldn't have done any better, Joe!' I jumped up, speaking softly but sharp, not wanting Clara to come down.

'Don't you look at me that way, like you are so superior, 'cos you're no better than I am. I didn't have no bootstraps to pull myself up by. We never had any boots in the old woman's charity house.'

He looked like I'd hit him, his eyes hurt, opening and closing his mouth.

'You're thinking she'd be here now if you'd come with me!" I said, glaring at him.

'I wasn't thinking that, Aggie.'

'You want to be rid of me now, don't you?'

'My own sister? Of course not. I said you can stay,' Joe said. 'As long as you want it, there's a place for you here.'

The anger was gone with my words. 'Oh, don't mind me, Joe,' I said quickly.

There was nowhere to go but upstairs to the sleeping children. I clicked the door shut and went round the foot of the bed to the window, where I stood listening to the rain beating on the roof.

'Charity.' The word had slipped out, leaving me wondering where it came from. Standing there, I was in two places at once, in two sizes: me at the window, thinking of me, little Aggie, back outside the Trap Inn in Chirk, being lifted off the ground by a giant with a ginger beard and fierce eyes, pinching my ear.

'She's one of the Parish Charity cases,' I heard someone tell him.

I was only asking for pennies at the back door of his inn. If I got enough, I planned to go to find my mother, wherever she was, and she'd hug me to her and say it was a terrible thing that had happened. When they took me away from her, she'd say, her heart was ripped from her chest.

216

That red-haired giant marched me down Chirk high street for everyone to see, then along the lane to the old woman's house. She didn't beat me, just took me back up the lane to that cold, cold church and made me pray with her. She sat on the bench, but I had to kneel with no cushion nor nothing and the stone was awful hard.

Behind me one of the children coughed and stirred. Children asleep are better, their little faces so peaceful. I couldn't stay. I didn't belong here, whatever Joe said. I was his sister, maybe, from long ago, but he was a husband and a father now. I should go somewhere else. But where? I lay awake a long time. I'd never have shouted at Joe if Iris had come back with me, but I couldn't blame her. If I had the chance to spend my life close to horses, I know what I would do. Imagine: every day practising, moving till that horse and I were one thing and the pace was inside me. Up on its back, I'd crouch, then stand, taking the rise and fall in my legs and up my body. My trick would be to stand on one leg with the other straight behind me or in front, straight up and touching my nose, like I used to do.

I had little use of that skill after the priest caught me that time when we were all together in his house in Chirk. He didn't like me. Maybe that's when he decided to split us up. Sometimes I showed off to the other girls in the old woman's house when they begged me to. Once she caught me with my leg behind my head, and she told me it was vulgar and unchristian. That's when she sent me to Mr Gulliver.

Did she know about Mr Gulliver? Was that her punishing me, or did she not know at all? He went to church and Mrs Price was one to think the best of everyone. Except me. Hannah was her favourite and she was the bad one in that house, the thief and a clever thief. She hid things under my bed so the old woman thought it was me who'd taken them. Hannah never said anything when I was punished. When I smashed the woman's china bowl against the wall in a temper, I said, 'That new girl did it!' The old woman brought out her whipper. I didn't say anything or feel anything except I was glad it wasn't me being whipped. Hannah squeezed my hand when we heard the swish of the whipper, 'cos we were friends.

That new girl never said a word.

43

WHEN I WENT down early the next morning, Clara was outside the back door holding Archie's rags down under the scummy surface of the tub with a wooden paddle.

'Drowning someone?'

She turned, wiping her forearms across her brow. 'Oh! I forgot to tell you: I heard in town that someone from Plas Newydd's baby was dead and the mother drowned in the river. What was her name now?'

My stomach flipped over.

'Gwendolyn? That's it. First her baby died, and then she was found in the river but they don't know if she fell or... you know. Was she a friend of yours?'

'Fell, most like,' I said lightly, picking up Joe's shirt, turning it and flinging it back over the wooden horse. I knew Clara was looking at me like she wanted to say something and not knowing what or how. 'I hardly knew her,' I said, my eyes on the shirt.

When I don't know what I'm thinking, I pace up and down. There's nowhere to pace in a house crammed with children and washing so I took myself outside.

Clara followed me to the porch.

'Go up that path to the woods. It's pretty up there,' she said. 'I'm sorry I forgot to tell you.' She hesitated and took my hand. 'And I'm very sorry about your friend.'

I followed the path gradually uphill, turning my feelings into words.

The baby died... but they do... often... Gwendolyn, though: so proud of her little red-faced creature – Peg. Golden Gwendolyn: churning the butter, milking the cow, skipping down to the river. Then I saw her white legs on the straw with Moses on top of her. I stamped my feet hard on the ground. What had I done?

I didn't go far before I turned back, longing for warmth and walls closing me inside – not all this nothingness stretching all round. Leaving my muddy shoes in the porch, I took my shawl in to dry by the fire. The parlour was empty. Upstairs, the floorboards were still. The children must be asleep. Archie was screaming. I folded the scorching clothes, holding Joe's shirt against me and feeling the warmth of the linen.

'Take him before I strangle him, will you?' Clara said, coming through from the kitchen holding wailing Archie at arm's length. He was turning his little head from side to side.

'If he smells me, there's only one thing on his mind. Milk! Joe's in town for some meeting, though he'd be no help if he was here.'

There was no smell on me of that kind. This was a punishment, putting Gwendolyn's baby into my thoughts: those little waving hands with the nails so tiny. Babies know more than you'd think possible. Archie cried and cried, till Clara came and snatched him from me. She loosened her bodice and gave me a look that made me feel useless.

She sat one side of the fire, me the other holding out my sodden shawl to the heat. I hated that her hands were red and split, blood lines in the cracks.

'You should rub lanolin into those hands,' I said, remembering how Mary took my little hand in her big ones and rubbed grease into them till my fingers stuck together. Clara just laughed at me as though I'd never done a hard day's work in my life. We said nothing more to each other.

Archie, eyes tight shut, was sucking furiously, his free hand beating softly on her chest.

'Don't bite, Archie. Don't,' she warned. Archie stopped for a moment, then resumed his sucking.

'Terrible dangerous when their teeth come,' Clara said.

She leaned back and closed her eyes, leaving me quite alone staring at the blue veins on her bubby.

Rain pattered against the window, a flurry and a lull and then another flurry, a wind driving it. Archie sucked and sucked in the silence, and I was suddenly filled with a pain – not rage any more: a twisting pain, a sort of longing for something. The bubby and the baby. I wanted to be him and I wanted to be her.

I'd never have anyone sucking the life out of me like that.

PART VIII
Joe

44

W HEN JOE ARRIVED at the meeting in the back room of
The Hand, dishevelled after his walk along the river,
it was already full of investors, conversations excited by the
thought of money to be made. He sat in an upright chair
near the door, ready if needed. At the front of the room, the
important men were beginning to take their seats. Red or blue
was the colour of choice, the coats and jackets splendid in their
fit and fabric. Joe loosened a button on his own: a good wool
but a dull brown. Mr Davidson shuffled his papers and stood
to speak.

'Sir John, gentlemen, welcome...'

Sir John Myddleton, chief investor, sat in the seat of honour
right under Mr Davidson's nose. The men with the most
money sat near the front: the landowners, the coal mine
owners with an interest in transporting their goods on the new
canal systems, the slate quarry owners, the men with furnaces
producing iron ore. Toward the back were the farmers who
owned the land they had to purchase – the ones who were

eager to sell, the ones who were reluctant. There was still a need to persuade and convince.

Joe's interest in Mr Davidson's voice lessened as he became aware of a commotion drifting through the window from the courtyard: a yelling, a scuffling. He hesitated, concluding he would not be missed. He knew the content of Mr Davidson's speech – after all, he had been the audience for his rehearsal. Perhaps he should slip away to investigate. He crept to the door doubled over, straightening at the top of the steps. In the middle of the cobbled courtyard a tall man was snatching a whip away from a coach driver.

'Can I help?' Joe asked quickly, as the tall man raised the whip over the cowering driver.

'Could you string this man up and find me a new means of transport before the end of the evening?' The big man dropped his arm and the trembling coach driver crept away into the darkest corner of the courtyard.

'Certainly, sir,' Joe said.

The man took a step backward. 'Good!' He loosened his cravat and straightened his jacket. The light from the window above lit up eyes sharp as flint.

'To whom do I have the honour of speaking?' Joe usually found that these kind of phrases stood him in good stead, but to his surprise, the man burst out laughing.

'Plain John Williams. 'The Iron Man of Wrexham', they call me. I have coalmines there too.'

'I'll have a carriage waiting at the end of the meeting, Mr Williams,' Joe said.

'And who do I curse if it's not?' said the Iron Man. His face was craggy, his eyes deep-set, jowls dark and unshaven.

'Joe Begg. I work for Mr Telford.'

'Well, it's Telford I'm investing in, as he's to make my fortune!' Williams said, tapping Joe on the arm with the whip and galloping up the steps.

The unfortunate coachman sat on the step to the tack room, packing his clay pipe. He was a little fellow with stooping shoulders, as though he'd spent all his life hunched over his horse, driving into the rain.

'Madman,' he said. 'Hot and cold with no saying which and when. All I did was swerve round a deer that ran into the road in front of us. Up went the horses and over we went. No one can drive fast with a buckled wheel!'

Joe nodded his head sympathetically.

'He's set against me 'cos my daughter was his maid till last week – she ran off with a carter from Liverpool and left him in the lurch. Him with his massive house. Brynmo. Know it?'

Joe shook his head.

'For one man and a sick wife! Second wife, mind you. He's got a little girl with the maid – the other one, not my daughter, I'm glad to say. But when all's said and done, he's a fair man,' he added, turning his head and moving his jaw from side to side to assess the damage. 'Gives us all a fine pudding at Christmas time.'

***

'I've found a position for you, Aggie!' Joe said, crashing through the door. Clara and Aggie jumped from their drowsiness. His face was flushed from his walk back after a hot, smoky evening, his hair plastered to his head. He carried his sodden shoes and coat. He stretched his shoes with wooden shoe trees, and placed them in the hearth.

'What position?' The women spoke at the same time.

'A man with all kinds of riches: coal and iron ore on his land and smelters and brickworks and I don't know what else.' Joe rubbed his hands and held them to the fire, talking over his shoulder.

He straightened up, beaming.

'He's a sick wife and one of his maids has walked out, leaving him in a pickle. Aha, I thought to myself... and I told him: "I know just the person."' He beamed at Aggie. 'Perfect references from myself. He trusts me. They all do. They know me for Telford's man. It's all arranged. His man is to collect you from the bridge in town at noon tomorrow – he's staying here tonight and getting a broken wheel fixed in the morning. Mr Williams will pay you.'

'But where does he live?' Clara said.

'How much?' Aggie said.

'£5 per annum. That's fair. And – this is the best of it – you'll not be too far away at all. Over Wrexham way.' He beamed some more.

'Tomorrow's awful soon,' Clara said.

PART IX

Peggin

45

Eight months later

I STOOD ON THE riverbank at Brynmo, counting the weeks since I'd left Joe. I didn't have enough fingers, not even when I'd used every one twice, though I couldn't have been more than a day's walk away, as the crow flies.

December. A few leaves were still falling from the trees – ones which had clung on through the autumn storms. When the weather was at it stillest, the wind having suddenly blown itself out, they'd suddenly let go and spiral down, gold in the winter sun. If I were a leaf, I could float down the river until I bumped into Joe's bridge. It would not take long at all, not when the river was fast with the first snow melt. Behind me, beyond the house, everything was ugly, noisy and black with pits and furnaces and men doing their best to turn the world upside down. Here, all was peaceful. On the far bank a field of sheep grazed with never a thought of being anywhere else, nothing to worry about in their past nor in their future.

Brynmo, the grand house, divided the two worlds with its lawn stretching down to the Dee. It was more a castle than a house, with its endless windows and all those empty rooms. The wide halls had cold, marble floors. The oak table in the dining room was so long you could hardly see one end from the other. Mr Williams dined alone there, with his silver knives and forks and cut-glass goblets and linen napkins and the empty table stretching out for yards in front of him. No wonder he wanted someone else in the room, ready to move forward to clear the dishes when he flung his knife down. He ate quickly, churning with his mouth open so you could see the food.

Mr Williams' staff were all old or ugly, chosen by his sick wife, Mistress Enid, before she took to her bed.

'Woman's troubles,' Mrs Morgan, the cook, muttered, punching the bread dough down from its first rising on my second day there.

Mrs Morgan had creaking knees, her fingers were knobbled and twisted, worse in the cold, and that house was colder in than out most days.

She never said much, not to me, just muttered to the others in Welsh, but I could see the pain on her face when she rolled her pastry.

'I'll take the Mistress' tray up,' I offered one morning.

I took a wrong turn at the top of the stairs and walked the length of the corridor before realising my mistake. When I was back at the top of the stairs, there was Mr Williams, coat over his shoulder, shirt undone, hair sticking up, unbrushed.

'Oh!' His hand was on the thick bannister, his foot in mid-air when he saw me.

'Beg pardon, sir.'

He was caught, startled as a rabbit. His eyes were black like two pieces of his precious coal, he was unshaven, with more white than black in his whiskers and the neck of a man no longer young.

'I've Mistress Enid's breakfast, sir. I took a wrong turn.'

He stepped back up on to level ground and looked me up and down.

'Ah, Joe...' He snapped his fingers. 'The aqueduct... his sister?'

'Aggie, sir. Aggie.'

'Good, good.' He scratched at his head. 'Easily done. Left and right. Right and wrong,' he laughed and pointed along the corridor behind him.

Halfway down the stairs he called up.

'Aggie!'

'Sir?'

'Will you serve me at table, Aggie? Would you like that?'

Me, a maid, serve at table! I would like that.

'Yes, sir.'

He nodded and cantered down the rest of the stairs, swinging on the newel post like a boy.

I knocked on the door, put my ear to the wooden panel, and hearing nothing, knowing the eggs must be growing cold underneath the silver cover, I opened the door. How I didn't drop the tray I don't know, because there in front of me was a dog as big as a pony. His jowls drooped down black and heavy, quivering at the edges as he growled at me.

I swallowed quickly, trying to remember if it was better to look a dog straight in the eyes or look away.

'Shut the door! Such a draft!' the voice from the bed was quavery and small but sharp. The woman herself was tiny, white-faced and bonneted, with a grey, lacy shawl round her shoulders.

'Yes, ma'am, but –'

'Beelzebub! Lie down. He does not know you. His job is to guard me from harm.'

Her command was barely a whisper but the dog backed away, licking his lips with his eyes still locked on mine. In one bound that was barely a stretch, he was up on her bed, lying with his huge head in her lap. Mistress Enid patted the table by her bed, where I was to place her tray.

'Shall I pull back the curtains?' I asked.

The smell of dog and the stale night air tinged with coal dust was hard to breathe.

'No!' She shuddered at the thought. 'You may go now.'

From that day I took Mistress Enid's meals to her. Beelzebub was always suspicious, standing in my way and growling. When I ignored him, he followed me with baleful eyes. I'd the upper hand and he knew it and so did I.

Before she ate, I folded down Mistress Enid's sheets and plumped her pillows, hooking my arm through hers to pull her forward. Her bones were like a bird's and the sweat on her was like a horse.

One day she was sitting in bed with no cap, holding a silver hairbrush in her hand. I brushed her hair as best I could: the angle was awkward and she couldn't – or didn't like to – turn her head. Her hair was long and smelt of sheep. I wondered if I should roll it and pin it out of the way, but that would take me longer than I wanted to stay so I laid it over her shoulders.

She hardly had a word for me, but after I'd put the brush down on her dressing table and tied a fresh cap under her chin, she told me I might empty her chamber pot as though I was to thank her for the privilege. The pot was pushed under the bed, covered with a cloth embroidered in the corners with flowers, which did nothing at all to cover the stink.

Mr Williams was always busy, rushing here and there with his mind on the day ahead. He'd leave the house with his toast half out of his mouth whilst he put on his coat, both sleeves together to save time. His shoes, on the few days he wasn't riding, were unbuckled and flapping, but mostly he rode in long, black boots. His groom held his horse ready for him outside the front door at the bottom of the stone steps, a fiery coal-black stallion: what other would he choose? Like his owner, the horse knew nothing of walking, leaping from still to a gallop, the stones and earth flicking up from his hooves as he raced away.

Most days melted one into the next; only the days marked with an incident stick in the mind. One evening Mr Williams came into the dining room steaming from his ride, with his hair wet and his jacket sodden. He sat shovelling food into his mouth before he'd shaken free of the second sleeve. He told me to fetch a dry coat from his room. I'd never been into his room before. His wardrobe was large but held little: a few coats, some britches, but space for much more. I took a coat and stopped by the tilted mirror to look at myself: mousy hair under my cap, dark dress, white kerchief and a white apron tied round my waist. The face I was looking at was older, lines and creases at the mouth which were not there before. For a moment, I was shocked, before laughing at myself. No wonder there were lines! What an age it was since I'd seen myself reflected in the newspaper man's coach at Plas Newydd.

I remember thinking, as I helped Mr Williams into his dry coat, transferring meat on a fork from one hand to the other, that he still had the smell of the horse on him. I stood with my back to the oak panelling, waiting for the clatter of his cutlery and the scrape of his chair, so I could clear the dishes. I was taken completely by surprise when I was pinned to the wall, no time to breathe, no time to speak before he thrust his leg between my own, and all I could think of was him straddling that horse. Even then I was half-thrilled and half-outraged. He hadn't even swallowed his last mouthful of bread. He had to chew and swallow as he lifted my chin up with his fingers, though I was pushing down, and kissed me, pressing his lips hard against mine, forcing my mouth open.

He tasted like yeast. His eyes, when he pulled away, were smiling. He stroked my cheek, ran his rough thumb over my lips and walked away without a backward glance. I was left pinned in that moment: the kiss, the hand, his skin catching on my lips. Shocking, surprising... but good. I was alive, inside and out. And after all, what was the harm in what he did, not if I felt as I did?

Mistress Enid was standing by the window when I took her tray to her the next morning. One of the heavy curtains was pulled back, her grey shawl was round her shoulders, a white cap on her head. Her ankles and feet, thin and white, poked out under her night gown. A couple could not be more different: her weak and feeble, and him with more life in him than anyone I'd ever met. Beelzebub sat at her side, not bothering to get up when I entered. She touched his wide head lightly. Such a brute he was, with that bright, shiny tip just out of its sheath so you could not help but notice it.

'Today is a good day!' she announced, looking at me as though she'd never seen me before, though I'd been waiting on her for weeks. Today, of all days, I was uneasy, thinking of her husband's knee between my legs – though it was not my fault in the least, and only a kiss, so what was the harm?

'I will sit in this chair,' she said. I pushed the folding table from the end of her bed nearer to her, placing it within her reach. It was a work of beauty: embroidered flowers and peacocks caught behind glass. I shook out the white napkin and laid it over her lap, keen to back away and leave. When I sensed her grey eyes on me, heat rose into my face.

'Have you children?' she asked suddenly.

I shook my head.

I was held there for a long time, not knowing what to do.

'You may go now,' she said, her voice weary.

I sat on my cot in the attic that night. The owls were hooting, the lambs baaing for their lost mothers. The house was so big, but time for thinking was vast too. There was nothing here that tied me to anything else in my life. I was strange to myself. I wasn't Peggin and I was a different Aggie – which was what I wanted, I suppose. The blessing and the curse. Never in my life had I asked another for advice, always doing what I wanted, and never giving myself the time for regret. 'You can't put spilled wine back in the bottle!' as Mary used to say. 'What's done is done.'

One thing leads on to another. Everything could have been different. In everything that followed, I was not helpless nor blameless. I never have been.

46

NOT LONG AFTER that first incident, Mr Williams called my name from the hall. He'd a powerful voice that we heard clearly in the kitchen, where I was placing his kipper on a plate to take up to him.

'Aggie!'

Mrs Morgan just nodded. 'Go!'

He was in the hall in his coat, with the front door open.

'Come,' he held out his hand and pulled me down the steps. I'd no coat on but the day was mild, with spring now back again and all the flowers in the garden yellow as butter.

'Where are we going?'

'You'll see!'

'What about the kipper?'

'Never mind the kipper!'

He took me round the side of the house to the stables. The stable doors were open with no horses inside. The groom, an old man with bandy legs, was leaning against the gate to the field. He straightened when he saw Mr Williams.

In the field in front of us the black stallion was nosing round a smaller chestnut. Her ears were flat and every time the stallion danced round her, she stretched out her neck to bite him. But he was too quick for her. He'd a tickler as big as a log. Up he went and in, holding her down with his teeth in her neck. Poor thing, she was barely able to stagger under the weight of him. Mr Williams was looking at me: his eyes were piercing my skin, wanting me to look at him. My blood was pounding and I was almost laughing, but I stared straight ahead of me.

Mr Williams gave a cheer, punching his fist in the air.

'Keep them together for the day,' Mr Williams said to the groom, as he led me back to the house. He said nothing, just winked at me as I scraped my shoes.

'Now, where's that kipper?' he asked, rubbing his hands together.

I knew what was coming. I did. The show outside was a message for me. He'd not have taken me out otherwise. I had no unease about it at all. I liked him. He liked me. Where was the harm?

That first time, and only that time, he took me into his room. The moment the door shut, he threw me down onto the bed, untying my cap and tossing it over his shoulder. I closed my eyes so I couldn't say what his eyes were like, but there was gentleness in the way he was with me. He could have been rough but he weren't. He was older, an expert. It didn't take long.

I weren't worried about him looking at me, and he didn't worry about me looking at him when I opened my eyes: grey hair on his chest, nipples like redcurrants and little moles and tags of skin all over him. His stomach was paunchy, his buttocks flat, and his legs scrawny.

He wasn't a surprise to me, I was. I wasn't afraid, nor in the fighting mood. My head went quiet and my body got noisy. Afterwards I wanted to lie there, on those sheets that smelt of lavender, horse and sweat, and I didn't want to move, thinking about the soft slipperiness which wasn't like anything in life I'd known.

Mr Williams sprang up. I heard water pouring from the ewer into the basin, the huff and puff and the cloth on his skin, but I closed my eyes again.

'Up, up!' he said, throwing me my cap.

I was slow, sitting then standing, pulling down my dress and fastening my apron.

'How old are you, Aggie?' It didn't seem odd to ask.

'Not yet thirty.'

He nodded and bent to fasten his shoes.

Mr Williams was away that night, then back, then gone again, and the disappointment was new, lying awake listening for the great door opening and slamming far below. In the mornings, I woke with my eyes gritty and heavy. On the third morning I found a letter addressed to me on the kitchen table. By the feel of it, I believe it had been read. The neat writing was unmistakable.

> Aggie,
>   We hope you are well. I am so busy here, I will not be free to come to you but if you could come to see us, we would be pleased to see you.
>   In haste,
>   Your brother Joe.

I folded the letter carefully. So, he was too busy and I was not? I pictured him sitting in his office, dipping his quill into the ink, writing quickly before folding the paper along the same creases, pushing his chair under the desk, taking his coat from the hook. He'd leave the letter for the post-boy to collect the next morning before walking back to Clara with one less thing on his mind.

The back door opened and a woman came in, shaking the rain from her shawl. She'd the kind of face which looks cross, her forehead creased and her eyes cast down. Mrs Morgan pointed a thumb at me. 'That's Aggie!' she said. 'Mrs Jones. Come to help,' she said, pointing her thumb the other way. Mrs Jones looked up at me, the lines smoothed from her brow as she smiled. She might be nicer than she looked, but I was not concerned with her. I busied myself with Mistress Enid's breakfast tray.

'Mr Williams is not here this morning, is he?' I asked. 'He will not need his breakfast.'

Mrs Morgan shook her head, as Mrs Jones propped her shoes up on a log by the stove to dry.

'He'll be back late tonight,' she said.

My heart jumped.

'Well, brother,' I thought as I picked up the silver tray to take upstairs. 'I would like to see you and Clara, of course, but you catch me at a moment when I have much to occupy me here, I'm afraid.'

***

Mr Williams did not come that night. Nor the next, but the third night he came to my room in the middle of the night with beer on his breath and I went from sleepy to wild in a trice, twisting and thrashing and beating my arms on his back and clawing at him. He slumped down on me heavy and spent when I was still wanting. I could not rouse him or even shift him. He was crushing the life out of me and snoring like an animal. I pummelled his back with both fists till he sat up, belched and left the room, not even closing the door.

That was the worst time and there were plenty more – some good, some bad – till I got eased into thinking this was how it would be.

I wrote to Joe explaining that I too was busy but would come when I could. I hoped the bridge was progressing and that Clara and the children were well. Writing brought them close. I would like to see them. There was much to tell them of my life here, though also much they did not need to know.

47

Had I thought this would never happen to me? Did I imagine I was too old? Heavy, swollen bubbies, dark nipples, no bleeding for weeks. Of course, I knew. But I didn't want to think about it, so I didn't.

Mr Williams caught me one day, staring into the long mirror in his room. I'd been sent there with an armful of clothes to hang in his wardrobe. I didn't hear him coming. I had one hand on top of my belly and one under it.

I felt him standing behind me.

'Yes!' he cried. 'Yes!' He galloped round the room like a child on a hobby horse.

'I thought you'd be angry!' I said, as he took me in his arms and patted my stomach.

'Angry? Why ever?' he said, bending to cup and kiss my baby before his face went serious. 'I'll take the best care of you, Aggie. The best. You will want for nothing.'

He danced out of the room, then stuck his head round the door, serious again.

'It would be better if you were to stop attending to Enid's needs, Aggie. And not a word of this outside this house. Not a word. Not to your brother, nor anyone. Understood?'

I nodded, surprised because I had not thought to tell Joe or Clara but now it was in my mind, I wanted to. More and more each day. I had not wanted this and never thought it would be my life. But now suddenly, I did. Mr Williams was pleased and I found I was too. Clara and I would have had so much to talk about. She knew I did not want the life of a mother, that I had no liking for children. I could have asked her everything I wanted to know. I would not have been so alone, because alone was what I felt, more and more. I had missed my chance to see them and now it would be impossible.

Mr Williams was kind. He brought me fruits which I did not know, a pineapple from a friend with special glass houses, figs, and calf's-foot jelly, which he'd heard was good for a woman in my condition.

Mrs Morgan never said anything to me and her looks were unreadable.

They'd a new woman to attend to Mistress Enid's needs, tall and thin, with such a long neck sticking out of her kerchief you could not believe it. Her head was small and she never blinked. I intended to warn her about Beelzebub, but Mrs Morgan thrust a posy ring into my hands and told me to do the flowers from now on. I'd no feel for it. Crocuses were simple in that blue china ring, but daffodils and tulips never looked as good as Elizabeth's displays in the niches of Plas Newydd.

I don't know who I'd have turned to in a crisis. Not Doctor Gerrard, a friend of Mr Williams, who looked hard at me when I took the brandy into Mr Williams' study one day, laughed, turned to Mr Williams and told him he might anticipate the event after Christmas – January or February.

Event. I did not like to think of the event itself. There were dangers, I knew that, though the men never thought of them – bleeding, terrible pain and death. Clara's own sister Gracie had died.

I woke determined to write a letter. Mr Williams might have to give me pen and paper, but he could not stop me writing. I asked him while serving his breakfast.

'Who will you write to?' he asked, with a frown.

'My brother's wife.'

'But you will not tell her,' he said. 'And she must not come here to see you.'

I felt a heat rising inside, half panic and half anger.

'You said I could have anything I asked for. I only want to send a letter. I had no intention of inviting her here!' And to my fury I felt tears in my eyes. Tears are what a man thinks he knows how to deal with.

He jumped straight to his feet and mopped at my face with his napkin.

'Dear Aggie, you are emotional. Of course you are. But you must stay calm for the baby's sake.'

If he had said 'for your sake', I might have been more content, but he didn't. I began to see things differently. His care was for himself, for the baby, but not for me. I put on my shoes and walked down to the river and thought of the leaves. How quickly the water would take them from me to the aqueduct.

48

THE EVENT TOOK us all by surprise.

Traditionally on Twelfth Night, wassailers came up from the village – so Mr Williams told me as he was lying in front of the fire with his ear to my stomach. He didn't come to my room any more, though sometimes he took me to the sitting room after he had eaten, to massage my feet or talk to my belly.

'They come to take advantage,' he said. 'If wassailers get nothing from their landlord, they'll put a curse on the house! And I'm not risking that just now, am I?' he smiled.

'You don't believe in that, do you?' I asked.

'Of course not! But I've instructed Mrs Morgan to make puddings and prepare the ale and what-not, so we're ready. Best make yourself scarce tonight. Upstairs now, and no worrying, whatever commotion you hear.'

He kissed me on the forehead, leaning right over to reach me, and slapped my behind as I waddled to the door.

As the house was dark, I had a candle. My dress was long, but clear of my ankles. My shoes were soft and fitting. I do not know how, but somehow I tripped and fell on the stairs, unable to save myself. My first thought was the carpet on fire. I batted the flame with my palm, though really it was nothing. It didn't even burn my hand, but I'd left myself in the dark. I stumbled my way up the next flight of stairs, gripping tight to the rail, sliding my elbow up the wall to keep me balanced. My tinder box was by my bedside with the candle, so all would be well. In fact, my room was bright from the window: I looked out and saw the fields covered in thick snow.

Sitting on my bed in the strange white light, I gradually became aware of a wet warmth under me. Oh, the shame! I fumbled with the tinder. Three attempts it took before the candle lit and the room flickered orange. I sat on my hand, pulled it free, examining it for blood under the light. Clear. From far below I heard the thud of the front door knockers and the chant of voices.

'Wel, dyma ni'n dŵad...' Something like that. The wassailers had hardly begun before I doubled over in terrible pain, and my mind doubled up too, knowing what was about to happen. A month earlier than I'd expected – I was cold with fear, terrified that the fall on the stairs might have harmed the baby.

I remember crawling to the top of the stairs and shrieking as loud as I could. Beelzebub must have heard me, because he startled howling. Next thing I remember, I was being hauled back into the bed by Mrs Jones. Old Mrs Morgan appeared too, in spite of her knees and then, later, when the pain was beyond the endurable, Doctor Gerrard arrived with snow on his hair. His hands were so cold. He took my pulse, nodded and left the room. This was women's work.

An event it most certainly was! After hours of an agony there are no words for, my babe was born, tiny with a waxy shell and blood – his or mine, I do not know – and joined to me by a rope of gristle. I held him, sticky and hot as he was: he was mine. My boy! The very moment I thought that, he was wrenched from me, leaving me to cry with all the strength I had left. Mrs Morgan told me to hush: Mrs Jones was only cleaning him. I thought it was a twin following, but it wasn't – just a rush of thick blood, caught by someone in a bowl.

Mrs Jones cleaned me up, changed the sheets and brushed my hair. My knees were shaking and my arms, every bit of me. Mrs Morgan brought my baby back, still tiny but wrapped like a little grub with only his face showing.

'He's so small,' I said.

'Come a bit early, I'd say,' said Mrs Jones. 'Couldn't wait to see you!'

I kissed him and kissed him and he opened his eyes and looked at me and I looked at him.

'Hello!' I said, and he closed his eyes and I didn't know what to say.

The door opened and there was Mr Williams.

His joy made me cry again and he was crying too. He took the baby as though he was the most precious thing in the world. And he was.

He was my baby, but from the first day Mr Williams called him John Stanley, though I didn't want to call him that and he never asked me.

A few days later when I was singing to him, his name came to me: Luca, my father's name. All I could remember of my father was the trolley, the empty britches and the stink of him, and that was sad. That decided me. My boy was Luca and that would make my father proud, if a dead person can be proud. I would be proud for him.

I did not think it would be so when I saw Clara with Archie, but nursing Luca was the best feeling ever, and then not the best because it hurt so sometimes when he sucked all wrong. I had to pull him away but he cried so much I had to shut my eyes and think of the sheep in the fields: a lamb nudging at its mother's belly, tail shivering, while the mother grazed with no concern at all. I bathed him, I changed him, I dressed him and shared all my thoughts with him. In truth, it wasn't all like that either. Once when he would not sleep, I shook him in a fury and I hated myself worse than I ever have before. When he did sleep, I loved him more than I've ever loved anything – it hurt so much.

Eventually, my feelings settled. I stopped bringing myself to tears. I thought of my own mother more than I had ever done before. She must have done for me what I did for my baby, been so tired she could weep at the end of the day, though she had Joe to help her. Suddenly, I desperately wanted to see Joe. I could not see my mother or show my son to her, but I could show him to Joe. Surely Mr Williams would allow me this one small wish?

I had to wait to ask him because he never came to me as he had before, nor did he kiss me again after the baby was born. His interest in his son dwindled, only showing his joy in snatches between more important things like making money, going to meetings and whatever else kept him out of the house. When he had time, I loved to see him taking the baby to show him the bird's nest in the roses round the window, though I knew that Luca was not seeing the birds or the roses at all but the way the light hit the glass. It made me feel a pang inside when Mr Williams wriggled his nose against Luca's and blew onto his little tummy.

'I want to write to Joe,' I said to him one day when he was making faces at the baby. 'Could I have pen and paper?'

We were in the drawing room, the windows open to the late spring air. I always stood with my back to the big painting of Mistress Enid above the mantelpiece, looking down her nose at me.

'I want him to visit me here.'

He turned, staring out of the window before handing me back the baby.

'Very well,' he said. I thought I'd have to work harder. 'You should. Of course. Tell him to come but do not say why. Keep it short.'

He handed the baby back to me and took paper and pen from the drawer of the desk by the window.

I composed the letter upstairs while Luca was napping. I made no mention of the baby, nor could I make a hint because I knew the letter must pass Mr Williams' eyes or it would not be sent. I took the letter to him in the dining room as he was eating. He read it quickly, all the time one hand suspended in the air, food halfway to his mouth.

He nodded, handed it back to me, continued eating and still chewing said:

'Remember, Aggie: from now on, John Stanley will be my child who you are looking after. Well, John Stanley *is* my child who you are looking after.'

He glared at me and I held his stare, neither of us wanting to be the first to look away.

In my mind I spoke to him loud and clear: 'He's *my* child. Do you hear me? *My* child.'

I don't know if he could read my thoughts but he waited until I turned away, tossing my head in fury. There was nothing I could do without risking making things worse for myself.

49

NOT FOR NOTHING was Mr Williams known as the Iron Man. He was clever, and once his mind was made up, he was unbending. The day Joe was expected, Mrs Jones came to the room and took the baby from me straight after his feed.

'I've had six myself, all grown now, but you don't forget! I know what I'm doing,' she said. She was more kindly than her looks suggested. Her skin, too heavy for her bones, sagged in folds under her chin and her cheeks were like cracked leather.

'I'm to look after the baby while your brother's here,' she explained.

'But –' She was gone.

I dressed in the gown Mr Williams had bought me before I was too large to wear it, green as apples. When he was attentive to me, he said green was the colour for me. The overskirt parted in the front like green curtains to show the petticoat. That dress weren't nothing fancy like Mistress Enid, with skirts so wide you wondered how she could walk through the door, but it felt fine slipping it over my head, fingering the lace on the cuffs. Walking round in it feeling it tickle my ankles was nicer than walking through long grass.

I brushed my hair and pinned it back, left off my apron and went downstairs to the kitchen for them to admire me. Mrs Jones was standing at the table chopping the head of a cauliflower. I stopped mid-twirl.

'Where's my baby?' I asked.

'His father has taken him to see Mistress Enid,' she said, without looking up at me – words that turned me to stone.

Mrs Morgan, at the other side of the table, was crimping the pastry edges of her pie.

'She'll be happy for him,' she said. 'All that trouble she had, she could not give him what he wanted.'

If those words were meant to make me feel reassured, they did not, but I had no time to agitate before I was distracted by knocking on the front door upstairs.

'Joe!'

I turned and sped up the stairs. Fine dresses are not meant for speed. I opened the door just as Joe had his hand raised to knock again.

For a moment I did not recognise him, disguised in a grey wig rolled neatly at the sides. His grin was wide as his face.

Before I could utter a word, Mr Williams was at my elbow, pushing past me to hold his hand out to Joe.

'Begg, welcome to Brynmo. Step into the drawing room. Hope the aqueduct will not fall for the loss of you for a day! Aggie, take your brother's coat. Did you make good speed?'

He whisked Joe into the dining room. At least we did not have the picture of Mistress Enid staring down on us in the drawing room. I hoped Mr Williams would leave us, but no, he pulled up a chair. The talk was of the aqueduct and canals opening up the markets, me sitting silent with the anger building up inside me.

'You're sourcing the iron arches from Hazeldene at Kynaston, I understand,' Mr Williams said with that raised eyebrow that I knew, but Joe did not.

'The contracts are signed.'

'I've experience myself, you know. I supplied all the iron at Ellesmere.'

'I know you did, sir. I congratulate you.'

My eyes were sending thoughts like darts, but Mr Williams would not look at me. Did he not think I would be bored stiff with their talk? I was about to interrupt when Mr Williams turned to me with his sly expression. 'Enough of men's talk. I'm sure your sister has things to ask you.'

I waited but he did not go, sitting back and crossing his legs.

'Haven't you important things to do?' I said. 'You are usually such a busy man.'

It was not possible to keep the edge out of my voice, and Joe gave me warning frown.

Mr Williams laughed, tipping his chair back and folding his arms behind his head. 'Business will take care of itself today. You'll stay for lunch?' he said to Joe. 'All arranged.'

'How is Clara, and the children?' I began, hardly caring, I was so heated.

'They are all very well,' Joe said. 'Though Joseph skidded on ice in the winter and broke his arm. We had to take him to the bonesetter. It was a miracle he did not fall into the canal.'

'Oh, how terrible!' I could picture it all, him running from the house, the ice, the fall and the treacherous water. 'Poor Joseph.'

'He's better now.'

'Clara must have been –'

'Ah, yes: I must tell you our news,' Joe interrupted. 'We have another child, a little girl. Two girls now and two boys,' he explained to Mr Williams, whose face didn't change. I didn't even know what I wanted to say. I could only bow my head and stare at my own hands.

There was a tap at the door and Mrs Jones appeared.

'Excuse me, sir, but your child needs attention.' She looked straight at me. 'Aggie's the best for quietening him.'

For just those few moments, I had not thought of him. Now I heard Luca's distant cry, the milk came gushing into my bubby.

Feeding a baby with your mind whirring with things unconnected to him is not fair. Luca sensed it, not latching on right, crying and sucking in a half-hearted way, then ferreting some more.

'Come on!' I said, exasperated.

'Try the other side,' Mrs Jones suggested.' Babies feel the hurry in you,' she said.

Lunch was already on the table when I returned: a beef pie and a fish dish and all sorts. I could not eat a thing.

Joe stood and beamed at me.

'You're looking well, Aggie. Not pining for us then?'

How could I say anything but with my eyes? Joe is not good at understanding eyes.

'I should give you all my messages. Clara sent good wishes. Josephina sent something – where is it now?' He patted his pockets and passed me a fir cone with a tiny person pinched from clay sitting on one of the seed scales. Thankfully, he went on talking and did not see me gulp at the sight of that tiny, lonely figure.

'And Archie sent dandelions, which I threw into the river before I reached Llangollen!' he laughed. 'Joseph would have made something, but he's only the one arm to work with. The other is still in a sling.' His face went serious. 'Ah, before I forget: there's sad news from Plas Newydd. Miss Carryll is taken ill.'

'Mary? No. How ill?'

'The details I do not know,' Joe said and then turned to Mr Williams to explain. 'Plas Newydd. The two ladies. You'll have heard of them.'

Mr Williams nodded, winked in a way I did not like, and continued shovelling his meat into his mouth with his knife.

'Mary Carryll is their housekeeper, brought from Ireland,' Joe continued. 'As I was told.'

'She was good to me,' I said. While the outside of me must have looked like it always did, inside I was boiling. Suddenly, forcefully, I wanted to see her. I needed to go. To make things right. Tell her how things had turned out; tell her she was right and I was wrong. But I couldn't. My heart was beating a fury in my chest.

Nothing of any consequence had been said, we had not been left one minute by ourselves before Joe was leaving, totally unaware of what had happened. There's a terrible limitation in men, that they cannot see anything beneath the obvious – a limitation that creates an unbearable fury. As Mr Williams opened the door to usher Joe out, I heard the distant wail of my baby. Immediately, milk gushed from me with great force. I looked down quickly to see dark patches spreading on my dress. I pulled my shawl round to cover them, holding the ends tightly in front of me.

'Excellent victuals,' Joe said, words that I wished he had not spoken. I saw Mr Williams biting his lip. 'No wonder that my sister is looking so well,' Joe continued, shaking Mr Williams' hand warmly.

'Your brother's coat?' Mr Williams said to me, steering Joe to the front door with an arm across his back. Helping Joe into his coat whilst keeping my chest covered was awkward.

'I will come to you as soon as I am able,' I said on the top step, Mr Williams at my elbow. 'Promise to tell me immediately if you hear Mary is worse. I will come. This is important to me, Joe.' He nodded, frowning as though he caught the urgency in my voice, but didn't understand. 'Kiss the children and Clara… and the baby…' I added quickly, releasing the shawl deliberately to fall to my side, showing the stains. I stared fiercely at him.

'I will. Of course I will,' Joe said, smiling up at me, oblivious.

50

I HEARD NOTHING FROM Joe in the weeks that followed. Each day I asked Mr Williams if any message had come for me. The answer was always the same. 'No. Expecting one?'

More and more he made me wild with his mocking. However, I must be pleased because Mary could be no worse. Joe would have told me. He had promised. I spent much of the time walking to and fro, patting Luca to bring up his wind, thinking about her and remembering the times she came to me when I was poorly, wiping my face with a cool cloth, giving me rowan syrup when my throat was sore.

'Think how sweet the birds sing and they just love the berries, don't they? You take this and we'll have you singing soon just as sweet,' she would say.

She was fierce was Mary, when she needed to be, but fair. When I'd done something mean, like I often did, she would scold me and give me some horrible job like washing out the stinking chamber pots or cracking the ice in the well for water in the winter till my hands bled. She'd send me to bed but then she'd come to me and rub lanolin into my hands,

'Peggin!' she'd say. 'There's goodness in you, Peggin, but you keep it so well hidden, it might as well not be there.'

I could still hear her voice in my head: 'Never give up – *ná scaoil do bheannacht leis*. My mother's motto and a grand one, and I'm not giving up with you!'

And then she did.

Luca was growing chubbier every day, as I grew thinner. My clothes were falling off me and he was bursting out of his long slips. I fed him in my room – just the two of us, out of sight – before Mrs Jones took him down to Mistress Enid for a short while. Mr Williams did not like to see him feeding. If ever he chanced to come across me, he'd look away, expecting me to pull the baby off me and cover myself quickly. Doubtless, he did not like to be reminded of the bubbies he'd fondled.

One day he came striding into my room without knocking, holding out a gown of thick white satin, square necked with little sleeves trimmed in silk.

'Dress him quickly,' he said, throwing it at me. 'I'm to take him down.'

'Take him? Where?'

'To Enid.'

The gown had a fusty smell to it.

Once he was dressed, Mr Williams took him and held him in the air. 'There's my boy. Who's my boy?' The way he said it had Luca smiling and Mr Williams smiling too.

What an agitating hour that was when they were gone, sitting chewing at my nails and listening to every sound in the house: the birds scratching their feet on the roof, the distant bleating sheep, the rumble from the pits, doors opening and closing, the clock in the hall striking the quarters.

When three quarters had passed, I jumped up, intending to go down to the kitchen. That way I could pass near to Mistress Enid's door. I could see from the other end of the corridor that it was shut, and though I lingered at the top of the stairs, I could find no reason to go closer.

'Ah, there you are.' Mrs Jones craned her neck up at me from the hall below. 'Saved me a journey. A message for you from your brother – Mrs Carryl's took worse. She's asking for you. You're to come down and meet the new girl while they're busy with the priest.'

'The priest?' My thoughts were tumbling. Mary worse. Asking for me. A priest?

'For the naming.'

We had not agreed a name! A new girl, what girl? Had the girl brought the message from Joe? Deep inside I felt a thumping like the sound of the pit. I continued on down to the kitchen, where a girl was sitting on a stool drinking milk. She'd a pale face with mousey hair pushed up into a little cap. Her eyes were blue and sad. She looked down, her shoulders rising up, but she said nothing.

'Catrin's come to feed the baby,' Mrs Jones said. 'She's plenty of milk but no baby.'

Catrin pressed her lips together; again her shoulders rose. She held the mug in her lap. The skin round her fingernails was picked raw.

It was strange, as though I was hearing through water, the words reaching me and the sense lagging behind.

'But I've plenty of milk!' I said.

Mr Williams rarely uses the bell to summon someone.

'Aggie!' he called from somewhere above. I met him on the stairs as he was running down, with the baby wriggling and crying, held out from him.

'I've plenty of milk for my son!' I said, taking Luca. 'Send the girl away.'

'Ah! You've met.' He scratched his jaw, irritated, having to explain the details. 'I thought you wanted to see… what's her name…' He clicked his fingers in the air. 'Mary. I gather she's asking for you.'

How could he know that? Had Mrs Jones told him? I had not thought she would pass on a message intended for me! My heart was beating a warning. I clutched Luca tight.

'I'm taking him with me.'

I hadn't finished speaking before he was shaking his head. He stood firm, feet planted wide. 'John Stanley stays here. The cart will be ready early tomorrow.'

'I'll only be gone a day –'

'You may go for as long as you want, Aggie.' Having made his point, his voice was lighter. 'That's what the girl's for! Think of her. She lost her baby. Let her think it is not for nothing.'

Even in my arms, my baby was crying, tossing his little head from side to side as though the dress was scratching him.

'Take him away, will you? I do not care for his hullabaloo.'

I turned quickly, pulling out my bubby from my bodice even before I reached the top of the carpeted stairs.

'Hullabaloo, is it?' I said to Luca as I sat cross-legged on my bed, leaning back against the wall with the cushion under my arm. I settled him in my lap, with my knees wide apart. He stretched right across me now, his little fingers waving in the air, his arms and legs plump and firm, his lips chafed with all that sucking.

'Hullabaloo! Coming from the mouth of a man who roars if his food is late, too cold or too hot! I should not say bad words about your father, Luca, but he is a bully and a beast and I am sorry. I should not have given you such a man for a father. Your name is not John Stanley, it is Luca. I am your mother and I should know. He says I may not take you. I could stay, my darling, and not go at all, but I must. I will not be gone long, I promise you that.'

All the time he was feeding, my mind whirled in two directions: Mary was asking for me, and who had ever wanted to see me in my whole life? But then I heard Mr Williams' words: 'You may go for as long as you want.' And that sad girl! It was not impossible that he had made up the message from Mary to be rid of me. Surely not. Mrs Jones had taken the message and she was not the deceiving kind – although she would always do as the master told her. I could not blame her: she could not risk her position.

The truth was hard to face. Now Mr Williams had what he wanted, it would be better if I disappeared. He did not know me, not as well as he thought he did. I would not be so easy to be rid of. I was Luca's rightful mother and nothing – no, nothing – would part me from my own son. I would go to Mary. I must. But I'd return immediately.

Luca had stopped feeding. His eyes had closed and his arms were heavy at his sides.

'I promise, Luca. I promise.'

51

PASSING LUCA TO Catrin the next morning was so painful. Her eyes had pity in them too, as though she felt for me. Immediately she unfastened her bodice.

'I've just fed him!' I told her.

She flushed but I could not think of her, I could not. Her bubbies were small, hardly there at all! She would never be able to give him what he craved.

Outside, the trap was waiting to drive me to the coach to take me to Llangollen. I sat out on the top, but I do not remember that journey at all. All I could think of was Luca. I should not have left him. I should have stayed. But there was nothing I could do now.

I tried so hard to think of nothing at all that by the time the coach drew into The Hand, I was numb, not feeling the ground when the coachman handed me down. It took several paces across the cobbles for my mind to wake up.

Not for a second had I thought that Clara might be there to meet me. I walked right past her as she turned through the archway, seeing her and not seeing her, then doubling back.

'What are you doing here?' I said.

'Meeting you!' she laughed. 'Mr Williams sent a message to Joe.'

We hugged – briefly, because something wriggled as I pressed her to me. I pulled away quickly.

'Did you not know?' Clara said.

'Joe told me. I'd forgotten.'

'Baby Nelly. Your mother's name and my mother's too. No argument there.' She pulled back her shawl to show me Nelly's face. I never would have thought that I could be undone by such a small thing. If only I could have poured my heart out to Clara, but I could not. I gulped, my legs weak under me. Clara pushed me towards the steps to the hotel, where she sat me in a chair in the bar and fetched me water.

'You should not have stayed away so long. You must come home and stay with us. You're awful pinched looking. Is everything alright, Aggie? You seem different.'

'I am different,' I started to say but I could not get the words out for fear of choking. I had to go and see Mary, which was why I had come.

'I must go up to Plas Newydd,' I said, finishing my water and standing up. 'There is something important that I have to say to Mary. I'll not be free in my mind until I have. I'll come afterwards.'

'I could walk with you?' Clara offered, but I shook my head. 'I should warn you, Aggie,' Clara said, carefully. 'I don't know what you did to those ladies, and I don't want to know, but I heard that the girls there are not to allow you in.'

I walked up the lane, thinking that I wouldn't have wanted to have me under my roof if I had been the Ladies. I had betrayed them to a newspaper man for money. And what had they done? Nothing but run away to be together. If I had to choose a person to run away with, rely on, spend my life with, it would not be a man – that's for certain. Although I might consider Joe. Then I thought of that blank face blinking at me, failing to pick up the unspoken messages, the questions he didn't ask. No, not even Joe.

I was walking up the lane past the chapel, wondering how I was to get to Mary's room without being seen, when my skirt caught on a holly branch sticking out into the lane. Unpicking myself from those prickles, everything came flooding back: the crystal meant for Gwendolyn's baby, which I took and buried under this bush because if I couldn't have it, no one else could. Spite. Mary knew it was me. She knew what I really was. Such shame I felt, standing there in the lane, having done such a mean and senseless thing. Desperately I wanted Mary to see me now and know that I wasn't that person any more.

I crouched to move dead foliage and crizzled holly leaves, soon clawing at the earth. A stick would be better. It was slow work, unearthing nothing but stones and a worm. The faster I worked, the more I feared I wasn't going to find it – when suddenly I felt something hard. I picked it up, clearing away the mud coating it with my thumb, stopping when I saw the glint of glass. I stowed it in my pocket and continued up the hill.

I should have come after dark when there would have been less chance of being seen, not in the glare of a sunny June day. There was a beech tree at the end of the lane where I could stand, peeking out over the garden. The wide front door opened and Big Duckie appeared. Shorter than I remembered, and fatter, her hair cropped and white, she wore the same grey suit and long skirt, but had a broad red ribbon with a large star brooch around her neck. She stopped and was turning, the light catching the star, when out came Little Duckie, bare-headed, in matching costume without the ribbon or brooch, thinner than when I'd last seen her. Little Duckie picked up the handles of the wheelbarrow on the raked path in front of them and followed Big Duckie to the herb garden. It made me smile, remembering how they were forever changing the things around them that they could change: lots of little beds and hedges, and in the centre a sundial and another font, like the one from Valle Crucis.

If I ran across the courtyard I'd be seen; someone was always looking out of the kitchen window. If I went down to the font and the Cufflyman, I could go round that way, up the steep bank, and from there speed to Mary's room.

Her window was open, the curtains half-drawn. I pulled myself up onto the ledge and swung my legs round. Her bed was in the same place, the iron bedhead looping patterns on the white wall, with the crucifix above: that little Christ looking down on her. I eased myself down, drew the curtains together behind me and ran straight to the door to bolt it. If anyone should come, I'd spare them the shock of finding me here. I tiptoed to her bedside. Mary's face was yellowy and felt like wax when I touched it. She didn't stir. I sat down on the bed, careful not to sit on her. Her face was so lined. I'd not noticed that before, nor the fine whiskers on her chin. Her lips were bluish and dry and a heat like a furnace came from her. By the bed, on her little table with the woven mat, sat her Bible: old, with the black leather cover frayed at the corners. I flicked it open. There in a spidery writing were the words 'Mary. On your 10th birthday from your mother. *Ná scaoil do bheannacht leis.*'

I whispered the words, though I didn't know how they would sound in the Irish: *Ná scaoil do bheannacht leis...* never give up. I turned to Mary, but her face was just the same.

Next to the Bible was a bowl with a cloth over the side. I wondered who had held it last. I dipped the cloth in the water to wipe her forehead. Her eyes flickered under her eyelids, where the skin was thin as a dragonfly's wing. While I was thinking that, her eyes opened suddenly, wide and staring, then closed, then opened again.

'Mary, it's me, Peggin. I wanted to tell you I'm sorry for all the grief I caused you, and how you are the best person I ever met. I can't stay for long or I'll be discovered and they'll have my guts for garters...' I paused, wondering if she could hear me, watching to see if her lips quivered, but I could not say they did. 'It was all my doing, Mary, no one else's: mine. Me alone.' I sat quiet for a moment, then I grasped where I thought her hand might be under the bedclothes. 'I have something to tell you, Mary. I don't deserve it, but everything is coming good for me. I've had a baby. Me! Peggin! A baby boy. You're the first person I told.' Her eyes were closing. 'If he'd been a girl, I'd have called her Mary,' I added, as I thought it.

From out in the corridor, I heard voices and the snuffle of a dog at the door, along the line of light, then nothing.

I waited a few moments in the quiet then bent and kissed her, straightened her old hook rug with my foot, pulled the sheet up over her shoulder, and unbolted the door – all without a sound.

The yard was empty. I hauled myself onto the sill, swung my legs round and dropped on to the earth below. Bent double, I ran to the path and raced down the slope to the river, holding my skirts so I did not trip. I didn't stop running till I reached the stepping stones in Llangollen. Lifting my skirt to hop over, I heard a small splash and looked down to see the crystal in the shallow water. I bent down and picked it up. I didn't put it away in my pocket again until I reached Joe's front gate.

52

I STAYED THAT NIGHT with Joe and Clara. The children's welcome should have been enough to make me forget the low spirits I had after leaving Mary, and it would have, had I not had my mind always on my baby. I'd never left him before. Guilt and fear mixed in a terrible confusion, so strong I could think of nothing else. I could not enter into their games, nor be engaged by the things they brought me to see: a bird's nest, a horseshoe, a stick whittled by Joseph to a fine point.

After tea, a squabble broke out between the children as to who should be the one to sleep next to me.

'It's my turn!' Josephina said. 'And I don't kick!'

'I'm the eldest,' Joseph said. He had the look of his father around his mouth when he was determined.

'I never had a turn,' Archie wailed.

'That's 'cos you wet the bed,' Joseph sneered, whereupon Archie thumped him and Joseph slapped him back.

'Quiet!' Joe thundered. 'Aunt Aggie will sleep downstairs and be done with it. Bed, all of you, now.'

He ordered the children away with a look on his face I'd never seen before. Aging doesn't happen in a rush, I know that, but I'd never noticed before how thin Joe's hair was, creeping back, leaving his forehead bigger and more furrowed. It was better that I should be alone. Archie might not be the only one to wet the bed, my bubbies were throbbing so.

I lay there in front of the dead hearth, my nose full of the smell of damp coal dust, my mind like a butter churn. Round and round went all those little pieces from the day: Mary's eyes, her bony shoulder, that crucifix with the dried blood drips over her head... I couldn't settle. But they weren't the reason why I got up and tiptoed to the kitchen. I had to do something. I took a bowl from the sink and leant forward over it until my bubbies felt heavy and full. There in the moonlight I squeezed until the milk dropped, easing myself by thinking of Luca sucking on those little bubbies he did not know. My eyes brimmed with pity for myself. When I had finished, I carried the bowl to the back door. If someone heard the catch, they would think I had gone to the privy. I left the dish just outside the door, certain it would be empty by morning: a hedge-pig would snuffle his little nose and catch the scent on the night air.

I woke heavy and leaking again. Clara was already sitting in the dawn light feeding baby Nelly. I threw off my shawl and walked over to her to show my soaking nightshirt.

'Did I wake you?' she said, without looking up.

'Look at me, Clara.'

Clara was so surprised, she jerked Archie from her nipple.

'Aggie! Why didn't you tell us? How...? Where....? What's happened?'

'I can say nothing more.'

We looked straight into each other's eyes.

'Here.'

She jumped to her feet, handing baby Nelly to me. Nelly squealed, but my milk squirting on to her lips soon settled her, though my bubbies were hard as stone. I closed my eyes. The relief was sweet agony.

Clara steered me to the rocking chair.

'Don't tell anyone – not yet,' I said. 'I must go back to him.'

'I… we hoped you would stay longer,' Clara began.

I shook my head. 'There's a girl will feed him, but…' I gulped, unable to make my fear real in words. 'I have to.'

Clara squeezed my shoulder. 'I won't tell anyone. I'll make up some reason for you going. Joe won't question anything. The children will question everything.' We smiled. 'I'll walk with you to the early coach, soon as you've finished.'

Clara turned back at the bridge. I stopped in the passing point as a wagon rumbled past and as the noise died away, I heard the steady thump-thump of the paddles in the mill. At the end of the bridge I looked up the lane to the old mill house, where men were loading sacks onto the wagon.

I'd not thought to see anyone I knew, and even when a man all floured like a loaf stopped a distance from me, staring, I didn't know who he was. And then I did.

I drew myself up and stiffened inside.

'Peggin!' His voice was the same. His hair was dusted white but the black was underneath and his eyes were the darker for being in a white face.

'Moses.'

I was not going to say anything but when he said nothing more, I blurted, 'What are you doing here?'

'Working,' he said. 'I help at the mill when it's busy. I take the ferrets out other times.'

He stared into my face a while longer before looking down. His boots were dusted too, with the creases white.

'I don't go to Plas Newydd no more,' he said. 'You heard, did yer?'

'I'm sorry.'

He nodded, then looked up.

'Her sister had me. We're wed. I'm a better person now, Peggin. I got a little girl and another baby on the way.'

'Replacements,' I said, and then tasted the old bitterness on my tongue. 'Sorry, Moses. I shouldn't have said that.'

'I don't blame you,' he said.

We stood a long moment in silence until I turned away, walking on up to The Hand with no idea if he was looking at me or had moved away.

It wasn't till later, as the Wrexham coach swayed its way down the road and over the bridge, I wondered if I should have said, 'And I did *you* wrong, Moses! But I'm a better person now too.'

53

No one knew I was coming and that was a fair distance to walk from the coach. Before I reached the turning to Brynmo, colour was fading out of the sky and the shadows were growing darker as I turned up the long drive. A thrush was singing its heart out from the top of the larch. The pits and furnaces were silent and even the sheep were quiet. Up ahead, light flickered from the living room. Why would a fire be lit in this hot weather? No time to wonder. Luca was the one thing on my mind. By the time I reached the house, I was running, with my bubbies hard and throbbing. He would be in the kitchen, most like, with that poor girl, Catrin. Luca! Please be hungry! But would he know me? Surely he would. I was barely gone at all.

Mrs Jones opened the back door to me.

'Oh!' she said, surprised. 'You're not expected so soon.'

Luca was up over Catrin's shoulder, grizzling. As she turned and he saw me, he hesitated a bare moment before reaching out his little arms for me.

'Luca! My boy!'

Catrin passed him and backed away. *'Newidais i fo.'*

'She changed him,' Mrs Jones translated.

I was so full of joy, I couldn't keep still but danced round the room, holding Luca tight so our hearts were knocking together.

'I'll feed him here,' I said, hooking a stool out from under the table with my foot, shrugging off my shawl and unfastening my bodice.

'Thank you,' I said to Catrin as soon as he'd latched on. The relief was so good I was groaning. Catrin half smiled, before looking away.

Behind her, Mrs Jones and Mrs Morgan exchanged glances.

'I'm not needing to eat,' I said. 'In case you were thinking about that.'

Mrs Morgan shook her head.

'Mistress Enid will have him when he's fed,' Mrs Jones said quietly. 'She's had him down in the living room today.'

I looked up slowly, not understanding, not wanting to.

'After Mistress is done with him, you can take him for the night,' Mrs Jones hurried on, with her eyes on the table top she was wiping. 'Or Catrin. Makes no odds,' she added.

My mind was racing as I carried Luca slowly upstairs. I should turn, now, run out of the house, back down the driveway, all the way to the place where the coach would pick me up the next day. I had no money. But Joe would pay them – everyone knew Joe Begg – all would be well.

'I've slept under a hedge before and I can do it again. I will keep you safe,' I whispered, as I walked on down the carpeted corridor to Mistress Enid's room. Luca's skin was so soft. He smelt of my milk.

I knocked and walked straight in. Beelzebub, lying stretched over the gold counterpane, lifted his head gloomily. Mistress Enid sat upright on her button back chair, in a pale grey dress cut low in the front to show her powdered, bony chest. Her hair was pinned on top of her head, giving her a stiff-necked look. A glittery necklace and dangling earrings are not suitable for holding a baby at all. I could only hope he would grab them and pull until she screamed.

'Ah!' she said. 'You have brought my son.'

'My son,' I whispered as I passed him to her.

I had just time to see her nostrils pinching, her earrings shivering as she took Luca and turned away from me.

I walked as calmly as I could to the door and closed it quietly behind me, leaning back heavily against the wood. What had I done?

Up in my room, I did not light a candle but stood at the window watching the tree branches, motionless and black against the sky. The air was stifling – trapped since I left, only yesterday morning. I opened the window to let sound in: nothing came but a deep silence, until my ears caught the distant rush of water. Inside I was heavy as lead.

I do not know how long I sat in the dark on my bed before I heard the heavy tread I was expecting. Outside the door, the floorboards creaked, the latch lifted.

'Aggie?' Mr Williams stood in the doorway with Luca humped over his shoulder. The candle in his hand made Mr Williams' face orange and ugly, his eyes dark, his nose large.

'What are you doing? Have you no light? I did not expect you back so soon.'

He held the candle up with one hand and put his other up to catch sleeping Luca as he tipped him forward. He stood for a moment clearing his throat.

'You know me, Aggie. Not one for shilly-shallying – blunt, to the point.'

He paused but I said nothing.

'John Stanley is my son. This is his home. Now, and always will be. Enid, my wife – this is her sadness and was mine – is unable to bear children. She will be a wonderful, attentive mother to my son. I am not an unfeeling man, as you know, whatever the world might say. You are free to stay here under my roof or go, as you please. Either way I will give you what you want.'

He nodded as if content with his speech, turning to go, but stopping to say: 'You have my word on that.'

I took Luca, shaking inside. This was not the worst. I was not dismissed, which I had feared so greatly I had not been able to think the words. And then, even more unthinkable, I might never have seen my son again. Mr Williams' power over me was hard to accept. Every part of my body cried out against it.

He had given me a choice, which was better than no choice at all. Go or stay.

'What do you think, Luca? What do you think I will do?'

I traced my lips to and fro over his downy skin.

'Whatever that woman tells you, Luca,' I whispered, 'you are and always will be my own son. No one can change a lie into a truth. No one.'

PART X
Joe

54

A T THE TAIL end of October when the preparations for the Grand Opening of the aqueduct were reaching fever pitch, Joe was overseeing the reconstruction of the steps down to the Dee. Over the months of construction, they had become treacherous. He himself had lost his footing, only saved from greater injury by clutching the sleeve of a workman passing in the other direction. His mind was on the inconvenience of a painful back, which stabbed at every step, and a weakness in the legs at such a time. However, all might have been considerably worse.

His next task was to make an inventory of all the damaged stones unused and left for collection by the stone mason in town. He would need to check his ledger. Letters were also piled on his desk for him to attend to later. He flicked through the pile. Right at the bottom was a smaller note in familiar spidery writing.

His hand shook as he opened it.

Dear brother
    Im in Chester. Its not too far so you mite visit if your not busy. Or I mite visit one day.
    Your sister Iris

For a fleeting moment, Joe was alight with hope. Chester was not far as the crow flies! A journey, nevertheless. He sighed: an impossibility until after the opening. He turned the letter over. She had left no address, no means of contacting her except through prayer, which could not always be relied on for achieving results.

That same day, after the stones were listed and valued and were piled ready for collection, Joe returned to his office to find a reporter from the *Chester Gazette* had been ushered into his office, anxious for further details of the Opening for his paper. A coincidence indeed, but not until after he had left did Joe think he might have asked for a special message to Iris to be included as a favour to him. She might see the paper, of course, and would certainly be aware of the event and wish to be there to celebrate. She knew of Joe's part in the enterprise. Aggie had told her, and Iris had sent the note to him at the aqueduct's office.

Being so preoccupied with all the last-minute details to ensure a fitting opening for such a monumental achievement left Joe little room to agitate about his sisters. Only when he knelt by his bed, barely able to keep his eyes from closing, did he plead that Iris in Chester and Aggie in Wrexham would be guided by God to attend the Great Event. In his mind, he pictured the routes they would take, knowing the roads as he did. Surely they would follow the pull and converge in this place on this auspicious day.

On the evening before the Grand Opening, Joe finished his work, closed his ledger, placed his pen neatly in its groove, and pushed his chair under the desk. Instead of walking up the path home, he walked on along the newly cleared canal bank, and took the steps down the steep riverbank. The Dee was flowing fast, yet unruffled, oblivious to the historic event happening far above it, pewter in the autumn dusk.

Many times before, Joe had stood with his hand on the stone of the first of the 18 vast pillars. Figures in books, however neatly written, removed him from this real miracle. For a while he leaned on the stone with his eyes closed. He took off his hat and tipped back his head to see the solid, navigable canal in the sky. Only one man had been lost in the final construction – which Mr Davidson had called a 'bloody miracle', sending Joe to the funeral to represent the aqueduct. The wailing of the man's children as Joe stood by the graveside would not leave his dreams.

Downstream a heron stood, still as stone himself, neck stretched, alert for a fish. Now that was something Joe looked forward to: fishing again, feeling the force of the water against his legs. Soon there would be the space to think about all unfinished business.

He pictured both sisters laying out their clothes, ready for the next day. Please, God – please, he whispered. A bat flitted across his vision – here and gone. A sudden worry came into his mind. Would he recognise Iris? It had been so long since he had seen the little girl who had dragged him through the hedge, the little imp who had snatched the button from his hand. Aggie had reported that Iris' hair was a lighter colour. Like Nelly's possibly, though he could hardly recall his mother's hair before he had last seen it, when it was thin and grey. It was possible that they might meet before encountering him; Aggie would know Iris, for sure. Since he had heard from a colleague in the iron ore trade that Mr Williams and his staff from Brynmo would be present, he had every confidence that Aggie would be there. This could be a Grand Opening indeed.

55

26 November 1805:
The Grand Opening of the Aqueduct

EARLY THAT MORNING, unable to sleep, Joe tiptoed out of the bedroom, his clothes over his arms, to dress in the chilly living room. He closed the front door soundlessly, walked up to the humpback bridge and looked down on the barges moored ready on the far side for the procession. He stood watching as the dawn light painted the barges, red and green and yellow emerging from grey. Shadowy horses shook themselves awake and began nibbling the grass verges. Ducks pulled their beaks from under their wings, stretched their sleep-stiff legs and began their morning preening.

Joe continued his walk across the old bridge, down and along the far side of the river, opposite his house. All must be perfect. He had inspected the night before but there was always a possibility that there was something he had overlooked. Outside his old office, he stopped to run his finger down the shoe scraper to dislodge any traces of mud. Beyond it, the viewing platform was festooned with bunting. This would afford the best view of the procession and was where the dignitaries would stand later in the day. He would be expected to stand with them, though he'd be content to stand back, knowing how the front by the rail jutted out over the riverbank, supported by wooden struts. Today, the fluttering inside Joe was less intense than when he had watched the first barge cross a few months back. He'd had to stand next to Mr Davidson as the horse began its slow journey, dragging the barge across, high above the River Dee below. His fear was that the horse would sense the space beneath its giant hooves and panic. Or that somehow the vast bridge itself would shiver under the panic of the horse and fall spectacularly into the river below. Or the water would drain away, leaving the barge beached in an iron trough in mid-air. Even seeing the horse's blinkers did little to calm him. He'd felt so sick, he resorted to a violent coughing fit, covering his face with a handkerchief, much to Mr Davidson's amusement.

The aqueduct was now emerging from the grey dawn: a solid trough of dark water with a walkway by its side, flanked by a wall topped with iron railings. 126 feet above the river, 18 arches. He thought back to the diagrams in The Eagle, held down by his river stones, over a decade ago. A drawing made real. 'A miraculous feat of engineering,' the papers were saying, and it was. Joe took a last look around at the empty platform. A lone clinker marred the neatly swept boards. He picked it up and threw it far over the edge of the platform. It had a long way to fall.

Hastening back past the office, he stopped to tuck a coiled rope further under a step. By the time he reached the humpback bridge back over the canal, the horses were being harnessed, their brasses catching the first rays of wintry sun. He stopped in the middle of the bridge just long enough to utter a quick prayer: 'Thy will be done, oh Lord. May there be no hitches.' For a moment he allowed his sisters to come to his mind. 'I have not the time to think of them, oh Lord, but please make them come.'

Clara was examining her reflection in her tin mirror above the fireplace when Joe returned: a grey over-gown with a panel of white cotton petticoat, lower at the bosom than she was used to.

'Is this fitting for the wife of the great Joe Begg?' she asked, turning towards him. 'Oh Joe.' She shook her head. 'Try not to think about what might not happen. Think about what *is* happening.'

He shook his head. 'I wasn't... I am!'

'I'm so proud of you, Joe!' Clara cut in. 'We are all so proud of you. Get washed and dressed in your finest. Your shirt is ready on the bed.'

Josephina danced into the room. She was pretty in blue, her dress low cut and her hem high enough to show some of her her white stockings.

'Oh Lord!' Clara covered her eyes as her daughter twirled.

'What?' Josephina stopped. 'Pa?'

'Very nice. Very nice, dear,' he said.

'You'll have to cover up,' Clara said. 'It's cold! I told the boys we'll meet them down by the river for lunch – are you listening, Joe? And if anyone should get lost in the crowd, we'll come back home and wait. Hurry Joe! We don't want to miss a moment.'

Upstairs Joe fastened the buttons on his coat and pulled down his cuffs.

'Joe!' Clara called. 'We're going!'

He heard the door close, and waited a few minutes longer before leaving himself. He stood with his back to his closed gate and looked left and right. Perhaps he should ensure the barges were ready, that everyone was aware of the itinerary, then perhaps he could take the steps down to the riverside to explain to any people who had gathered there that they would have no view of the crossing unless they climbed up – though of course the bottom of the arches was the best place to appreciate the scale of the construction.

Down by the Dee, Joe thought immediately that he should be up near the canal. He should make sure that the humpback bridge, the obvious place for a jam, was being marshalled correctly. It would never do if the dignitaries were held up, throwing the whole schedule into confusion.

Annoyingly a cart belonging to some of the entertainers was crossing the humpback bridge as he arrived, in spite of his yells and arm-waving. The driver stopped.

'Dignitaries only allowed over the bridge. You must leave your cart in the field back on the lane,' Joe directed him. 'What were you thinking?' he berated the youth who had been instructed to turn away such traffic.

As the boy took the reins to help pull the mule round, it lifted its tail and delivered a large trail of steaming manure.

What a beginning! This he should have foreseen. He turned, hearing his name called by a man from the construction team. The lower steps near the river had needed shoring up after slipping under the traffic of people. He personally had organised repairs but Joe should make sure it was to his standard. Joe thanked him.

'Sweep it up!' he shouted at the boy, before hastening back down the steep steps. The crowd was growing. No longer could he skip up and down, but had to stand aside as the people came up, then thread his way against a constant stream.

The steps were solid. As Joe turned, he saw a woman six steps ahead of him: the right size, yes, the same gait, a red shawl over her head! His heart leapt.

'Aggie!' he called. 'Excuse me. Apologies. Excuse me.' He wove through the crowd. At the top he caught sight of her still ahead, nearing the humpback bridge. Just as he passed the closed gate to his house, Mr Jessop and Mr Telford were strolling down Mr Telford's path. He would not have stopped for anyone else.

'Ah! Begg.' Telford lifted his cane. 'Remember Begg, Jessop? This is my man-of-all-work! Do you recall when I was yours?'

'I do! I do! And look what became of you!' the older man beamed.

'Sir.' Joe stopped, snatched off his hat and stood with a rigid smile on his face, willing himself to be still and to keep his eyes on the two men.

'Quite a day!' Mr Telford said. 'And they said it couldn't be done, eh?'

As Telford opened his gate, the crowd parted, applauding, the boys and men throwing caps in the air. Joe turned, frantic. She had gone... and then there she was again – that red shawl, right in the middle of the arched bridge. He ducked and dodged, up and over, until he was right behind her.

'Aggie!' he called, catching her sleeve.

A woman with rounded cheeks and close-set eyes turned, angrily shaking herself free.

'Beggin' pardon, Ma'am. My mistake.' She smiled graciously, leaving him with a heart beating so fast he could barely breathe. He leant against the wooden wall of his old office, hand to his chest, calming himself.

All around him a large crowd had gathered. When he looked over, he could not see his house for the people standing where those horses and carts had once dragged the stones from the quarry. They'd have a reasonable view, though not as good as the important people gathering on the platform: Mr Telford, Mr Davidson, John Simpson and John Wilson, the master masons, and he must join them. An honour, of course, if only his legs had not felt so watery. Joe checked his fob watch. All was ready. And right on time. Mr Davidson's nephew had been chosen to run to give the signal to the first barge. A fast runner, so Davidson said, though Joe had considered his own son would have been faster.

The boy had gone. The sky was bright and the trees in their autumn finery, all shades of russet, yellow and green. The first leaves spilled down in little gusts of wind and settled, twirling, on the water. The surface looked to be still, unmoving, but when a yellow star-shaped leaf settled on it, Joe noted the speed as it moved toward the aqueduct. The crowd hushed in anticipation.

From under the humpback bridge a lone duck appeared, pursued by a snub-nosed, glossy black barge rimmed in red, pulled by a black shire horse in a harness bright with brasses. A scarlet band connected the blinkers across his broad forehead. The barge passed slowly, silently, with Mr Davidson's brother-in-law sitting straight-backed at the tiller in a bowler hat and waistcoat. Joe lifted his hand to salute the bargee and surreptitiously covered his eyes, occasionally easing the fingers to peek at its progress.

'Pa, quick!' Joe felt the tug of Joseph's arm, pulling him to the platform to marvel at the barge making its slow progress to the far side. Joe forced himself to look. The banks on either side of the Dee were packed: the masons, the erectors, the men who had riveted or bolted the ironwork in place, their wives and children, plus scores of assorted onlookers. A muffled cheering floated over the rush of the river as the barge cleared the aqueduct to join the Chirk canal. Joe put his arm round his son and squeezed him tight.

'When did you grow so tall?' Joe asked.

'When you weren't looking,' Joseph answered, with a grin.

A second and third barge passed. Everything was going according to plan. No hitches. The procession was underway. The queues for rides across the aqueduct wound round the offices. Joe shuddered. Nothing would induce him to ride across, though to his horror Josephina had told him in the kitchen a few days previously that she and Joseph had walked across and back.

'And if you stand on the wall and hold onto the railings, you can look straight down to the river!' Josephina told him excitedly, as Joe had sat heavily on a chair, cold sweat breaking out on his forehead.

Jugglers, tumblers and acrobats, stilt walkers, chestnut vendors, cake purveyors and meat pie sellers – they were all there, as he had arranged, to please the crowds.

Near the old offices, barges were lining up for the procession, the horses biting at their bits and tossing their heads. Joe stopped to watch two women in long grey suits being helped down into one of the barges. The ladies from Plas Newydd: one small and round, the other thinner, both in identical tall hats. A taller woman was handing them down to a bargee wearing a fine blue waistcoat. In place of the usual coal were plump red cushions. Mary – it could be no other, the woman Aggie was so anxious about – looking strong and healthy in her dark green dress and plaid shawl, her hair pulled back from her face. How pleased Aggie would be. Surely she would be here to see this? He looked to right and left but there was no sign of her.

For a moment his attention was taken by a juggler in the gaudiest yellow trousers. Children crowded round him as he tossed balls high in the air: one, two, three, four, five; catching them behind him, in front, under his leg. Strange to think that he, Joe, had been able to juggle like that when he was only a lad. He knew that it was so, yet the lad Joe seemed someone else entirely. Even the stilt walkers ducking under the branches of the trees seemed strangely familiar in their long red silk pantaloons. He smelt the earthy chestnuts, the sweetness of cakes; he heard the music: a brass band behind him, a penny whistle, and far away someone singing, and was filled with a sudden melancholy inside.

A woman brushed past him, bringing him back to himself. She was weaving her way towards the bridge at speed. He hardly noted her, and then suddenly he did. Aggie! He knew she'd be here! He pushed through the crowd after her, but she was already ahead of him and there were so many people, he lost her. And then there she was once more, right in front of him – but once again, when she turned, she was nothing like Aggie.

***

Hope did not disappear until much later, when it was dark. The fireworks were over and the crowds were leaving, making their way down the dark road with faces lit only by an occasional lantern. A faint scent of chestnuts and gunpowder lingered on the chilly air.

Joe loosened the buttons on his waistcoat and sat on the edge of the canal. He could not go inside. Not yet. A cloud unveiled the moon behind him, casting a dark shadow on the water: a hunched figure, the rim of his hat resting on his shoulders.

'That's me,' Joe sighed.

Neither of them had come. Not Aggie. Not Iris.

Eventually, cold to his bones, Joe settled his hat back on his head, though it was only a few paces to his front door. In the porch, he hung up his hat and coat, took off his boots and opened the inner door.

Clara was standing by the fire.

'I begged her, Joe. The man was at the gate, impatient to be gone. She'd begged a ride on a farm cart coming down this way, but she'd to do his bidding and when he said they'd to go, she went. You missed her. But she left this and swore she'd be back to claim it one day.'

Clara held out her hand.

On her palm lay a red silk-covered button.

PART XI
Peggin

56

I'VE NEVER FELT attached to anything so strongly before that it tied me down, making a prisoner of me. So long as Luca fed from me, I was allowed to stay under Mr Williams' roof, but I knew the kind of man he was. He might call himself fair – I called him heartless. He'd turn me out without a reason, so I must give him no reason, bite my lip and keep the things I wanted to do secret. Not that he ever thought about me these days. Too busy making money with his coal and his iron.

I knew the first barge had crossed Joe's aqueduct 'cos I heard Mr Williams telling Mistress Enid when I went to collect the baby one summer evening. Beelzebub was sprawled on the bed. He never moved now, just followed me round the room with his gloomy eyes. Mr Williams was marching up and down, quite unable to keep still with such exciting news. All his wife's attention was on Luca, toddling about with his legs wide, three steps and down he'd go. Mr Williams stooped and picked up Luca, dancing round the room, hoping his son would take more interest than his wife in his news.

'We'll be rich, my boy. You'll be rich. And don't you forget your old father who made you rich!'

That was a truth. If Luca stayed with his father, that would be so. He would be poor if he came with me. I couldn't leave him, but I couldn't take him away. If the Williamses mistreated him... but they didn't. They adored him. But a mother's love... isn't that more important than anything?

Mistress Enid never went outside herself, but held the opinion that fresh air was good for a child. So long as I didn't take him to a place with other people and a chance of contagion, I might take him out. When he was small, I used to tie Luca in a cloth round my chest. But when he grew into a sturdy toddler, I carried him on my back. I swear he grew heavier by the day, and eager to be on his legs. Most afternoons, I took him out when Mistress Enid had her rest upstairs.

A nearby farmer, who rented land from Mr Williams, grazed his sheep in the field up-river. On early spring days I took Luca to see the lambs. He loved them. When I sat him down in the grass, he liked to pick daisies, pinching them between his little fingers, though it was a problem making sure he did not eat them. We kept away from the edge of the river, though he grew to love the ducks more than anything.

One day when we went through the hedge to the field, I saw a girl in the far corner. It was Catrin. She picked up the lamb at her feet and started swinging it from side to side – it was red, wet and glistening in the spring sun. Its head was tiny, its limbs long. She held it to her chest, clearing its mouth, lifting it to her face as though she was kissing it, long and hard, before she flung it over her shoulder. Only when she turned did she see me.

She had blood on her cheek.

'Is it dead?' I asked. She nodded.

'Sad,' I said.

She shrugged. 'Luca! remember me?' She went to chuck him under his chin but he turned his face into me. 'I s'pose there's only one part of me he might remember, and it's not my voice.'

'You look well,' I said. She was so pretty with her flushed cheeks and her fair hair tied back.

She smiled. 'I'm better now. He looks grand. *Ti'n edrych yn dda!*' she said to Luca.

'I thought you could only speak Welsh.'

'The Welsh words came back first after... after my baby.'

She looked at me and smiled and I felt so bad. I had never thought of her loss at all, that girl with the bitten nails and the tiny bubbies. I wanted to say how sorry I was, but all I could do was blurt out, 'What are you doing here?'

'My uncle rents the field. I help out sometimes. You should bring Luca up to the farm. We've a cow and geese and a pig. It's only iron and coal he'll see at Brynmo!'

Most days after that we went to meet Catrin – except when it was raining, for there's nothing more terrifying than rain to Mistress Enid. I had to take care to wash Luca and make sure there were no farmyard smells on him. He liked the cow best, with her big, wet nose and huge eyes. He liked to pat her, banging his hand on her neck and side. She was a poor-looking creature with a bony ridge along her back, her belly hanging, her diddies wizened. Not like Gwendolyn's cow at Plas Newydd.

That summer was the best I had ever had. Every morning I was happy to wake, and at night I thought about Catrin and how she was a friend. I had never had a friend before.

The letter from Joe about the 'Grand Opening' came just as Mr Williams announced he would lay on transport for his staff who wanted to attend, apart from the few who must stay to guard the pits and the furnaces or to see to Mistress Enid's needs. That would be Mrs Morgan, who was old, and Mrs Jones, who didn't like crowds. Catrin's uncle, the provider of Brynmo's milk and eggs, his wife, their son Aled and Catrin his niece would be travelling in Mr Williams cart, she told me. At last I would be able to show Luca to Joe and Clara!

Early in the morning of 26 November, I nudged Luca awake so I could feed him before we went out into the cold. I dressed him in his wool undergarments, his warmest padded jacket and trousers. I slipped my flannel petticoat on under my dress and took my thickest shawl. The carts would be ready at 7 a.m. I dressed, pulled on a bonnet, loaned for the occasion by Mrs Jones, and picked up Luca, who was sitting at my feet, rolling his favourite little leather ball and crawling after it.

Mr Williams met me on the front step.

'Aggie. Where do you think you are going with my son?'

I stopped, confused. Outside Mr Williams' coach stood, harnessed and ready to go. Behind it was the open cart and the mule with the hanging head. Catrin sat in the back next to her cousin Aled, with a basket on her knee.

'My son is not going into a crowd. Think, woman! The very idea! Out of the question. You will stay here with him.'

'But…'

'But nothing, Aggie. Isn't this what you are wanting – time with my son?'

I did not have time to write a message to Joe before the carts were rumbling down the drive into the chill of the morning, leaving me standing on the top step. Catrin turned round but there was nothing she nor I could do. Luca had his hand on the ribbon of my bonnet. No need to loosen his grip. Let him pull it off.

In the kitchen I gave the bonnet back to Mrs Jones without a word.

She took it, pressing her lips together.

'I shouldn't have raised your hopes,' she said. She turned to Mrs Morgan, who was sitting by the fire, one leg stretched out in front of her, the other bent so she could rub her swollen ankles. 'You said he wouldn't let them go, didn't you?'

Mrs Morgan nodded. 'Happened before, didn't it?' she said. 'The other girl – before you came – she took off with her baby and never came back. Baby girl, mind you. He's not going to let the boy out of his sight.'

'What baby?' I said.

Mrs Morgan changed her attention to her other foot.

'Little girl, the other maid. Nearly broke the mistress' heart when she went.'

I clutched Luca to me so tightly he started to whimper.

57

CATRIN TOLD ME a little about the opening celebrations – the fireworks flashing colours, exploding and drowning the bleating of the terrified sheep and the mooing of the cattle all around. We were sitting in her Aunt Jane's kitchen, Luca toddling over the floor chasing the cat. It was no farm cat, but a great fur ball with only three legs. He made us laugh.

One day we stayed to see the pigs fed. Luca was safe in my arms, not frightened at their screaming, but his eyes were wide and he was silent. When Catrin tipped the swill into the trough, the pigs pushed and struggled as they gobbled, with their heads and feet deep in their food. Luca bounced up and down in my arms.

'Dirty beasts. Look at the feet. Chewing with their mouths open!' Catrin gave a great mimic of a pig smacking its lips and shaking its head.

I shouldn't have stayed so long. I had to run as fast as I could across the field to return Luca to Mistress Enid on time. The wind was blowing against me and I had to hold him tight to my chest, and that child was heavy.

Mrs Jones was at the kitchen window, watching for us.

'She's sent for him already!' she warned, as I kicked off my boots and ran up the stairs.

Mrs Jones came after me with the water; she took the top half, I took the bottom and Luca screamed between us as we forced him into his long smock and fastened the straps to him. She liked to hold him like a small dog. Luca hated it and I didn't blame him.

I had to calm him before I took him to her. No milk no more but a dab of honey on the nipple to catch him and then the sucking soothed him.

'You're late. Wherever have you been?' Mistress Enid in the stuffy living room with the fire alight had a face as cross as I'd seen it. Her grey eyes were sunk but glittery.

'We've been out!'

'In this weather?'

'Fresh air is good for him.'

'He'll catch his death.'

'I wrap him warm, Ma'am.'

'This must end. No more risk to my son until spring unless you have my permission. Put him down.'

Her nose twitched. She held her handkerchief to her face.

'What is that smell?'

Telling the truth was dangerous, I knew that. 'He likes the animals. I took him to the farm, Ma'am.'

'You did what?' Her voice was sharp enough to cut.

'It weren't no risk, Ma'am. I'd never put my son in danger.'

I shouldn't have said that, but the words were out before I could stop them.

'Go!' she said. Her voice was ice.

I thought the first time I said he was my son, I would be sent away. Now I knew I would. When I went down to the kitchen with the bowl of dirty water washed from Luca, I had the heaviest feeling. Mrs Jones raised her eyebrows as I walked through the kitchen to empty it in the courtyard. No one spoke.

I wasn't surprised that Mrs Jones was called upstairs instead of me when it was time for Luca's milk. She brought him down and he reached out his arms to me.

'I'm not supposed to...' said Mrs Jones, handing him to me. She stood biting her lip, anguished.

Mrs Morgan' s face was set grim.

I took Luca upstairs with me, changed his rags and sang to him as he lay in the bed.

Lully, Baby bunting,
Father's gone a-hunting...

I don't know how I knew those words. Perhaps my mother sang it to me once. His eyes closed, I snuffed the candle and sat a long time looking at him in the silver moonlight.

***

Mr Williams called me downstairs early the next morning. He stood in the living room impatiently tapping his crop against his leg, staring out of the window.

'Ah, Aggie.' He spun round but he would not look straight in my eye, glancing at the portrait of Mistress Enid above the empty fireplace.

'You know me for a fair man, Aggie. A blunt man too. There is no easy way to say this. My wife has decided that our son John is of an age not to need you. He is to have a girl to look after him, more appropriate to the task. I do not know if it would be better for him to be separated completely because I know he is very attached to you – or if he should continue to have contact.' His eye quickly caught mine and then flicked away. 'I will leave that to you to judge. I have found you employment, Aggie. An acquaintance of mine over Mold way, Probert – he's a coal interest there and needs a woman to look after his elderly mother. I have no hesitation in recommending you.' He pressed his lips together then stepped forward as though to take my hand, but I pulled back, keeping my head up staring straight at him until he looked away.

'How am I to see my son?'

'Details to be arranged!' He flexed his crop in both hands.

There was a tap at the door and Mrs Jones appeared with a bundle of my clothes, which she placed by the door.

'Everything's ready, sir,' she said, backing out hastily.

'This had to happen one day, Aggie. And this is the day. I will take you to my carriage, which is waiting outside for you. Don't make a fuss, Aggie.'

He urged me down the stone steps with a hand on my back. At the bottom I stood firm as though my feet were planted, until the coach driver came up behind me and took my arm. I would not be dragged into the coach. I shook him off and walked forward, climbing in without his help.

I perched on the edge of the seat as we moved away, with one thought in my mind. Catrin would help me. I leant out of the window and called up to Samuel, Mr Williams' driver.

'Could you stop when we pass Bryn Tydden farm, please? Just for a moment.'

'I mustn't. Mr Williams told me straight there and no stopping,' he called down to me.

'But you could take a message for me later on the way back?' He said nothing.

Not until we had sped past the turning to the farm did I sit back, a terrible feeling of helplessness washing over me.

I had not even had chance to say goodbye to Luca. She had him. I kicked out at the seat opposite me in fury. Why had I not dodged Mr Williams' grip and thrown my bundle at him, knocking him right down the steps, run up the stairs to Mistress Enid's room, and snatched Luca? Before she'd had time to shriek or ring her bell, I would have been racing for my life across the fields to Catrin, who would have taken us in, slammed the kitchen door and bolted it. Her uncle would have chased Mr Williams off with his fierce dogs and his pitchfork. I would have stayed there with her and all would have been well.

I slumped back against the hard velvet ridges of the seat.

The carriage drew up outside a large brick house in Mold. The ride had only taken about an hour but I felt as though I had travelled to another country. The driver stayed on top of the coach. He would not be opening the door for me, unless to pull me out. I preferred to jump to the ground myself to speak to him.

'Stop at Bryn Tydden, Samuel,' I implored him. 'Tell Catrin where I am. Tell her to come to me. Please.'

Just saying her name affected me so, I had to take deep breaths to control my shaking before walking up the short dark path to the front door.

58

I DO NOT want to think of those many dreary months in Mold, looking after an old woman I did not know and who could not know me because she knew nothing. Her needs were similar to my son's. Each time I changed her rag, bathed her or fed her thin gruel, watching it dribble from her mouth, I thought of Luca. Each evening I had to make her presentable for her son, who had no interest in me. He stayed a bare five minutes, not allowing me to leave the room. Heaven forbid that he might have been forced to touch her or do something for her.

At night I wept for Luca, holding a little piece of his shawl to my face, kissing it and kissing it – Mrs Jones must have ripped it off to hide with my clothes. I slept with it in my hands and when I woke and dressed, I stuffed it down my dress to have it next to my skin always.

Snow fell in those weeks. The house was icy, apart from Mrs Probert's room, where the air stank and a fierce fire burned day and night. Each day she grew lighter. Her bones were appearing through her skin, which thinned to parchment.

I slept in the coldest attic room, at the front of the house. If I stood at the window, I could see the carts in the street and the occasional person trudging through the snow. I slept in all my clothes and barely washed, for what was the point?

Downstairs there was a housekeeper, a widow with a sad face and no talent for cooking, though that was her job. We were the only servants.

And then one day, eight long months since I'd left Brynmo, I glanced out of the window to see Catrin walking up the front path. Never have I been so glad to see someone. We fell into each other's arms at the back door. The driver had not given her my message. I could not blame him for that, for who would risk their job for me? Catrin had missed our visits to the farm, and worried that something had happened. She decided to visit Brynmo herself. Taking the eggs as an excuse, she banged on the back door, which was opened by Mrs Jones, who invited her in. As she sat by the fire, Mrs Jones told her I had gone, but no one knew where. A girl came down the stairs carrying Luca.

'Just a girl, staggering with the weight of him and such a cross face on her. I don't know why she carried him, because he can walk now, Aggie. When he saw me, he struggled, so she put him down. He ran over to me, Aggie. He did and I hugged him.'

Catrin and I were both crying and clasping at each other, and that was some comfort.

'How did you find me?' I pulled back to ask.

'Mrs Jones asked the groom, who asked the coach driver. He was ashamed he hadn't given me your message, because he was scared of Mr Williams' temper. So here I am, Aggie. My cousin Aled brought me. He has business here and comes each month. I cannot stay long. Next time I will ask him to drop me earlier so I may spend longer with you.' Catrin's eyes were excited. 'I want so much to see you again.'

She came back the next month, unfortunately at the same time as the doctor was visiting the old woman. I saw her arrive and waved from the window, and managed to rush down to the back door to speak for the shortest time.

'I'm coming this way this time next week,' she said, taking my hand in her own. 'I'll bring news of Luca. I promise.'

Short as it was, Catrin's visit saved me and changed everything. I knew if she said she was coming, she would come. There was something to hope for. I would be able to get away next time, I would, even if I had to place a pillow over the old woman's face to do so. Anyway, I thought, what difference could it possibly make to her if I was in the room or somewhere else with Catrin.

***

Through those long seven days following it was hard to see the point of the old lady living. Every day I was feeding her and giving her sips of water to keep her all the longer from her grave. There was only one way she was going. This was wrong, I thought to myself as I sat with her, her eyes unseeing as if ice had frozen them over. Sometimes I'd put the food in her mouth and she'd forget to swallow until I held her chin up: it felt as though her jaw bone was sitting in my hand.

She said nothing. She did not know me. But then she did not know her son neither. He didn't say much.

'How are you, Mother?' When she didn't answer, he told her about his day, which was always the same.

'I went to the works, Mother. Sent three carts of coal to Howell's furnace. Dick's off sick so Evan took his place. I had a nice piece of beef for my supper.'

And then he ran out of things to say. He sat there and sighed. Sometimes he'd stare at her. Once he waved his hand in front of her face, waited a minute, then slapped his thighs and said, 'I'll leave you now, Mother. You get some rest.'

Rest is all she did.

Snow piling up on the window ledge outside the old woman's room gave the air a heavy yellowish tinge. I saw Catrin coming down the path from the window. I tucked the bedclothes round the old woman, plumped her pillows and left her, racing down to the front door and pulling Catrin in with my fingers pressed to my lips. Catrin nodded, pulled off her wet shoes on the bottom step and tiptoed up to my attic room. As soon as the door shut, we bent double, stifling girlish giggles until I said, 'She won't hear us! There's no one who will hear us.'

Catrin's shawl was wet and cold with fat snowflakes. I flicked at one and it landed on her cheek.

I wiped it off her, tipping back the hood of her cape so I could see her face, fresh and pink and smiling. She unfastened the neck and I threw the cape on to the hook on the door. We stood there staring at each other, both smiling, and then not. Eyes have never been more powerful. We took each other's hands and because hers were freezing cold, I rubbed them between my own.

Catrin winced. 'I caught my finger in the pig bucket.'

She showed me the purpling bruise, pouting like a child.

My room was so small we only had the choice of standing or lying face to face on my narrow, lumpy bed. As we lay down, we clasped hands again. Gradually, our faces drew closer until our foreheads touched. There was a long moment of stillness when we could have pulled apart, either one of us, only neither of us did. Slowly and at the same moment our faces moved until our lips touched gently. Hers were warm but chapped with the wind.

We didn't know what to do, nor what we were doing. We loosened each other's clothes. I had never thought before what a beautiful thing a shoulder is, the roundness of it, the fine line of bone running along to her throat. I pressed deep into that dip at the base of her throat until she stretched back for me to trace my finger up and over the rising line of her jaw to her lips. And then she bit me, her eyes springing open, teasing and mischievous. We were playing and not playing, and it was wonderful.

Suddenly I heard a banging on the front door downstairs and we froze.

Holding my dress to my chest, I stood on the box to look out. Catrin's cousin Aled was walking back along the path, hunched against the falling snow.

'Is it him?'

We fastened our clothing at once, bumping into one another as we bent and stretched. I listened at the door, opening it silently and tiptoeing down.

'We will be together again. Soon. You, me and Luca,' Catrin whispered at the front door, throwing her shawl over her head and scurrying off down the path.

That night I lay awake for a long time thinking about what had happened, reliving the moments over and over. Catrin and I. Together. Friends. More than friends. And as I was remembering the strangeness and the preciousness of it all, I thought of the Duckies' bed: that smooth cover, the red pillows, those deep carvings on the bedhead. I squirmed with the memory, wanting to bat it away, but it would not leave me. I remembered the newspaper man's hand on my arm. I saw his eyes, greedy for my words, and then that purse, heavy in my hand. Extraordinary Female Affection. His words, and they were true words, and words that should mean just what they said, good and rare, but he didn't mean them like that. He meant them to read as though they'd been printed from smuts, not ink.

'You Judas! … blood money… I have no words…' Spit had flown from Mary's mouth as she danced round me, her eyes wild with fury. I had stood there, laughing at her.

That was the most terrible thing I ever did.

59

I DON'T KNOW EXACTLY how long it was before the old woman died. One morning I took her the gruel. I didn't say 'Good morning' because there was no point. I stood the bowl on her table while I pulled the curtains back. She was sitting just as she always was. I did not know anything was different until I put the spoon to her mouth. Her eyes stared, unseeing, but they always were that way. I stood back and looked at her. She was very still. Quickly, I wiped the gruel from her chin and ran out to call for help. All I felt was a lifting of my spirits.

That was not the end of my duties, but the beginning of the end. I had the room to clear, the sheets to wash. When she was gone with the undertaker, I flung the windows wide and found it was spring. I helped prepare the food for the few friends who came back after she was buried in the churchyard. I served drinks. I stood back. I helped men into their coats and hats, I washed up the plates and glasses and swept the room.

Mr Probert called by and handed me money, telling me I was released. I waited for him to thank me, but he did not. All my work was unseen, the evidence buried in the graveyard.

I had one thing to ask of him.

'Sir, could you see a way to find me a ride to Brynmo?'

He looked up, startled that I would ask anything of him, but he nodded. The next day I was in the coal cart, riding back along the road to Brynmo.

I knew exactly how long it was since I had seen my son: fourteen long months, two weeks and three days. He'd be in britches, not gowns: a little man. My heart was knocking against my chest so hard I thought my ribs would crack as I hurried up the long drive. I went round the house, past the stables to the back door.

The excitement was like a fever, but underneath lay a fear of what I might find. My hand was raised to knock when the door was opened by Mrs Jones, who jumped and gasped. She had a harness in her hand with Luca on the other end. I ran towards him but, he turned away, struggling to run from me until Mrs Jones let the leash drop.

'Luca!' I knelt, hoping he would run to me when he heard my voice. Instead he buried his face in Mrs Jones' skirts.

'He's forgotten me!' I wailed.

'No, no,' Mrs Jones said, ushering me in. 'Come John, it's your Mama come to visit you. Be a big boy.'

I wanted him to be my baby but he was four now, dressed in a loose yellow shirt with a wide collar buttoned to his trousers, which reached down to his ankles. His hair curled over his collar, but his face was a different shape. I stood, not knowing what to do.

Mrs Morgan was rolling pastry on the marble top.

'You sit now, Aggie. He'll come to you. Give him a moment. He knows his name as John.'

I would never call him John. Never.

'He'll be punishing you for leaving him,' Mrs Jones added, trying to peel him from her skirt.

As if I needed more punishment. This was so unfair, but who could explain to him all this was against my will?

'Come on now, John,' Mrs Jones said. 'Don't act the baby!'

I picked up his ball, which was lying near my stool, and started throwing it from hand to hand. He peeped at me. I pretended to throw it, my eye following it through the air, but when I opened my other hand, there was nothing there. I frowned and looked around me. I pretended to heave like a cat with a fur-ball, took my hand from my mouth, and there was the ball.

There's nothing like a trick to have any child interested. I took the ball from his ear. I pretended to swallow it and found it in my sleeve. He still stood a distance away from me. His face was suspicious but he did not look away. I could not rush him, although I wanted so badly to fling myself at him and hug him to me: tight, tight, tight.

Mrs Jones and Mrs Morgan were talking in Welsh, so I did not know exactly what they were saying. I knew it was about me by the way they kept looking in my direction, their old eyes full of feeling. Mrs Jones slipped away up the stairs.

I reached for a piece of pastry which Mrs Morgan had cut from the edge of her pies. She nodded. I rolled it into small pieces and left them in a pile in front of Luca. I took one and squashed it flat, fashioning it into a shape like we used to do.

'What's that? Hmmm. I think it's a duck!'

He took a step forward. He could reach the table now without his stool. He picked up a ball of dough, squashed it and busied himself pushing and pulling the edges.

'A fish?' I guessed. He shook his head, his eyes willing me to get it right.

'A sheep?' He shook his head.

'A pig?'

'A pig. A pig!' He shouted, running in wild circles round the kitchen.

The game lasted until the dough was brown and greasy and Mrs Jones was back in the room.

She shook her head to Mrs Morgan.

'I'll ask him later.' She turned to me. 'We've no one to help. The girl he hired for John – for Luca – walked out on us.'

For a moment I could not breathe with a rush of hope, but then I talked firmly to myself: never hope too much, then you'll be safe.

'I'm too old,' Mrs Jones said. 'He's a handful now, aren't you, John Stanley? I've no liking for the harness but if he runs, I can't catch him now.'

When the bell rang from Mistress' Enid's room, Luca, who obviously knew what it signalled, ran to the far corner of the room, dodging the moment Mrs Jones stepped near him. Catching him by the arm as he streaked past, I pulled him to me and hugged him. Oh, it was a moment to treasure, but I knew he must go. As I began to ease him away, he clung to me, his legs pinched round my waist.

'Be a good boy, John,' Mrs Jones said, helping me loosen his grip. I held his arms as she pulled a comb through his hair, though he tossed his head from side to side.

'You'll see your mama later, but only if you behave,' she added. 'Then,' she looked at me, 'your mother upstairs might give you a sweetmeat?'

I hated that he thought of her as mother.

'She's good to him in her own way,' Mrs Jones said, leading Luca away.

She came back into the room nodding.

'He's calm now,' she said to me, 'If you want to stay to help look after him, you'll have to accept things as they are. Mr Williams is away. I'll speak to him when he returns.'

I wanted to be with Luca, of course I did, but I did not want to stay. I could not bear the thought of Mr Williams' face when I begged for his compassion. I was in his power again, unless I could think of another solution.

Catrin.

As I set off across the top of the field, I replayed her words on the doorstep in Mold, over and over. We would be together! How exactly it was going to be, I didn't know. She hadn't been able to come to Mold again in the last few months, so we'd had no chance to plan, but if Catrin and I could be together somewhere, Luca would be with us somehow.

Before I had reached the gap in the hedge, I heard the pigs squealing. My heart beat fast. It must be feeding time. The noise rose to a frenzy as I squeezed through the gap. Catrin was bending over at the back door, fastening her boot. Her head was bare and her fair hair long down her back. She picked up the buckets and walked toward the sty. She would not hear me above their noise. As she tipped the food over the low wall, I walked right up behind her, standing only a pace away, smiling, waiting for her to turn and throw herself into my arms.

'Catrin!'

She turned, shocked then delighted, but her smile slipped as she placed her hand on her belly. She was pregnant.

60

WHEN YOU HAVE a wound that is scabbing over, it is best not to scratch it even if it is irritating beyond endurance. Wait until the skin heals over, as it will. As Mary used to say, nothing lasts forever.

I stayed at Brynmo because I did not know what else to do. I found I had not the strength to leave alone, to abandon my child. Mr Williams said I might stay on so long as I obeyed his rules. I must have no contact outside Brynmo without his permission. Any infringement and I'd be dismissed and I would never see my child again. I had no doubt he meant what he said. I couldn't believe I'd ever felt anything but loathing for this man.

Clara married her cousin Aled in the local chapel. I didn't go. Her baby was born. I did not want to see it. It was easier that way. I did not write to Joe and I don't know if he wrote to me. If he did, I received nothing. I thought of him. I thought of Baby Iris. We were connected and always would be, though we were apart and that's how it was. Fledglings may begin together in the nest, one might drop to the ground below, one gets pushed out, but when they are ready to fly, they go their separate ways and you cannot put them all back into the nest no matter how hard you try.

Being at ease with how things are is the best you can be in this life.

I had Luca to myself at nights. He slept in my bed mostly, preferring to be with me, as I preferred to be with him, though he did have a little bed in my room and a bigger nursery was being prepared for him downstairs. I stayed awake as long as I could each night, paying attention to each place on my body where his skin was against mine: his cheek on my breast bone, his hair brushing my chin, his shoulder tucked into my armpit, my knees folded under his legs. We were together like one thing.

In the daytime I took him when he was tired or fretful or ill, or when the Williamses were entertaining, as they did more frequently. Mistress Enid was so miraculously restored by a child to pretend was her own, though I could not be surprised that Luca was a better medicine than everything the stuffy doctor prescribed. At her insistence, I dressed him in silly, fussy clothes: long trousers, a waistcoat and shirt, and shiny shoes, like a little gentleman. He hated to be fiddled with. He'd scream at me and hate me as I made him ready for her. Once, when I was wrestling tangles from his long hair, he spun round and would have hit me had I not grabbed his wrist. His eyes were like flint – his father's eyes, and I could not bear it. We didn't know what to do next, staring at each other in horror until we both crumpled with shame and misery, crying as we hugged.

Mistress Enid was not unkind to Luca. He softened her. When I left him with her, he would turn happily and be the boy she wanted him to be, which was not the boy I wanted him to be. She did not speak to me, nor look at me.

I thought about escape, churning the possibilities over and over, but there were problems every way I turned. Having no money, where would I go? I couldn't go to Joe, Joe would be the first person Mr Williams would think of. He'd be after me at once to take back what he believed was his. I'd be arrested as a thief, and the law would be on his side. Oh, if only Catrin had not deceived me... the rage I felt against Catrin was greater than the rage I felt about Mr Williams, which I knew was not fair. When the anger eventually vanished, I was left helpless.

On more than one occasion I thought of my death, not dwelling on the death itself, but thinking more of the funeral. The chapel would be empty but for Joe, Clara maybe, possibly Joseph and Josephina, Archie and little Nelly – who would be five now – crying and wiping their noses on their sleeves, but Luca would not be present. He'd be cross-legged on the green carpet in the drawing room with a book in his lap, being scolded if he rustled the pages. He would never know who I was, because who would tell him? I could never leave him believing Mistress Enid had given him life from that stiff, bony body. But in the end, I could not think of myself as dead, being so alive inside as I was, with this son who needed me.

***

One morning, not far into the new year, I was in the kitchen preparing Luca's breakfast just how he liked it: honey and bread soaked in cream. A man banged on the kitchen window, waving a letter and nodding. I was the only person in the room. He nodded again and pointed so I opened the back door.

'Aggie Begg? I must deliver this into the hands of Aggie Begg and none other.' He was out of breath and red in the face. His horse, flecked white, stood on the cobbles behind him. Mr Williams' stallion whinnied outrage at an intruder from his stall across the courtyard.

'You led me a merry dance!' the man said. 'Asked your brother's wife. She sent me here but she weren't sure. Long time since they heard from you,' he said, but I only half heard him because I was reading the note:

Peggin,
Mary died. Funeral Thursday
St Collen at 11.
Sara

I slipped the note up my sleeve as the horse's hooves clattered on the cobbles as he rode away. I took Luca up to the dining room. All the time my head was empty of the things near me and full of things far away. Sara. She had thought to tell me when I would never have believed she would. How glad I was that I had gone to see Mary. I could not be sure if she ever knew I had been, but told myself that she had.

Plunging hands into scummy water on a cold February morning was a way to bring myself back to the things that are real. Making a plan gave me something to think about. This was Wednesday. The funeral was the next day.

I would go to Mary's funeral and my son Luca would be with me. We would never return to Brynmo. I must think carefully. Mr Williams would follow me, without question, so I could not go to the obvious places: Joe or Catrin. They must know nothing. Who then: Iris? I had found Browns' entertainers once. I could again. Moses? Surely he and his wife would help me for a while. The Ladies at Plas Newydd? Would they be able to forgive me? Probably not. Not after such a terrible betrayal.

I must lay a false trail but not tell anyone that what I was telling them was untrue, or they would reap Mr Williams' wrath. He might have all the power, but I had the wits I was born with and that must be enough. I would do it. 'Details to be arranged,' as Mr Williams had once said to me.

The moment I had finished the first wash and the sheets were pegged out on to the drying racks, I slipped away, telling no one I was gone, leaving the water on the copper to heat for the second part of the wash. If I hurried, I'd be back before it was ready. Mrs Jones was occupied upstairs. Mrs Morgan lived inside her own world more than she ever did, and would not notice if I was there or not.

As I walked across the field, I rehearsed my lines in my head so when I actually said them they would be true to me. The day was raw and grey; a cold wind pushed against me. The hedge shivered its bare branches. Underfoot, the puddles in the ploughed troughs were skimmed with ice, which shattered as I walked. As I squeezed through the hedge, Catrin came walking toward me, head down, with a bucket in her hand. Seeing me, she dropped her bucket with a clatter. I asked her straight if she would help me. She gulped and nodded. The following morning, I told her, at first light, I would be walking along the road toward Wrexham with Luca. They had a mule cart, didn't they? She nodded. The cart must happen to pass and offer us a ride to Llangollen. If ever Mr Williams should ask them if they knew anything about my escape, they must deny it.

I stepped forward to whisper: 'I'm taking Luca to my sister in Manchester. I know I can trust you never to tell anyone.'

She nodded and reached for my hand, her eyes pleading, but I could not look at her and was soon stumbling back across the field, my boots heavy with mud.

As I hoped, no one had noticed my absence.

Mrs Morgan's first batch of sugar buns was in the oven; the second was rising under cloths near the steaming copper. Half the water had already boiled away. I filled the tub and picked up the pile of soiled clothes, releasing the smell of Mr Williams as I did so.

'Never again will I breathe in the stink of you! Never!' I promised myself as I scrubbed at the stains with fury, opening the cracks on my knuckles. I threw the clothes over the wooden drier, licked the salty blood on my hands and then I waited. I had to time this just right.

At the sound of the tins being knocked against the kitchen table, when the smell of fresh buns was stronger than soapy water, I tipped up the tub, deliberately soaking myself.

'Look what I've done!' I wailed as I ran into the kitchen. 'I'll have to go up and change.' Mrs Morgan paid me no attention. As I passed the table, I snatched two buns from the cooling tray and tucked them under my shawl to smother the smell.

The hallway upstairs was very quiet and the door to the drawing room open. I couldn't leave a trail of mud across that pale green carpet. I looked to left and right, kicked off my boots and slipped inside, walking straight to the mantelpiece, where I took the silver candlesticks, pulling out and leaving the white candle stubs next to the gold clock. All the time, Mistress Enid looked down at me from her picture. The candlesticks must be worth a lot of money. I looked up, wanting to jeer at her, but a little smirk on her thin lips made me pause. No, I will not give you the satisfaction! To take my son was one thing, but to steal items worth money was another: a servant stealing from her employer! If I were caught, I would be sent to gaol or transported to Australia for certain, and I would never see Luca again. I placed the candlesticks back on the mantelpiece and pocketed the stubs for no reason other than the fact that I could.

By nightfall everything was in place. The buns were wrapped in Luca's clothes, which were tied into my own. Luca's room was still not ready downstairs so I settled him in the cot in my own room. Although my voice was tight when I sang to him, he did not seem to pick up my nervousness at all.

I sat on my bed waiting. Bless him. In sleep he was still my baby, though he was six now – the age I had been when I was split from my mother in Chirk. I was taking him with me. His blond hair curled round his cheeks and with his eyes closed, there was little of Mr Williams in that sweet face.

All night I sat there, listening to the clock chiming the quarters far away downstairs. Roosters are unreliable timekeepers, but as soon as I heard the first call drifting across from the farm, I took a candle stub from my pocket, lit it and roused Luca. Half asleep, he stepped into his clothes and walked himself down the stairs, still drowsy enough not to ask questions. I slipped the bolt, opened the big door, and we were gone.

PART XII
Joe

61

THERE WAS STILL much to do after the opening of the aqueduct. Having acquitted himself so well, Joe was appointed to oversee the construction of a water line from Pontcysyllte to Llantisilio, and the tenting of the banks where there had been earth slippage during heavy rain. Halfway across the Llangollen bridge, taking plans for the tenting frames to be approved by the committee, he met the new post-boy.

'Saved me a trip, Mr Begg,' he said, sorting through his leather bag as his horse twitched water from its ears. The rain which had soaked his cape hadn't dampened his good cheer, though the same could not be said of his miserable cob, with its lowered head and quivering bottom lip.

Joe was late. He paid the post-boy, glancing down at the spidery writing on the letter – smudged by the rain, yet familiar. Not wanting to risk blotching it further, he waited until he was inside The Hand to open it.

Dear Joe
     I left the Browns. I had a fall. They were
not kind. Im wating a ride. I am comming soon.
Ive nowere else to go.
     Your Sister
     Iris

Iris! Left the Browns. Not kind, the Browns? How dare they not be kind! She had nowhere else to go, she said. Of course she must come to her brother. Most certainly he was a kind man. His mind was racing with the beat of his heart. His prayers were answered! Iris could be the answer to Clara's prayers too, helping with the children and in the house. Excellent! Finally, his promise would be fulfilled. Or, strictly speaking, *half* his promise.

Joe slipped the letter into his pocket and pushed open the heavy doors into the back room. The meeting had started. An empty chair had been left for him at the front, though if he stayed near the back of the room, he could make a quicker exit. He took the tenting plans forward to the convenor and signalled his intentions to sit at the back, which he then did, attempting to listen to the agenda being announced, with his mind scanning the letter again: I'm waiting a ride. I've nowhere else to go. Iris. Come to me, little sister, he thought. Come to your brother, Joe.

Never had Joe been so aware of how men loved to hear their own voices, how they spoke round and round in circles, rarely reaching the place they had intended to reach. There was much deferring to a man of higher position: 'After you, sir, my learned friend,' and 'No, after you, most distinguished colleague.' The moment the first man stood and began to fasten his coat, Joe stood too, pulled out Iris' note, nodded his head to anyone who was looking and pushed back through the doors. On the top step, he stopped to read it again, though he knew what it said:

Im wating a ride.

Today or tomorrow? Next week? That she would come, he was sure. She had promised Clara that she would return for her button. That it had meant so much to Iris – a little red button, silk twisted over the padding by his own hands so long ago – made Joe's heart warm in spite of the rain falling.

St Collen's church bell was tolling sorrowfully over the town. Joe checked his fob watch. Ten to eleven. A group of women, shawls over their heads, were making their way past The Hand to the steps leading up to the church. Behind him, the door opened and the publican Euan Edwards appeared, with his elderly father leaning on his arm.

'Are you coming, Joe?' he asked, guiding his father down the steps. 'To the funeral? The Ladies' housekeeper… from Plas Newydd.'

'Mary…' he blinked. 'I heard she'd recovered. I saw her myself at the opening of the aqueduct.'

'That was four years ago. Still, 84 is a good age, eh, Father?'

If only Joe had not stopped to reread the letter, he'd be over the bridge and on his way home and no one could blame him for not attending, for he would not have known. Now he did know. Aggie would be very upset. He'd promised to tell her if he heard that Mary was taken worse, but he had heard Mary was recovered. He would go and pay his respects. Afterwards, he could write to Aggie and tell her and she would know him as the thoughtful brother he was. All those letters he had written and not once had she replied. That had hurt him, though Clara told him to leave Aggie be – that she would write when the time was right, whatever that meant. All that hurt must be laid aside. He must go for his sister's sake, if not his own. This was the right thing to do.

Turning back up the hill, he fell into step with Euan and old Mr Edwards.

There would be no need to go inside the church; standing outside would be sufficient. The rain was falling harder and the women in front of him, three deep, pulled their shawls over their heads and hunched like rooks. The drip-drip from the protruding stone at the top of the tower changed to a steady stream, hitting the ground where the moss grew over the stones. Joe moved under the shelter of a dark yew.

He knew when the heads turned to the right that the coffin had arrived at the lychgate; he followed its progress down the path by the movement of the crowd. Standing on tiptoes, Joe caught a glimpse of the wooden coffin and the hands of the pallbearers. One of the mourners moved aside, giving him a better view. The two ladies whom he'd seen with Mary at the opening led the procession. 'The Duckies,' Aggie called them. They were holding each other's arms, dressed identically in black, the older one short and stout, the other thin and straight-backed. Both wore tall black hats with veils over their faces. The churchyard was silent apart from the bell and the soft patter of rain.

Joe moved back, bowing his head. How strange it was to mourn someone you never knew, though in that moment, with a tightening in his throat, he was overcome by a sadness as though he was mourning everyone, including himself.

The last of the followers disappeared into the church and the doors closed. He noted the freshly dug grave by the path, ready to receive Mary. Wooden boards held back the earth on either side. The sexton and his boy stood in the shelter of the church wall, ready with their shovels.

And still the bell tolled.

No need to stay, every reason to go. He'd slip away and no one would notice.

PART XIII
Peggin

62

WE HAD NOT been walking long down the dark road before the birds started waking; the grey sky grew paler and Luca started asking questions.

'Where are we going? Why? I'm hungry.'

The buns quietened him for a while and just as he was beginning to moan, I was thankful to hear the clip-clop of the mule and the rumble of cart wheels behind us. I peered into the gloom. Between the mule's ears I saw just one person sitting in the cart. Catrin was not there. Aled waited for me to haul myself up next to him. He was not in a talking mood and neither was I.

A fine rain began to fall. I covered Luca as best I could and stared down the road ahead, thinking only of the thump of hooves hitting the road. If I thought of anything else, I would be undone.

Just before we reached the Llangollen bridge, Aled jerked back the reins with a soft 'Whoa!'

The sky was lighter but a thin drizzle coated everything.

I shook Luca awake and jumped down, turning to lift my sleepy boy. Aled said not a word but shook the reins and turned a wide circle to trot back the way he had come.

'Where are we?' Luca asked, looking around. 'Where are we going?'

The bell was tolling. My shawl was soaked through, heavy. Even so, I pulled it right over my head, not wanting anyone to know me. The bridge and the river were so exciting for Luca, he wanted to stop and marvel every few steps.

'We're late,' I said. 'You hear that bell? That's for someone who was good to me. We're going to her funeral.'

'What's a funeral?'

I hardly knew. This was the first one I had been to. 'And then we're going to get the coach and go to London.'

'London? On a coach?'

Luca's eyes were wide with excitement. 'What are we going to do in London?'

'I don't know. We'll find out where we get there.'

'What about Father? Is he coming to London?'

I took him by the hand to make speed across the bridge.

'No more questions. We've got to hurry now.'

In St Collen's churchyard, with the bell tolling and the sparrows chirping cheerfully in the hedge behind, a crowd had gathered. I moved quickly round to the far side of the graveyard, standing back near the lychgate. Luca was taken by the gravestones, digging the green moss from the stones with a stick, but when the crowd pressed forward, I picked him up so he could see.

At six years old he was a weight, taking my mind away from the mix of sadness and shame for what was past, and not knowing what was to come. The coffin was lifted on to the shoulders of six men in frock coats. It was not a smooth journey for Mary because the men were of different heights. I didn't like to think of her being bumped about. I wished she could know I was there.

I shrank back, wanting to see but not be seen by the two Duckies behind the coffin. Big Duckie was shorter than I remembered, fatter and older, and Little Duckie, her beloved, was so thin and sad. Seeing them made me sadder too, thinking of Mary. Luca was slipping from my arms so I put him down, but kept his hand in my own. He picked up his stick in the other hand, happy to be jabbing at the moss. All the others from Plas Newydd were following: Bethan, Sara and Elizabeth, all more solid somehow, heavier; Jeremiah in his best suit; and Mr Stour in a dark outfit that looked too big for him, followed by his boys, grown men now. Walter came after them, never big at all but now shrunk and bent and shuffling, without the strength to pick up his feet. Moses was way back down the line with a young woman, like Gwendolyn in the way she walked, but her hair dark as her clothes.

The church doors closed.

It is strange that you can somehow feel when someone is looking at you.

Over on the far side of the graveyard, under the yew tree, stood a shortish man, staring straight at me. My heart leapt. Joe! No! This wasn't meant to happen! Joe would be the first person Mr Williams would think of when he came looking for us. I shook my head, sending the message as urgent and loud as a person can with their eyes.

63

Joe

STILL THE BELL tolled.

Joe was about to leave when he noticed a boy standing by the lychgate. There was something about the way the boy was looking up at the woman who stood with him which made him think of Joseph when small: that same tilt of the chin. He looked more closely at the woman – it was Aggie! Just as he had forgotten to think of her, here she was! He was about to run over to her when she looked up sharply, stopping him with a shake of her head. Her face was tense. Joe stood certain and uncertain. He touched his own chest and shook his head too. She nodded. What did she mean? Was he to walk away as though he had not seen her? She nodded again as he started to move, his eyes never leaving her as hers never left him. To turn away, not understanding, was the hardest thing: doing what was right when it felt so wrong.

Joe walked quickly down the hill. What had happened, why it had happened, he could not fathom. What could Aggie have meant, warning him off? She might follow him later and explain. Surely she would. And Iris might have arrived already. To think that both his sisters might arrive on the same day, the three of them together in his own front parlour.

He was almost running by the time he reached the bridge – empty now, most of Llangollen being crammed into St Collen's Church. The Dee was racing with the recent rain, the mill paddles thumping quickly.

A black horse galloped onto the bridge ahead of him. Hooves clattered on the cobbles. Joe stepped back into the passing place. Though there was plenty of room for a single rider to pass, there was a wildness in the man standing up in his stirrups, leaning forward. White foam flecked Joe's lapel as the horse streaked past. He was wiping it off when the man leapt from his horse.

'Where is she, Joe Begg? I'll find her, wherever she is!'

'Mr Williams…' Joe stuttered. Fury burned red in Williams' cheeks. 'I don't know. I haven't seen her –'

Mr Williams grasped Joe's neck, pressing him back against the bridge. He could not swallow.

'You do know! Tell me now!'

'I can't. No.' Joe felt the edge of the wall on his back. Only his toes still touched the ground, the water roaring beneath him. He struggled to prise the fingers from his throat, jerking his head sideways, unable to speak.

'Up there?' The grip loosened a fraction. Williams cocked his head on one side. 'That bell got anything to do with it?'

Joe said nothing. Williams let go of his throat and held the lapels of Joe's jacket, pulling him close to his face.

'Thanks, Begg.' Dropping his hold, his foot was in the stirrup before he turned and walked back to Joe.

'That's my boy she's got, Joe. And my boy is my heart,' he said, thumping his chest with his fist.

He turned away, mounted the horse and was off from standstill to gallop.

'No!' Joe said, breaking into a run back to the end of the bridge, though he knew he could do nothing.

'I didn't say anything!' he told himself. The mill paddles boomed in his ears. The boy. Aggie's boy… was Mr Williams' boy… He chewed the tip of his glove, hardly noticing the cart crossing the bridge, nor seeing the young woman handed down when the cart stopped, nor her limping back towards him. She stopped. They looked at each other.

'Joe?'

'Iris?'

64

Peggin

I WATCHED JOE EVERY step of his way until he was out of sight. He'd be walking down the hill to the bridge, desperate to know what I meant. Poor Joe. He wanted so badly to gather us back into his brotherly care.

I do not know when Luca's hand slipped from my own. I was distracted for only a few seconds. When I looked to where he had been, he wasn't there. I heard a cry – 'Mama!' – and at the same moment saw Mr Williams striding back towards the lychgate, with Luca over his shoulder.

I must have screamed, because Mr Williams swung round. I ran like the wind after them. The gate was still swinging shut. I do not know if anyone was there to witness, or no one. All I could see was the black stallion waiting and Mr Williams swinging himself up into the saddle holding Luca tightly in front of him. Luca wasn't struggling. I threw myself at them, pulling at Mr Williams' coat, clawing at him. He was up above me, looking down.

'Let go, Aggie!' he said, but I wouldn't. I hung on with all my might as Mr Williams flicked his reins and started to move away. I saw his crop strike me across the knuckles but I did not feel it.

He turned back and spoke over his shoulder.

'You are responsible for this, Aggie. You.'

And they were gone.

I stood there numb, not moving, fingering a shred of cloth from Mr Williams' coat. My knuckles were bleeding.

I didn't cry out.

I didn't do anything.

The rain beat on to my head, ran down my face, dripped off my chin.

I remember picking up my shawl, stumbling back, sitting on a tomb.

I don't know how long I sat there.

Sometime later I must have lifted the latch at the church door. I pushed it open, treading into the dips where the stone floor was worn with the years, and slid into the back pew.

I sat there, still as stone, in that empty church. They had all gone. Mary. The Duckies. The priest. Everyone. A faint musty scent hung on the cold air.

It takes a lifetime to understand your life. Not just your lifetime, but the other lifetimes around you. That's what a lifetime is for, I thought: the amount of time it takes to make some sense of it.

The church door opened behind me. Outside, a crow was cawing. The sound took me to another time, another place: the stairs in the priest's house. I was on the step below my mother, who was looking down at me with the baby in her arms, and the bird was laughing silently outside the window.

My mother could not take me. Perhaps she thought I'd have a better chance at life away from her. She let me go because she had to. She made no fuss because she did not want me to carry her pain.

Oh, Luca.

The church door behind me closed with a heavy clunk. I half turned to see a woman limping down the aisle, sliding into the pew beside me. Someone crossed the church behind us to slip into the pew on my other side. Joe. He took my hand, squeezed it, and reached across me to take Iris' hand. He placed her hand in my lap, mine over it and covered both with his own.

65

A WEAK FEBRUARY sun was sinking behind the hills and the cold was tightening everything when I knocked at the front door of Plas Newydd the following afternoon. Visitors knocked at the front door. But that's what I was, a visitor. Sara opened the door. Her eyes opened wide as if I was a ghost.

'I've come to see the Ladies,' I said. 'Thank you for sending the note about Mary.' She would not meet my eye. 'Are they in the library?' I asked. She nodded.

'I'll see myself up. I know the way.'

I lifted my skirt to climb the carpeted stairs, and tapped on the door.

'Who is it?' It was Little Duckie's voice. I walked in, closing the door behind me.

The Duckies were sitting in their usual chairs, still dressed in black. A book was open in Little Duckie's lap. They looked surprised, not shocked, then tired, old and sad.

'Peggin? Could it be you?' Little Duckie spoke first.

I nodded.

I had not thought of the words, but I knew what I had come to say. I stayed where I was, just inside the door.

'I came to Mary's funeral.'

Big Duckie's mouth twisted side to side. She had an egg stain on her black dress.

'It's too late to say to Mary what I wanted to say. But it's not too late to thank you for the chances and the lessons you gave me. I never was a good pupil but I am a better one now.' I looked down at the twisted fringe of the Turkish rug, breathed deeply and looked up, talking straight, first to one, then the other. 'I'm sorry for what I did. I knew nothing then and now I know more. That's what I came to say.'

I was turning to go when Little Duckie called out.

'Don't go, Peggin. Stay and sit with us and we can be sad together for a while and talk of Mary.'

Big Duckie shooed a cat from the little green button-back chair and smoothed the velvet pile to silver.

'You sit here, Peggin. Tell us about yourself now.' She looked so much older, with the brightness gone from her eyes and her skin like gauze.

'Is it tea I'll send for, beloved? Or should we take a sherry?'

I sat stiff on the chair, wanting to be gone but needing to stay a while.

I told them of my brother and my sister waiting for me. I told them we had not been together since we were split apart all those long years ago: Joe going one way, my mother and the baby the other, and me another, sent to the old woman who looked after unwanted children in the parish.

'And how old were you then, Peggin?' Little Duckie asked.

'I was six,' I said.

Big Duckie looked at Little Duckie.

'And then you came to us, didn't you, Peggin? And served us well for so many years,' Little Duckie said.

'She did,' Big Duckie agreed.

'Mary was good to you, Peggin, was she not?'

'She was.'

'Do you recall the time she kicked out at you when the cat stole a rabbit and hurt her foot? I think she blamed you.'

'She did.'

'And she asked you what you'd learnt from the situation and you said, "I'll never kick a table in my life!"'

The Duckies both smiled and shook their heads.

'She told us that, did she not, beloved? I can hear her now. Mary was a good mimic of you, Peggin,' Little Duckie said.

'She was,' Big Duckie agreed. 'She was.'

The cat sat with its back to me, licking its front paw. I had to look down at my hands, held together in my lap, to bear their kindness.

'Do you recall all the songs you sang for us, Peggin? It was a sweet voice you had. What was it now – "The Cruel Mother"?'

'I don't sing any more,' I said.

'Oh, you should. You will. But maybe not that song,' Little Duckie said, reaching across and touching my knee.

'I have to go,' I said, standing up. 'That cat will be up on the chair, curled round and sleeping before I even get to the front door.'

'She will. She will.' Big Duckie said. 'Thank you for coming by, Peggin.'

I stepped toward their table, reached into my pocket and placed the crystal in front of them. They looked up at me and nodded.

'Ah, the crystal!' Big Duckie said. 'You see, beloved, things are seldom lost for ever.'

'Peggin,' Little Duckie said, smiling at me. 'Such a pretty name.'

Acknowledgements

THANKS ARE DUE to numerous people who helped me with this novel. Firstly, to my brother Andrew and cousin David, who took me first to Plas Newydd, where the idea took root. Thanks too to the museum in Oswestry and the information centre in Llangollen for their help. I am indebted to Elizabeth Mavor's book *The Ladies of Llangollen*, published by Penguin in 1971.

Thanks to my writing buddies, Rebecca Lisle and Amanda Mitcheson; to Pip Morgan, who first knocked the book into shape; to my old friend Roger. My greatest thanks to Carolyn Hodges, my brilliant editor, and everyone at Y Lolfa.

Lastly, I want to thank Chris for everything.

Christine Purkis
March 2023

Also by the author:

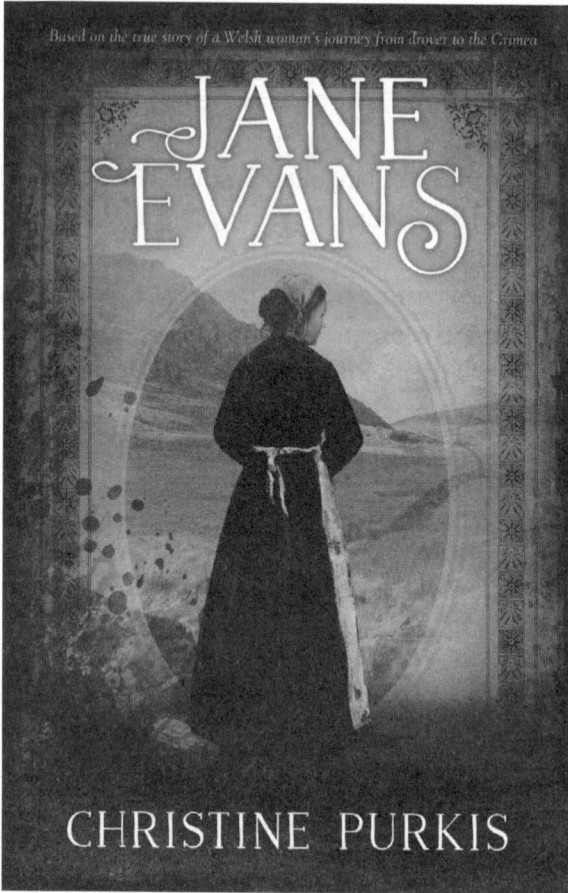

Based on the true story of a Welsh woman's journey from drover to the Crimea

JANE EVANS

CHRISTINE PURKIS

Fleeing with the drove to escape her harsh life, Jane ends up nursing in inhuman conditions in the Crimea. Can she survive the dangers and return to Wales – and to what welcome?

£9.99

Also from Y Lolfa:

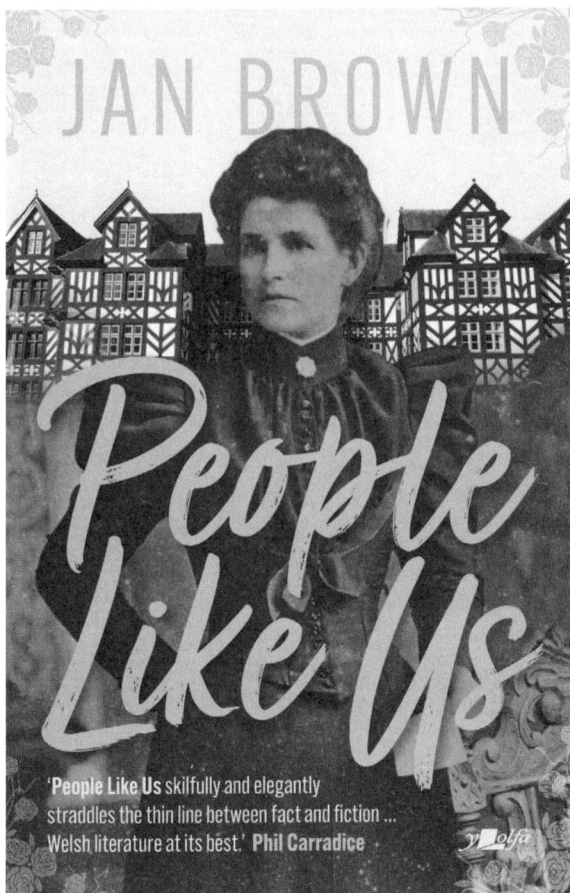

A poor girl rises to become Cook at Gregynog Hall. Her courage sees her battle to avoid losing control of her life, the fate of many women at the turn of the 20th century.

£9.99

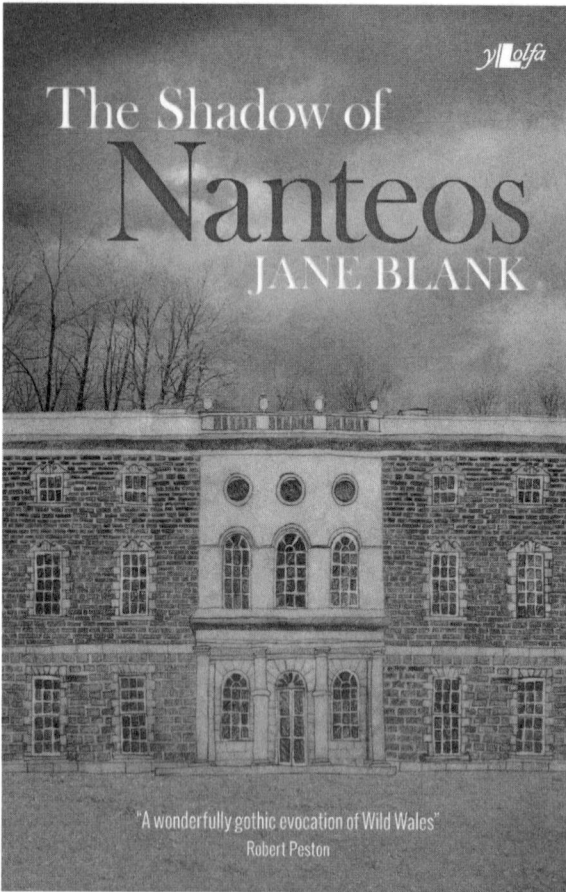

The Shadow of
Nanteos
JANE BLANK

y Lolfa

"A wonderfully gothic evocation of Wild Wales"
Robert Peston

A historical love story based on the lives of the Powell family of
Nanteos mansion near Aberystwyth, set against the background of
the mid 18th-century Cardiganshire lead wars.

£8.99

NANTEOS:
The Dipping Pool

JANE BLANK

'Beautiful and original... Branwen's story is as memorable and moving as *Tess of the d'Urbervilles*.' Helen Garlick

y Lolfa

Visceral and hard-hitting historical novel, continuing the story of the infamous Powell family of Nanteos mansion and of the violent, secretive world of 18th-century Cardiganshire.

£9.99

"A family history powerfully reimagined as an absorbing and moving fiction."

In The Vale
Sam Adams

Historical novel set in the Vale of Glamorgan at the time of the Napoleonic Wars. A poor curate and the youngest son of a powerful landed gentry family both fall for governess Sarah.

£9.99

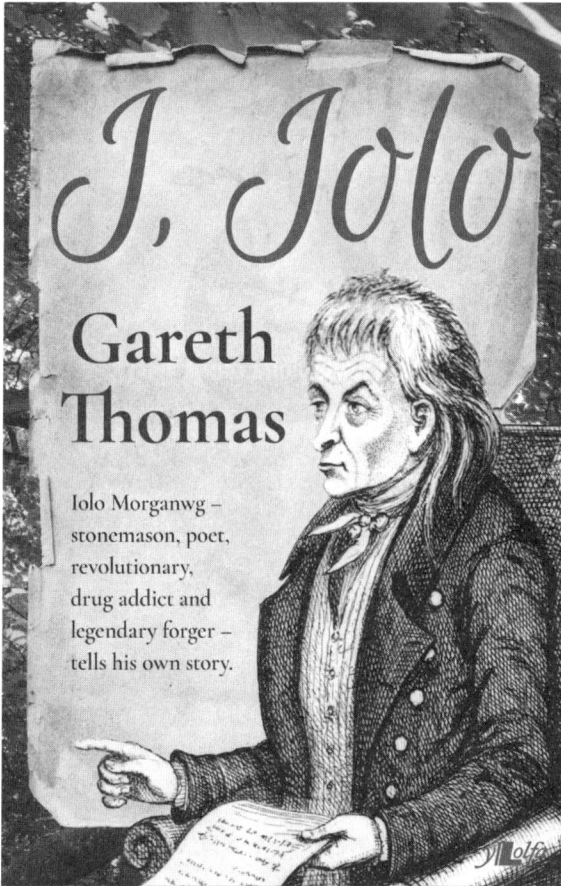

The tale of Iolo Morganwg: real-life stonemason, scholar, hymnist, revolutionary, druid, failed businessman, drug addict, and perpetrator of the greatest act of literary forgery in European history.

£9.99

Ask for a print quote!
www.ylolfa.com